GOD'S CHILDREN ARE LITTLE BROKEN THINGS

GOD'S CHILDREN ARE LITTLE BROKEN THINGS

Stories

ARINZE IFEAKANDU

A PUBLIC SPACE BOOKS

A Public Space Books
PO Box B
New York, NY 10159

Stories from this collection appeared, in earlier forms, in the following publications:
"God's Children Are Little Broken Things" in *A Public Space* No. 24
"Alọbam" in *Guernica*
"Happy Is a Doing Word" in the *Kenyon Review*
"The Dreamer's Litany" in *One Story*
"Michael's Possessions" as "Redemption Song" in *Redemption Song and Other Stories: The Caine Prize for African Writing 2018*

A Public Space gratefully acknowledges the support of the National Endowment for the Arts, the New York State Council on the Arts, the Amazon Literary Partnership, and the corporations, foundations, and individuals whose contributions have helped to make this book possible.

Library of Congress Control Number: 2021941866
ISBN   9781734590715
eISBN 9781736370926
Distributed by Publishers Group West (PGW)

www.apublicspace.org

9 8 7 6 5 4 3 2 1

For Mum and Dad.
And for Mma, Dodo, and Ogonna,
in loving memory.

SET ME AS A SEAL UPON YOUR HEART,
AS A SEAL UPON YOUR ARM,
FOR LOVE IS STRONG AS DEATH.

—SONG OF SOLOMON 8:6

CONTENTS

THE DREAMER'S LITANY

On a warm Saturday night full of starlight, the man walked into Auwal's shop and asked for a recharge card. "Scratch it for me," he said to Auwal and then took his time tapping in the numbers. He sat on a bench outside the shop, asked for a bottle of Star. "Sorry, sir," Auwal said, "we no sell alcohol, sir," and the man chuckled and muttered something, his eyes roving around Auwal's face, seeking his eyes. Auwal looked away, and when the man asked where he came from, he said, "Cotonou," although he had moved to Brigade from a village two hours away, a village of greenery that stretched all the way to the horizon so that land and sky became one bluey-green parchment. He felt guilty about the lie for which he saw no reason except for a niggling feeling that he did not want to be known by this man.

"Cotonou, Cotonou." The man looked clueless. "Cotonou, them no dey speak English?"

Auwal shook his head. "No, no. *Français. Comprenez-vous le français?*"

"Ah! No sell me with French o!" The man had a shrill giggle, and the way his hands fluttered to his lips, light and delicate, the rapid blinking of his eyes: Auwal thought of Idris then, lithe, fragile

Idris with eyes like small pearly nuts. But this man, this man with a hairless head and an Igbo accent and an air around him of something disruptive, something waiting to disrupt, was not exactly like Idris.

"I no fit sell you, fa," he said, laughed. "French, good. Fine language."

"True. Very sexy language. I lie?"

Auwal shrugged, smiled. "I fit buy you Star from person, him dey sell contraband."

"Don't worry," the man said, rising, switching to Hausa. "It's getting late." He extended his hand and Auwal took it. The man lingered, his baby-soft palms rousing in Auwal an awareness of how calloused his own were.

Still holding Auwal's hand, the man said, "My name na Emeka, Chief Emeka," and in that moment Auwal decided that he would never call him Emeka, would never grace him with the intimacy that a name bestows. Because he knew that this man would return, timid as a rat, half pouncing, half scuttling. He could see it in his easy friendliness. An Igbo man like him would have no reason to smile at you, Auwal thought, except he wanted something.

"Chief," he said. "I am Auwal."

He did return, Chief did. Not the next day, nor the day after. He returned a week later, when Auwal had forgotten all about him. Auwal's daughter, Aisha, had just resumed school, the private nursery school Maryam had picked out, its colorful walls painted with ABCs and fruits and animals, a school where the teachers taught in English, and to mitigate the expense of her textbooks, workbooks, socks, and sandals— everything she said she needed, he bought—he'd been opening the shop early and staying late. He knew the humiliation of lack, of wearing old, stitched-up school uniforms, knew the hunger for the industrial smell of new textbooks, for their smooth glossiness. That hunger had ruled his childhood, so that even though he owned his small store, his dream was to own a huge one that sold almost everything, a store that would be the heart of Brigade; soon, he would start doing trips to Cotonou for cheaper goods.

Chief returned smiling, bustling with unwarranted explanations—he'd had to travel suddenly, he said. He came bearing gifts: "I bought this shoe for fifty thousand naira! Can you believe it?" He laughed, settled onto the bench with a casual familiarity. "I brought it home and my woman said it looks like a boat. A boat! What does she know?" He shrugged. His eyes gleamed with contentment, a blind contentment. How could he not see that his presence here was like a rope around the neck, tightening, tightening? Auwal was wary of what this attention meant and wary of what his response might be, he had a life now, a life he loved and was working hard to make better.

"You can have it," Chief said. "There is a perfume in the bag, too. It smells really nice."

He came every other night, making his visits later and later, when fewer people came into the store. He sat on that bench and talked, speaking Hausa, and Auwal was surprised and flattered in spite of himself, he'd not expected Hausa to be, for this man, a language of tenderness, he'd expected it to be a language for business, a language to be used and discarded and reused. Every night, before Chief left the shop, he bought provisions worth more than what Auwal sold all week, and Auwal wondered what he told his wife when he returned home all those nights, bearing the same things he had bought only a night before. Auwal imagined that on his way home he flung the provisions out his car window, he seemed like that sort of man, ebullient and careless, a man whose path flowed with the oil of abundance.

He told Maryam about Chief, that there was a man who came in every other night and chatted with him and bought things. "He seems nice," she said. She'd just placed a tray of tuwo shinkafa on the mat. She sat beside him, Aisha seated across from them, her baby doll in her hand. To her, Maryam said, "Put that away and wash your hands," and to Auwal, "Is he trying to do business with you or something?"

"If he intends to do that," Auwal said, "he's not made a move yet."

Maryam nodded. "You should probably ask him what he wants, don't you think? Someone doesn't just drive from Sabon Gari to

Brigade almost every night for nothing."

"It seems like a rude thing to ask a man," he said. "'Why are you being friendly to me?'"

"Why are you overthinking it?" She frowned. "It seems like a very sensible question."

And so a night came when Chief stayed his longest and talked about everything, from football to business to children. They spoke in Hausa, and the more Chief came to know about Auwal in that language, the more Auwal wanted to share. Auwal told him that he was ready to have a second baby with Maryam, especially now that he would be traveling often for business. "She go need small man or woman to play with, I lie?" And he laughed for no reason, and Chief said, "I dey imagine the thing you dey carry do am. E go fat like yam."

Auwal paused before saying, "E big pass yam," grinning and looking directly at Chief, he was both scared and curious, and Chief must have seen this because he stood up and shut the doors. The noises of the road had stilled, darkness thickened, fewer people in the street. Chief knelt in front of him. Auwal's chest heaved. Because even though he could easily squash this man between his palms, something existed between them that leaned heavily on Chief's side, a beam of power. He sat there, saying nothing, spreading his legs when Chief caressed his knees and thighs, his dick hard as a tree in his jeans. Chief unzipped his trousers, gasped "Odogwu," and Auwal asked, "What does that mean?"

"It means you're *the man*," Chief said before lowering his head and wrapping his lips around Auwal's dick, making him gasp. At first Auwal closed his eyes, but soon opened them. He stared down at Chief, his bobbing head, the frenzied movement of his right hand as he stroked himself, the hunger and dissolute need in his eyes whenever he looked up at Auwal, the mere fact of him kneeling there on that rough floor, this man who smelled and looked like money: it all filled Auwal with a wonderful feeling of power.

———

Auwal felt a watery helplessness after that first night with Chief, and to feel alive again he reached for Maryam with a ferocity devoid of desire, a ferocity that terrified him and made him desperate. There was nothing pleasing in his movements, he wanted to take her somewhere, and the fact that he could gave him a small and simple assurance. After he slipped away, he lay on his back with his face to the ceiling, her hair pricking his arm, her breathing light as the evening breeze. It was especially hot that night, there hadn't been electricity in days, and he could make out their belongings hanging around in corners, like indistinct specters waiting to unfurl. Their entire life packed into that tiny space. He swiped at a mosquito buzzing in his ear, twirled his drenched shirt in rapid-flying circles around Maryam, like a fan, the sweat pouring out of her body was warm and smelled faintly of soap and powder. Chief had smelled of something foreign and sweet, like a sugary fruit dipped in expensive alcohol.

The thought jolted him, and he left the bed and stooped beside his daughter's mat. The windows were open to let in some breeze, but the heat from the day's sun seemed trapped in the air. The moon sprayed silver light on Aisha's face. He felt her to make sure she had not wet herself, caressed her hair. Her face was dark and peaceful, and he wanted so much to gather her up into his arms and hold her close and smell her hair, which Maryam took care to oil and comb, and be made whole by her innocence. Having her was the biggest miracle of his life; everything she did made him quiver with love, her smile, the excited voice in which she recited her three-letter words, the way she gripped his finger even in sleep.

The next night, when Chief lingered, Auwal began closing the shop early. "My pikin and my wife dey wait for me," he said, his eyes averted. "E don late."

"I go drop you," Chief said, and he stood from the bench outside and walked into the shop and embraced Auwal, holding him long. His head stopped just below Auwal's chin, and Auwal was overpowered by that scent.

"No, Chief," he said, extricating himself from his hold. "This thing no good, Chief. I marry, you marry. We get small children."

Chief looked at his face, arms still wrapped around him, but loosely. "Auwal," he said, his eyes burning with reprimand. "Stop acting childish."

"Toh, let me be childish, kana ji ko? Let me be childish. Just leave me alone, haba mana." He hadn't meant to raise his voice but there it was: one moment he was flailing, without hope of being collected, and the next he was collecting himself and acting.

Chief stepped back, his face struck by the deflation of the rejected. And then he straightened up, his eyebrow rising to a supercilious arch, his eyes burning with disdain. Auwal had seen that look before, on buses full of traders, and at the market when he accidentally ran into an Igbo woman and she turned around and glowered at him. For a moment he feared that Chief would follow it with one of those insults, said in Igbo, that were particularly hurtful because he did not know what they meant. But Chief said nothing as he turned around to walk away. Watching him go, Auwal felt a slender pang of sadness, and he knew that the end had come too late, that something in him had already come alive.

He walked home that night, even though it was still early and he could have easily found a keke. He walked to feel the wind on his face, to be drenched in air. But there was barely any air in Brigade. On every street corner, crowds huddled together, so that the roads became a forest of white kaftans and jallabiya. People lay on mats in front of walled kulle, houses so sleek and shiny and gigantic, they seemed to stand in mockery of the many tiny houses surrounding them. One of the big kulle had forgone walls for a netlike fence, a fence crawling with red flowers. In the evening light, the house seemed to bleed. He imagined that Chief lived in a house like this, perhaps somewhere in Sabon Gari. It occurred to him, then, that he knew so little about this man. He didn't even know where he lived. He kicked a stone, small particles of dust rising to circle and kiss his feet. Continued kicking it down the street.

A group of boys stood at the bend leading into his street, smoking and talking in loud raspy voices. They quieted as he approached, watched him with lazily aggressive eyes. "Sannunku!" he called out with a learned familiarity reserved for alleys and street corners. "Ina wuni!" they hailed back. He longed for Kura, for winding paths choked by trees, for acres and acres of cornstalks, for solitude. In Kura, solitude had seemed like imprisonment, something to flee. In Brigade it was a luxury, afforded only by the wealthy in their walled houses.

At the gate, Aisha greeted him. "Yar Baba," he said, hoisting her into his arms; he threw her up and caught her, threw her up and caught her, her shrill laughter smashing the rock in his chest. When had he last seen her awake? Ever since he began closing the shop late, she was usually already asleep when he returned home, and when he woke in the morning, sunlight filling the window, the house would be quiet, Maryam already at the junction where she sold fries to early risers, and Aisha already at school. He carried her into the house. Maryam was squatting over a small mortar, her arms shaking with the intensity of grinding. He greeted her, "Salamu Alaikum," and it felt to him like an invocation. She stood up and took the bag he was holding. "Wa'alaikumusaalam," she said and smiled. He wanted to kiss her but Aisha was standing right there, distracted by the bag Maryam had taken from him but there nonetheless. He looked around. A single lamp stood in the middle of the room, its golden light dull. Only a few more months, he thought, and he would be able to get his goods cheap from Cotonou, and then he could afford a two-room apartment.

"Did your friend the Chief tell you what he wants yet?" Maryam asked as Auwal took off his trousers. She draped a white cloth over the mortar, sat on the bed. Very early in the morning, she would make two walks to the junction, carrying the mortar, carrying pans, carrying Aisha. It often broke his heart to see her lift heavy loads. At twenty-one, she was supposed to be finishing university. He recalled the night he had promised to sponsor her through university. It was a year into their courtship. He'd just moved to Brigade at the time and was visiting

Kura for her graduation ceremony. She'd broken her school's JAMB examinations record, scoring higher than anyone in all the years the school had existed, and so was going to get an award. The eve of the ceremony, she sneaked out of her parents' house to see him, she could not wait until daytime, she'd said, when they were allowed to see each other, and she definitely did not want to see him under the oppressive gaze of an aunty. At the primary school where they usually sneaked off to make out, she told him that she would not be going to university, that her father had decided that his limited resources were better spent sending her brothers to school instead. Auwal remembered that the crickets and toads seemed especially loud that night, that the moment she said, "My brothers don't even like school," she let her head fall onto his shoulder and began to cry. He put his arm around her shoulders. He would not let her dreams go to waste, he told her, how could her father not see that she was a star?

Now, when he watched her, he could not shake off the feeling that something essential had been squeezed out, could not stop blaming himself for it. Had he not been foolish in his optimism, he could have seen all the ways in which life could hinder a dream and so would not have given his word so easily, which, perhaps, would have made her fight harder for herself. He could have insisted that she go to university first, could have come to a deal with her father where they split the responsibility. He knew people who had done this. But he had not, partly because of fear: if he did not marry her right away, he'd thought, she would go to university and decide that she was too good for him. It was therefore safer to get married first. Now, though, they had Aisha, and school fees, and rent, and NEPA bills, and although they occasionally still talked about it, their plan to send her to university, she no longer spent the last hour before bed bent over a lamp, reading her old textbooks, keeping her brain awake, as she put it. It seemed she had folded her dream and tucked it at the bottom of her box, together with her certificates and medals and old photographs. Occasionally, she brought out those things and stared at them and caressed them, her demeanor charged with longing, and he imagined, in those moments, that she was mourning something lost and irreplaceable, that she hated him but did not know it yet.

"No, he did not come to the shop today," Auwal said, suddenly aware of her eyes on him. It was an easy lie, less chaotic than the one he would have to tell if she asked how the conversation around what Chief wanted had gone. The man was gone, that was all that mattered. Auwal could return to his life, this life, with its simple joys and its simple, uncomplicated sources of angst.

Chief returned a week after their fight, just as Auwal was closing the shop. He drove his black jeep right to the front of the shop, parked with a sighing of tires. He did not come into the shop but rested his back against his car, legs crossed, arms folded. Auwal felt a rush of gratitude. Chief was wearing a white dashiki. "You like?" he said, smiling, a pleased, self-mocking smile.

"E fit you," Auwal said.

"One of my customers, an Alhaji, threw a party today." He laughed, reached out and flicked something off Auwal's shirt. "Imagine a party without alcohol. Have you ever been drunk?"

Auwal closed his eyes, his heart heavy with memory. "It was not funny, wallahi." He walked around and got into the seat beside Chief. He caught an image of himself in the side mirror. His face was black, like soot, as were his lips, and his beard looked like an untended farmland, and his eyes did not look gentle but bore his loneliness and his anger. If he were a man like Chief, he would look for a man whose eyes were full of light and laughter, a man like Idris, and chase him to the ends of the world.

"Why me?" he asked, as Chief started the engine, as Chief's hand came to rest between his thighs.

"What?" His hand squeezed and caressed, and Auwal closed his eyes, his trousers tightening. The car eased onto the road, bobbing from the undulating cracks in the asphalt.

"Why you like me?"

Chief grunted and said nothing. He had managed to free Auwal from his zipper and was now stroking him, maneuvering the car with just one hand and just one eye. Watch the road, Auwal wanted to say, but Chief's hand on him felt like a warm bath. And he was having that feeling again, of sitting high up on a mountain and looking down at the world. It felt good, to be desired so, to be hungered for. All through their drive, Chief said nothing, except at the police checkpoint, where he tossed a fluffy blanket over Auwal's thighs, a blanket he reached for with a speed and ease too casual to be coincidental and said, "Cover it."

Lights barged in from both windows. Chief rolled down the windows, his face calm, revealing nothing. Auwal felt as though his heart would burst out of his chest—he was sure he'd be asked to take off the blanket. But there was something about the way Chief sat, something about the way his shoulders, his small shoulders, filled the backrest. Something about the way he looked up and said, "Sergeant!" as though he were friends with the men, even though they all knew who was boss. Cries of "Good evening, sir! Sorry about the light, sir!" and Chief zoomed off, his hand returning to its position on Auwal's groin.

The hotel in Sabon Gari was tall, at least ten stories, and seemed to be made entirely of shiny, glossy steel. It stood alone on a street corner, took up, in fact, the entire street corner. It was placed for privacy, Chief had said, but it roused in Auwal an image of a child forgotten on a playground. Chief spread his arms in a theatrical show of ownership— "My newest shop"—and Auwal thought how different Chief was, how he had slipped into a different persona. He was no longer the small, almost pathetic man who knelt on the dirty floor in Auwal's shop, fumbling in the darkness. He owned things, ran things, and when he walked into the lobby, bright and white with light, young men and women in orange shirts scattered in all directions, suddenly becoming busy. He walked with a swagger, Auwal beside him. He would never return here, Auwal thought, because of how out of place he felt, because of how the eyes that burned behind them as soon as they'd walked past felt hot with knowing, with sickened, hostile knowing. But he returned. Every other night. He returned to smoke by the window, naked, and listen to the city shake off its last flickers of life. The city was like a drunken man, it wobbled, garrulous and loud, and then a moment came when it tempered into a fitful somberness, slipping finally into a long, exhausted sleep. He loved it by that window on the top floor, had found that spot on the first night, when Chief brought out a cigarette and said, "You want?" and he thought, Why not? A ritual small and inconsequential. Watching the lights go out in all those windows, Auwal often imagined the bodies that came alive in the darkness, wondered if they burned with love. There was nothing loving in what he did with Chief. Every time their bodies came together, Auwal would reach out to grasp something intimate, but always it slipped away. In the beginning, he would lean in to kiss Chief, because it was what lovers did, but always Chief turned his face away, saying, "I don't like to kiss," so that Auwal was offered his neck, a neck he attacked with a sinking in his stomach and anger growing in his heart. This attack fired in Chief a wanton eagerness, so that his lips burst into loud obscene cries.

This is not the sort of surrender I long for, Auwal wanted to say. Outside the window tonight, a light precipitation fell, making the air soft. Auwal wanted to hold Chief, wanted to be held by him. If he moved away from the window and went to his phone on the dresser, he would see the five missed calls from Maryam—he had been counting— but he did not want to go home tonight and look her in the face and lie that he had been at the shop all along, or that he'd been hanging out with the other shop owners after closing.

"Auwal," Chief drawled, as though from a land of dreams. Auwal turned and faced him. He, too, was naked, was lying on the bed on his stomach, his chin propped up by his hands. He was staring at Auwal. A light of contentment shone on his face, and it made Auwal happy to think that he was the reason for this contentment.

"You know why I like you?" Chief said.

"Why?"

Chief smiled, his eyes traveling round Auwal's body, from his feet to his thighs, lingering on his dick, fluttering back up to his chest before settling on his face. "Because you be beast," he said, and Auwal thought how the edge in his voice could cut metal, how it cut him. "You"—he waved his hand in a motion that took in the totality of Auwal—"*You* be like wild animal." He laughed, a short offhand laugh. "And you dey fuck like wild animal."

Auwal stared at him, at the light dusting of hair on his back, at his face, his beard that looked soft and shiny black. "What do you mean, I be like wild animal?" he said.

Chief shrugged, as though he did not understand what Auwal was talking about and could not be bothered. He rolled off the bed and strode toward the bathroom, his hairless buttocks making small yo-yo movements. He was always that way, present but not quite, going from one phone call to another, forgetting Auwal. Auwal did not wait for Chief to return from the bathroom before snatching his clothes from the floor and the furniture, before slinking into them and leaving. He did not look at the receptionist, even though he could feel the boy's eyes on him, full of scorn and suspicion.

Outside the hotel, he stood for long minutes, watching the cars driving into the compound and the people spilling out of them, men with women who looked too young to be their wives and too clingy to be their daughters. A red jeep pulled in and a man in jeans and a white shirt jumped down, yawning and stretching. The car's other doors flung open, a boy emerging, as well as a woman in shorts, her face, though exhausted, shining with a simple beauty. And yet it was on the man that Auwal's eyes became glued, the man who had paused what he was doing, pulling out travel bags from the trunk, to squat and listen to what his son was saying. He threw his head back and laughed, a crystalline sound that made Auwal think of shattering glass. The boy looked confused, and then he burst into earsplitting wails. "Sorry, sorry," the man mouthed, looking chastened, pulling the boy to himself and rubbing his back. The woman stood there, smiling down at them, and Auwal felt something inside him leap, a small impersonal joy.

On his way home he thought of the man and his wife and their son. Where had they come from and where were they going? For how long had they been on the road? And then he thought of Chief, who looked nothing like the man, who dangled a promise before his eyes then withdrew, a reflection on a crystal-clear pool, there but not there.

It had begun to rain heavily, water splashing into the keke. Auwal wrapped his arms around himself, it was so cold. The sky was black and starless. He thought of a night in his childhood, when he was maybe sixteen. It involved Idris, as did every fond and every painful memory. A cold Friday after prayers, it was harmattan season, the wind rude and nefarious. If Auwal had not complained about the weather, Idris perhaps would not have driven his father's car to Sabon Gari to buy a bottle of Rémy Martin, which they drank in the car, passing the bottle, the windows rolled up and the speakers blaring the song of the season. They sang together, *No one be like you*, their heads getting lighter and lighter, their faces drawing closer and closer. They were happy the way only children knew how to be, without the shadow of tragedy. On their way back to Kura, Idris had had to pull over so that Auwal could vomit by the roadside. It had been late at night and they both had been afraid because the road wound through dense forest. "We will park at a motor park," Idris said, glancing at Auwal, after driving for a long time. "You can call your mother on my phone and tell her you're with me. Mine won't notice I'm gone." The breeze had turned icy, it seemed as though they were close to a great sea, but it was all trees and grass and night sounds. At the motor park, the car's lights turned off, the two of them nestled together in the back seat, Auwal thought for the first time, listening to Idris sleep, that he was in love.

———

When he got home, it was still raining. Maryam opened the door but stood in the doorway, blocking him. "Where have you been?" she said. "I've been calling your number."

"I was out with the men," he said.

She stared at him, something like disappointment in her demeanor. "You return home late, smelling of cigarette smoke and a strange perfume, and you don't even have the decency to be a little more creative with your lie." She paused, looked at him, her eyes, fierce and wet, glinting with a shrewd and wounded light. "It's not the Chief, is it? Tell me it is not the Chief."

The accusation startled him, partly because he'd not expected it but mostly because he did not know how much she was accusing him of. The family next door was watching a Hausa movie loudly, for which he was grateful, the sound of their television melding with the patter of rain. He shivered, from the cold and the wetness, from exhaustion and worry. "Can we talk about this later?" he said. "I am tired and cold, as you can see. And I'm hungry."

"There is nothing to eat," she said, moving out of the way. "Aisha had a *convulsion* this evening, that's why I was calling you. Aisha had a convulsion, it was so scary and I was calling you but you didn't answer. Something terrible could have happened to your child, Auwal, while you were doing whatever it is you do these days. Thank God for Baba Kabiru, who drove us to the clinic!"

Auwal stared at Aisha sleeping on the bed, swaddled in the white shawl they used when she was a baby. She must have asked specifically for it, she did so whenever she was ill or whenever they, for any reason, were being especially giving. He imagined Maryam rummaging through layers of clothing to dig the shawl out, imagined her confusion, her anger every time he failed to answer the phone. He touched Aisha's head, it was warm and sweaty, then took her hand gently in his.

"I'm sorry," he said to Maryam, who was still standing with her arms crossed by the door, now closed.

"Tell me," she said. "What is wrong? We promised not to keep anything from each other."

He remembered the first time he saw Maryam, during morning assembly in secondary school when she read the news. She was his junior at the time, and he was in love with Idris, and so he'd felt nothing but admiration for her, something close to worship. Idris used to tease him about it, He is such a fan, he once said to her. Many years later, and his admiration had not diminished. Before Chief, he'd been content with his life.

He could not tell her the truth, he knew, he could already see the ending: her shocked and disgusted face, her teary phone call to his mother, his eternal disgrace. "It's nothing you need to worry about," he said. "I'll do better, I promise."

That night, he dreamed of Idris. They were in Kura, on a hot, sunny afternoon, and a fight had just broken out on the field. Bala, a boy who hated Auwal with a virulence too sharp to be disaffected, who called him *dan daudu* every time his team lost to Auwal's, lay on his back on the ground while Idris sat on his chest, pouring sand into his mouth, the ultimate sign of defeat, of humiliation. Suddenly, they were no longer at Riga Field, suddenly Auwal was in his bed, while Idris sat in a chair facing the bed and fixed him with a long, unsettling gaze. Auwal woke with a pointed gasp, and for a moment he did not know where he was. Maryam woke up and, as though forgetting that she was angry at him, asked, over and over, if he was okay. She did not ask what the dream was about, but she sang to him. It was a song his mother used to sing to him whenever he was afraid, to ward off night spirits. She sang it, too, every time she massaged his scalp with coconut oil. As a kid, he'd had such luxuriant hair, an inappropriate crown on a boy's head. His mother took such pride in oiling and combing it. The other kids called him names, *na mata*, *dan daudu*, and they pulled at his hair, laughing when he lashed out at them. He never told his mother about the hair pulling and the names, because he sensed in her a need that surpassed any pain he felt. It had been, for as long as he could remember, just his mother and him. He knew who his father was—he passed the mansion painted entirely white every day on his way to school, sometimes his classmates would point and say, If your father lives there, why are you so poor? Is it because your mother is a whore?—but he had never spoken to the man, never spoken to his many half brothers and sisters, how could he when his father had denied him even before his birth? As a kid, he would sometimes wake up in the middle of the night to his mother's sniffling. One day, he promised himself, he would become something, a millionaire, and then nobody would ever treat him, nor anyone he loved, as nothing.

It was a dream he shared with Idris whenever they walked to the fountain on the outskirts of Kura. They would sit on a rock, watching the people who came to draw water from the stream, planning their getaway to Cotonou—"One day, it will happen," Idris often said, his voice solid with faith—Auwal totally forgetting that they were supposed to be fetching water for his mother. They would sit there until sundown, talking, Idris sometimes taking on the firmness of a teacher: "It's *beaucoup*, not *boo-coop*," and Auwal would repeat, *Boo-coop*, and they would laugh. "Will you go with your friend today?" Auwal's mother would ask. "Yes," he would say. "Then make sure you tidy up the house first." She used the other word for friend, *amini*, a word bursting with fondness and suggestion. When he thought of it now, it made him wonder.

The last time he ever saw Idris, the sky had been spread out and bare, starless but bright, flush with God's eternal presence. Idris, heady from the blunt he had been smoking, had blurted out, "Baba is sending me back to Cotonou."

Auwal had just taken the blunt from him and was about to take a puff, he was new at this and very slow and careful. "You are joking," he said, chuckling.

Idris shrugged, took the blunt back. His eyes were glazed and distant. Stop, Auwal wanted to say, but his heart had begun pounding. He hated it when Idris did this, treated something serious as though it were nothing. Auwal pressed his palms together, crushed his fingers. "Why is he sending you away?" he asked.

Idris threw his head back and blew out smoke. His left leg was crossed over the right and his body was a slender arch, a graceful arch. His shirt lay on the grass, breathing in the breeze. "Bala caught me with Ahmed, and he reported," he said, the smoke escaping from his lips and spiraling heavenward, an offering.

"Ahmed fucked you?"

Idris shrugged. "Don't sound so shocked. You fuck Ruqayat."

"She's a girl!"

Idris laughed, said something in French, shaking his head as he said, "Why does it matter? I didn't think you'd mind."

Auwal put his hands in his pockets to hide how much they were shaking but also to steady them, because they had begun to do the thing they did on a blustery Friday morning years ago, when he punched a boy for the first time and wouldn't stop punching until his teachers pried him off the boy's body. "When are you leaving?"

"Tomorrow, in the morning," Idris said.

At first Auwal said nothing, because this is what happens when one receives news of a death: the heart, like a spider, forms a web of denial to protect itself. Then he said, "First, you fuck another guy, and then you leave me."

"Don't be like that," Idris said. "Baba seized my phone but once I get a new one, I'll call your mother and you and I will talk all the time. Maybe you'll even have your own phone by then!"

Idris's words, said brightly, did nothing for Auwal. All he felt was the sting of abandonment. He knew exactly what would happen: Idris would make new friends, find a new boy to love, and forget all about him. He stood, picked up his shirt from the grass. Slung it over his shoulder. He did not touch the wheelbarrow full of jerricans of water, did not think of an explanation for his mother. He started walking home. Idris called out to him, his voice growing desperate with each distance gained. "Auwal, Auwal!" he called, and Auwal threw his ears to the wind, his heart welling. "Rabin raina," Idris called, their name for moments of reconciliation. Now, he turned around and, for a split second, saw Idris as the name declared, as half his soul.

"Don't ever call me that again," he said, his voice ringing in the thin clustering of trees. And then, to keep the tears from rolling down his eyes, he tightened his lips, reached deep for that cruelty that was at once familiar and strange, and spat: "Dan daudu!"

If he hadn't had the quarrel with Maryam, he would not have called Chief. He should have been on a bus to Lagos, on his way to Cotonou. But he'd fought with Maryam, and even though she sang to him after his dream, she refused to talk to him at daybreak.

And so the next day he called Chief and said that they needed to talk. He had never been the one to arrange a meeting, and it felt strange asking if they could meet. When Chief said, Sure, yes, it was after a pause. "Is everything okay?" he said to Auwal.

"Yes." Auwal pressed the phone to his ears. He could hear noises in the background, children crying, a woman's voice scolding. Chief said something, and it took Auwal a moment to realize that he wasn't talking to him, that he couldn't have been talking to him in Igbo. Auwal drew in air, steeling himself. He said, "Please we no meet for hotel."

"Why?" Chief asked. He seemed distracted, detached, but the question was pointed, the tone of a man who felt entitled to something, to everything.

"Because we must to talk." Auwal shuffled his feet, he felt a mild exasperation. He spoke English, decidedly, because to slip into Hausa would be to slip into a language that had become, for them, a language of fondness. "We meet for open place. You know somewhere?"

Auwal knew what he would say when they met, had examined the words and stacked them neatly in his head. He had rehearsed, also, his countenance, grim but not too grim, and hard, if need be. This thing happening between them had run its course, he would say.

But when he got there, he was thrown into confusion by the presence of a third party. A tall, light-skinned boy whose face he kept glancing at until a picture formed in his memory: the boy who sat behind the reception desk at the hotel. He seemed different here, in a deserted bar on a quiet street, a bottle of Heineken open before him. He was taller and broad shouldered. He couldn't be more than nineteen, although his eyes were already shrewd with something resembling worldly wise knowledge. He had acknowledged Auwal's presence with a nod and a handshake, now his attention was on his phone, his fingers busy. He had clean fingers and a face so handsome, it seemed unreal, as though God had taken care to sculpt every inch of it. Auwal felt ashamed when he imagined what the boy looked like under his shirt and shorts. The clarity of his imagination jarred him, it was obscene and naked, and he felt as though the others had seen it.

"Aisha had a convulsion last night," he said, to redeem himself, and then felt a twitch of shame.

"Was that why you left without telling me?" Chief said.

Auwal shook his head, sipped his Coke. He did not want to have that other conversation. He was grateful when Chief nodded absently and said something to the boy, whose name Auwal now knew to be Chima. Auwal had watched the subtle movements between them, had read their bodies for signs of something intimate. He had seen none. He watched Chief now, he was speaking in Igbo, his voice soft. He was begging. Auwal noticed, for the first time, how old Chief was, freckles of graying hair that he tried to hide by being completely bald clinging to the sides of his head like thin white dust. Once in a while, Chima nodded or grunted something, but his eyes hardly left his phone. At one point he sounded angry. "I've told you, this man, I'll do it when I'm ready," he said, and then said something else in Igbo, a string of words tossed as though to a child, his voice like an echo from the depths of a well. Chief glanced quickly at Auwal. "Biko," he said, to Chima, which Auwal knew meant *please*. Chima stood up, typing lazily into his phone and then slipping it into his pocket. He extended his hand and shook Auwal's, but he said nothing as he walked away. Auwal wanted to walk up to him and make a joke, to disassociate himself from Chief, and to show Chima that they were alike.

"Give me a minute," Chief said, rising.

Auwal nodded, pulled out his phone to see if Maryam had texted him. When they quarreled, which was not often, she often reconciled by texting him a short list of household things she would love him to get on his way home. There was none today.

Chief stayed outside for a long time, almost fifteen minutes, before returning to the bar. He plopped down into his seat and covered his face with his hands. "Bring your daughter to the hotel tomorrow morning," he said. "I'll call my doctor."

Auwal nodded, surprised yet pleased by the offer, muttered his thanks. Chief was still not looking at him. "I wan' tell you something," Auwal said, slipping into English. Chief looked up briefly, nodded, and Auwal saw pain and sadness in his eyes. To continue would be an act of cruelty, and so when Chief asked if they could leave, Auwal joined him in the car, even though he knew he shouldn't.

Chief drove slower than usual. Auwal was sure they were driving to the hotel, had already accepted the implications, but Chief parked under a tree a few streets away. The tree was large for a dogonyaro, its branches stretching out to form a canopy over the thin road. He left the engine running, placed his head on the steering wheel, his shoulders shaking.

Auwal felt a small panic. He placed his hand on Chief's back. He did not know if that was enough, wondered what would be enough. For weeks he had longed for this closeness. "Ina sauraran ka," he said. It was almost like that evening with Idris when they had cuddled to fight the cold.

"After everything I did for that kid," Chief said, the steering wheel muffling his voice. He shook his head. "I practically do everything for his family. Because of him." His voice thickened, like a bat or an assault rifle: "The ingrate."

He quieted, and Auwal heard the tree sigh under the breeze. He looked out and marveled anew at its branches, so immense they made him think of God. He was still rubbing Chief's back, even though there wasn't a need for it anymore. He sensed Chief's story was over, a short-lived lamentation rather than a story, but Auwal was waiting for something else, a resolution. When Chief straightened up, Auwal moved his eyes away, embarrassed at his happiness.

"I am not from Cotonou," he said without even deciding to say it.

"I know," Chief said, leaning close to kiss him.

The day was perfect before it shattered. First, morning, the sky unsure of its disposition, vacillating between gloominess and glaring brightness. Auwal stood in the hotel's lounge with Maryam and Aisha. Chief squatted in front of Aisha, asking her questions about school. Aisha, shy, hid her face behind Maryam's hijab, peeking out at Chief, smiling as she responded to his questions. Chief said, "Wise girl," and patted her head, and then looking up at Auwal and Maryam, said, "She's so intelligent. And well mannered."

"Oh, you don't want to see her throwing a tantrum," Maryam said, smiling politely.

The previous night, when Auwal told her that Chief had offered to take Aisha to his doctor, she'd relented—she still was not talking to him after their quarrel—before saying, "He's being so nice," in a tone and with a look on her face that suggested she did not trust this niceness, and for a second he fretted that she was on to him, and so did not pursue the conversation. But as they lay in bed later, she turned and turned until he sat up and asked what the problem was. She did not know the man, she said, but Lord knew Aisha needed a real checkup at a real hospital.

"You should come along," he said, a terrible idea, but he was willing to pretend. He was not new to pretense. Wasn't his entire life a play, and hadn't he put on, so far, a stellar performance? He had picked this life and sworn to be very good at it because there was no reward in loving boys, he'd concluded the evening Idris had told him he was leaving, it made you the most hated person in the world, and for what? Heartache, betrayal. Since Aisha's convulsion, the feeling had been growing in him that he was terrible at this, but how could that be true if Aisha got to see a good doctor because of Chief? Even Maryam would see it for herself, he thought, the usefulness of his association.

Chief said, "One of these days our kids should go out together." He took Aisha's hand. "You'd love to go to amusement park, wouldn't you?" Together, they walked toward the door, Maryam and Auwal following behind.

"You see?" Auwal said, trying to read Maryam's face. "He's not bad at all."

"I appreciate what he's doing for us," Maryam said, her tone too even to be interpreted. Auwal looked ahead at Chief, who looked boyish in blue shorts and brown sandals and a blue cap.

The hospital was a few streets away and smelled clean, unlike the clinic in Brigade, whose corridors were always crowded with people coughing. Chief's doctor held Aisha's hands and talked to her as though they were friends, and she did not immediately burst into tears the way she usually did when she saw a person in a lab coat. After they left the hospital, having ascertained that all was well, Auwal took Maryam and Aisha to FanMilk. They sat alone in a corner, the place deserted at this time of day, scooping ice cream from rectangular bowls. "Baba, can we come here every day?" Aisha asked suddenly, and there was a pause before Maryam laughed. Auwal laughed too, said, "Not every day, yar Baba. But we will return, inshallah."

That evening, he returned to the hotel, took the elevator to the last floor, marveling afresh at the magic of floating up unencumbered, at the plush red rug in the hallway when he stepped out. He had not been to his shop all day, and it did not bother him. He knocked, three gentle raps. When the door opened, it was Chima. "Yes?" he said, his eyes hard and unfriendly. He was leaning against the doorframe, one hand on his waist, his shirt buttons undone. "Yes?" he said again.

Auwal looked past him into the room. All he could see was whiteness, the walls, the sheets, the blinds. "Where Chief?" he said and looked Chima boldy in the eyes.

A moment dark with hostility passed between them. And then Chima laughed.

Chief's voice called from within, "Who's there?"

"Comot for my road," Chima said, almost brushing Auwal with his shoulder as he walked into the hallway toward the elevators.

In the room, Chief, seated on the bed, said, "I did not call you." He walked toward a table. He was wearing white briefs, he had to be the only man who still wore briefs, his singlet draped on his shoulder. He poured himself a drink, gulped it down, standing there by the table with his back to Auwal, poured himself another glass.

"That boy wan' kill me with fuck," he said, chuckling. His hands shivered, as though from the memory. "Do you know how many years this guy kept promising that we'll do it and then refusing?" He gulped down his drink, his eyes watering, and sat on the edge of the bed, his head just below Auwal's belt.

"You kiss him?" Auwal said.

Chief looked up, arched an eyebrow. "What?"

"Did. You. Kiss. Him?" Auwal, angry, had slipped into Hausa, English too unreal for his surge of feelings.

"Of course!" Chief looked exasperated. He stood up, walked to the table, and retrieved an envelope from the drawer. "Sixty thousand," he said, holding out the envelope to Auwal, and then, "It should be more than enough." Auwal had never heard him speak English the way he did now, slowly and clearly. It felt cold. "I can also introduce you to my friends," he added, grinning, the envelope held between them.

Auwal stared at the envelope without reaching for it. He thought of Maryam, what this arrangement could mean. He thought of the house just down the street from their current one, it had two rooms and a toilet inside and cost eighty thousand a year, thought of his mother in Kura whose arthritis was getting worse.

"I want you," he said, recoiling from Chief's outstretched arm.

Chief looked shocked, then amused. He stood so close now, Auwal could smell the drink on his breath. He unbuckled Auwal's belt, pushed

Auwal's trousers to his knees, and slipped his hand into his boxers. "You're a beast in bed, I no go lie." A chuckle. "You sweet, all your people sweet, but—"

"All my people sweet?"

Chief shrugged.

Auwal shoved Chief onto the bed, then lay on top of him, pinning him down and grinding against him. "Did he fuck you like this?"

Chief gasped, his body acquiescing.

"Fuck you," Auwal said.

For a moment, Chief lay there. And then he rolled off the bed, straightened himself with a haughty dignity, looked Auwal in the eyes, and said, "You are a fool." And then, "Ewu Hausa."

It was not so much the words as it was the force behind them— Auwal felt pummeled, blinded. This is not how this ends, he thought as he sank onto the floor. He began to cry.

"You have to leave now," Chief said.

He took the stairs. The lobby was deserted. Even the receptionist's desk was empty.

He walked into the road, past the tree under which, only an evening ago, he had felt the utmost happiness. He turned on to a quiet street. A dog stood by a heap of refuse, its nose buried in the pile. As Auwal approached, the dog halted, then lifted its head to contemplate the man ascending the sloping road. Slowly, it lowered its head, apparently deciding that Auwal posed no threat.

A great wind swirled toward him, blowing bits of paper and polythene off the rubbish heap, stirring dust, the darkness suddenly alive with things that spiraled toward his face, particles that flew into his eyes. It reminded him of the morning Idris was to leave for Cotonou, how windy it was as he ran to Idris's house to say goodbye, Idris's brother saying, "He just left, if you look, you'll even see the dust rising from Baba's car driving away."

HAPPY IS A DOING WORD

I.   They were ten when the plane crashed. Binyelum saw the blackened remains in his father's *Sunday Times*, they always read the Sunday paper together, passing pages between each other. Just look at this rubbish, his father would say, frowning at yet another headline about Hisbah ("Kano State's Hisbah Cracks Down on Private Schools, Enforcing New Hijab Rule," one headline had said), or, Sharp observation, my boy, which made Binyelum's head swell. The day of the crash, his father did not sift through the pages, deciding which he wanted to read first before sharing with Binyelum; he went straight to the page with the story, shaking his head as he read, muttering under his breath. Binyelum leaned against him, reading at the same time, the way he used to do when, littler, he would sit between his father's legs, asking what this or that word meant, how this or that word was pronounced. This is tragic, his father said, turning to him. Later, Binyelum ran to Somadina's house, waving the paper and saying, Look! It was evening, the sun, huge and yellow, rolling into the belly of the sky. Somadina followed him outside, to the dogonyaro tree across their yard under which they often sat, watching birds. Binyelum caressed the pictures, his eyes like a dreamer's. One day, he said, he too would fly, and he would not fall.

Binyelum and Somadina and the other neighborhood children used to sit under this tree and sing to the birds—*Chekeleke, give me one white finger*, they screamed skyward. Every evening, the birds erupted in noise as though, having returned from wherever they had traveled since morning, they could not wait to regale one another with stories about their day. Binyelum believed that he could tell each one apart, and he gave them names even though Somadina told him this was impossible: there were just too many, and they all looked the same, clear white feathers, pale yellow beaks, and long broomstick legs. See, Binyelum said, Sarah had a way of flapping her wings, like a thing about to reveal itself, regal and wild, but Rose was timid and loved the branch hanging close to Baba Ali's fence. That made no sense, Somadina said, and they fought, sometimes with silence, a few times with their bodies, rolling in the sand, over dead leaves, pulling at each other's shirts. By morning, they were friends again, playing catch, watching the birds.

But this was before. Before the plane fell from the sky. Before all Binyelum wanted to talk about was how he would be a pilot when he grew up. Before Hisbah seized the truck full of alcohol and ruined his father's business. Before the evening when, after playing ball, the boys formed a circle around him and he took down his shorts to show them he'd begun growing hair down there. They were all a little shy, until Nnamdi, who was the most senior, said, You be man now o, you fit give woman belle. Binyelum, no longer shy but proud, glanced at Somadina and smiled, as if to say, You see? The next day, they both climbed the short fence into Baba Ali's compound again and went into one of the discarded old cars littering the yard. It seemed ages ago, and not only yesterday, that they used to have their bath together outside, under the eyes of the entire world.

They returned there most days after school, making up excuses to wander off from the company of the other boys. Baba Ali's was the perfect spot, that yard with the dark, quiet house whose windows seemed permanently shut to the world. Baba Ali was never in town, and there was no wife cooking dinner in the corridors, no kids running around under the mango tree with branches that stretched to the dogonyaro tree outside, forming a vast canopy for all those abandoned cars. Who taught them to hide? They never wondered. They were only curious fingers in the mild dark. You like it? Somadina said, not in the voice that he would use with the girls and women years away, he'd not yet learned to treat pleasing someone else as an act that affirmed his power over them. He asked because he wanted to know, and Binyelum said yes, and it was not a performance of surrender at all; this was not a game of owning and being owned, not yet.

Had they been older, and cannier, had their minds been tainted early by the world's caprices, like the mind of a boy like Nnamdi, orphaned at three and passed around from one close relative to another distant one, they would have known how suspect they looked, two boys abandoning the gang almost every evening and wandering off on their own. But they knew nothing about the shrewd, untrusting nature of the world. And so there they were, alone in each other's company, shorts pulled down to their ankles, and suddenly there was sound, and light, and they were no longer alone: they lay there, awkwardly, all around them eyes gawking. I tell you, Nnamdi said, turning to the other boys, smug and knowing. They all stood there in silence, Nnamdi smirking still, and maybe it was that smirk that made Binyelum start begging. Abeg, he said, abeg no report us. Somadina looked from his crumpled face to Nnamdi's smug one, and to the wondering faces of a dozen sweaty, grimy boys, and it dawned on him how much trouble they must be in for Binyelum to plead that way. He, too, began to beg.

For days, Nnamdi hounded them like a potent cloud, taking their break money, sending them on errands, making them race each other so that he could see who the man was and who the woman. One evening, he pulled them aside and made them scale the fence. There were five of them, two other boys whom he'd brought along to look out, and this would become Binyelum's second lesson in growing up, having already learned shame the evening they were found: to always watch his back. Pull your knicker, Nnamdi said, and they both stood there and gaped at him, confused, until he frowned and said, Quick. Good, he said, now do that thing wey una dey do before.

In the same back seat as the first evening, it did not feel the same, did not retain that thrill of discovering something sweet. Binyelum looked down, crying. I no tell you to stop, Nnamdi said from his view in the front seat, and now Binyelum's crying made his body shake, and it made Somadina incredibly sad, he too began to cry. They disengaged, and no matter how many threats Nnamdi barked at them—I go tell your mother, I go report to your class teacher—they did not return to each other, did not look at each other, could not.

That night, Binyelum's mother brought out the belt she hid in the same trunk in which she locked her most expensive lace and Georges and Hollandais. Your body will tell you today, she said, as she whipped him on his back, his buttocks, his legs. She'd never beat him, nor his sisters, like that; in the past, she'd ask them to stretch their hand and spread their palm open, and it had been better because he could close his eyes and anticipate the sting, count the rest before the belt came down, one, two, three. This time, she flogged him all over, chanting that his body would tell him. He could hear his sisters crying in the other room. When his father returned, he woke Binyelum up and they sat together in the living room, the girls asleep on mats spread out on the floor, saying nothing, his father's head bowed for what seemed like eternity, his bald spot round and gleaming like the moon. Finally, he lifted his head. You are a man, he said, calmly, shaking his head— you are a man, Binyelum, my son. Binyelum sat there and cried: it was the strangeness in his father's voice, as though he could no longer recognize the boy with whom he read the papers on Sundays, swapping pages, laughing over the cartoons, solving puzzles, as though Binyelum had intentionally misled him all those years and now that he'd been exposed, there was nothing else to feel but crushing disappointment.

Somadina, on the other hand, went out and came in, not quite like before, but almost. When Nnamdi came to Somadina's house with the news, his aunt, Mma Lotanna, was there. And why are you only telling us this? she said. She spoke Igbo to Nnamdi, persistently, even though he responded in pidgin, and she stared him down with a fierceness. Somadina stood in a corner, watching. The next morning, smug and bouncy with triumph, he waited by the gate to tell Binyelum what had happened. How he told his mother about Nnamdi, about the back seat of the car in Baba Ali's compound. How, seething, his mother said, I si gini? You say he made you do what? How Nnamdi stuttered, then fled the room. How after she opened her Bible and showed him the wrong in what they had both done, she'd bought him ice cream. He waited until he almost missed the school bus, until his mother came outside and asked what he was still doing there.

At school, Binyelum stayed far away, as though Somadina had a smell about him, and the next morning Binyelum walked past him on his way to the bus stop, and no matter how fast Somadina walked, he never caught up with him, and no matter how hard he called, Binyelum never turned.

II.   The Christmas Baba Ali returned home with a woman, they were teenagers, seniors in secondary school. Somadina's father had gotten a job with AP Oil, and they had moved to a nicer house on a quiet street far away from Sabon Gari, a street where the taps spat clean water and the boys were gentle—that was how Somadina's mother had put it, *where the boys were gentle.* Somadina liked a girl in his class, Kamara, who was always beating him at physics and maths, and Binyelum continued to play on the same field, with mostly the same boys. He'd let Dave, a boy from school, suck his dick a couple of times, always at Dave's house when his parents were at work, the doors bolted shut, the curtains drawn, an awkwardness between them. Outside the walls of that house, they did not speak to each other, did not act like they had ever spoken to each other.

Baba Ali's new woman stayed, night after night, month after month. She set up a light-yellow kiosk under the dogonyaro tree. MTN,

Everywhere You Go, it said on the body of the light-yellow kiosk from which she sold recharge cards and milk and soap and egg rolls that were soft and sweet, and when the children congregated under the tree to sing to the birds, she shooed them away, the children; in the mornings and afternoons and evenings, women gathered there, talking, laughing, sometimes quarreling loudly, so that people rushed out of their compounds to gawk at them and point fingers. Baba Ali became a face that people saw every day, standing under the electric pole with the fathers and bachelors, a lean, clean-shaven man in the whitest singlet talking politics and football and smiling at the children as they walked to school.

It was Saturday morning, and the husbands had played a football match against the bachelors. Binyelum's father returned home, flopped down on the couch, his red Arsenal jersey around his neck like a towel, his round hairy stomach glistening with sweat. Binyelum got him a cup of water, which he gulped down, Adam's apple rippling.

Binyelum returned to his phone, Dave had texted, *come to the church*. He'd recently started attending choir practice with Dave. Last week, in the parish's bathroom, which smelled of Izal, he had been more worried that they were doing this in the house of God than he was about the fact that Dave was kneeling on the bathroom floor, on tiles that looked brownish with accumulated grime futilely scrubbed. It was one thing doing what they did at Dave's house with the windows and doors shut, there, it was secret and safe; in church, he felt the eyes of God on him, blazing with condemnation. Sometimes—especially on those nights when his father, cursing and staggering, had to lean on him to make it home, the entire street staring at them—he wondered if he was the cause of his family's misfortune, if his secret desires were too abominable for God's grace.

Before Hisbah seized the truck full of alcohol, ruining his father's business, his father's bar was the happening place. People went there for his special drink combos, and because whenever a dedicated customer asked for a brand of cognac they'd had on a business trip somewhere far away, he made real efforts to have such a drink in his next consignment. Whatever you call your business, son, his father used to say, be proud of it and aim to be great at it. After his goods were seized and destroyed, he became a silent person, sleeping all day and drinking all night. But something about Baba Ali's return had awakened him, making him join the men again at their football games and their early morning banter about the news.

I ma, his father said, looking out the door where the wind was lifting the yellow curtain. I was just there, looking at Baba Ali, e nekete m ya anya, and I hailed him, Odogwu!

Whenever his father got this way, he slipped into an elevated Igbo, untouched by English and garnished with the occasional proverb, the occasional unfamiliar word. Binyelum knew the story about Baba Ali. It had been whispered in the street ever since he was a child: how his wife had woken up one morning, dragged her bags outside, Baba Ali begging and crying behind her, how she'd gotten into a taxi and left. They had even made a song about it at one point, *Baba Ali, clean your eyes, no dey cry / Pluck mango from your big tree, chop life*, but the adults had scolded and whopped the song out of their mouths. Was he odogwu, Binyelum asked, because he brought home a woman?

His father looked at him, eyes yellow, sprinkles of gray hair on his chin and on his head, lines at the sides of his eyes; it struck Binyelum like a punch, his father was getting old. Baba Ali and his wife, Aina, had been very close, some people even said they were cousins—a detail he could not confirm, his father said—but love can do that to you. His father paused, eyes trained on the picture above Binyelum's head, a framed photo of his sister, Ngozi, standing behind a birthday cake with one candle in its middle. There was hardly a Sunday, his father continued, that they did not go to church dressed in matching clothes, hardly an evening that Baba Ali did not desert the men to go sit with Aina in the kitchen. Their life, already domed in joy, would have been perfect at the birth of their daughter, but they soon learned, after several illnesses, that she had sickle cell. They watched their child suffer, knowing that the suffering was a direct result of their love. After their daughter died, Aina left. The story went that she loved Baba Ali still but could not risk bringing another child into the world just to suffer, that Baba Ali had tried to convince her to stay, the two of them alone in their marriage, but, I guess, Binyelum's father said, face bright with contemplation, that not even they could survive the blow of such a tragedy.

He fell sick for months after, and we thought he might die. We had to rush him to the hospital one time because he could not move, had not eaten in days. Your mother and some other women had to care for him after he was discharged. And then he closed down his shop in Kano, which was doing very well, moving everything to Kaduna, to a branch that was only just starting out. But he kept the house, he'd lived there since he was a boy.

His father took a deep breath, released it slowly, his stomach rising and falling. You see, my son, he said, many people break after something like that, or they become bitter and hateful. But not Baba Ali, not the man I talked to and played ball with today, so eager for life. That is *something*.

Binyelum knew the story and all its embellishments, was used to his parents retelling tales with as much vitality as they'd told them the first time, but there was a solemness to the way his father told it this time, a tenacious optimism, that saddened him. His father was trying to motivate himself, he realized, by lifting Baba Ali as evidence of the possibility for life's restoration. Binyelum was not sure if he felt the same way, he'd begun recently to think that the forces of life were capricious and fickle; why, he wondered, did some people spend their lives struggling to scrape by while others wallowed in abundance?

At school, Dave had started to sit beside a boy, Somadina's cousin Lotanna, who seemed to have everything, staying back in class to talk to him at break time, holding his hand in the corridors. Dave's husband, their classmates teased him, but he laughed at the name, and soon everybody said it without accusation. Binyelum watched Lotanna talk to Dave, Dave's head thrown back in laugher—it annoyed him, how easy it was to fool people. Lotanna, polished in his school uniform that was always crisply ironed and in the way he spoke, without hurry, as though the whole world were his audience, and good as he was at playing midfield, at tennis and chess, and loved as he was by the teachers, was someone for whom trouble was glamorous and safe, someone for whom the world would bend.

Mma Lota, who was at the house most Sundays, came with the news that Baba Ali had died. When his mother poked her head into his room to tell him, Somadina looked up, grunted, and she said, What, it's my house, and sat at the foot of his bed, glancing at everything as though she wasn't in there every day.

You should come out and sit in the living room, she said.

Moving had been her idea, and though Somadina no longer hated her for it, he could not understand why she continued to be invested in gossip about their old street.

Did Somadina's mother know, Mma Lota said in the living room, that Baba Ali's new girlfriend left him as he fell sick? The poor man, had he not enough heartbreak, his mother lamented. May affliction not rise to us a second time.

I took food to him on Sundays, she continued. Mma Ayo did on Fridays, you know, small gestures here and there—it was the most anyone could do.

What happened to him? Somadina asked.

People say he had AIDS, his mother said. But you know how people like to make up stories. The poor man must have died of loneliness.

Loneliness does not kill people, Mummy, Somadina said, shaking his head.

She rolled her eyes at him. What do you know? You have not seen anything yet.

It had seemed, when they first moved out here, that he would never be able to breathe again. There were no boys his age playing football on the street, and his classmates spoke Hausa at break time, which he did not understand. He wanted to go back home, he'd told his parents. This is home now, they said. Now, though, he had friends who sat on the living room couch, on the floor, drinking Coke and eating chin-chin, playing PS and arguing in loud voices about *Merlin* or *Greek* or whether the guy in that video had actually put it in her ass; friends who thought his mum—the few times she'd dropped in from her shop to get something at home—was cool, the way she did not frown at them like most of their parents would have done.

And he had Kamara. His mother said of her to Mma Lota, She's a wonderful child, so smart and so mature, and the nnwa amaka. I did not know Somadina had big eyes like that.

Mummy! he said, raising a pillow above his head as though to throw it at her.

Kamara had only just started talking to him again. JAMB was around the corner, she'd been studying a lot and so hadn't gone with him to the party where he had a can of Star and large puffs of Faruk's blunt. When his friends dared him to kiss Mary, the only girl at the party, he did it. His friends cheered. When the bottle spun toward Mary, they dared her to take off her blouse, an earring, her skirt. No, she said.

It's the game, Faruk said. Don't ruin the fun. And then he said something else in Hausa, which made the other boys laugh.

The next day, Kamara showed up while he was shooting hoops and stood in the middle of the basketball court, arms crossed. Somadina walked toward her but she lifted her hand, halting him. Her friends appeared at the other end of the court, watching. Come on, he said, is all this necessary?

You tell me, she said.

I'm sorry—you want me to kneel down? 'Cos I will. He began to roll up his trousers to avoid staining them, but she said, Please don't embarrass me.

Binyelum scored 268 on JAMB, and his mother cooked his favorite, coconut rice, to celebrate, and his father was sober that evening, and they sat outside, shirtless in the heat, and talked aimlessly about things that had happened and things that were yet to come. With a score like that, his friends told him, he would surely get in somewhere. At the screening for the Defence Academy, Binyelum did not run into Somadina, and Somadina did not run into him. They took the written parts of the exam in the same hall, Somadina in front, Binyelum behind, the hall full of sixteen- and seventeen-year-olds in an assortment of school colors. Binyelum passed but did not get in. Ibadan released their list, and then Nsukka, and he was not on either.

It rained on the evening he got the *Daily Times* to look up Nsukka's list. He sat outside Mama Ayo's shop with the boys, heads huddled together, as they went through the names. Wait, is this the Somadina we know? someone said, pointing at a spot on the paper. They could not believe Binyelum had not gotten in, the boys said, and talked about how rigged it all was, patting his back, making encouraging speeches. It began to rain, the first rain of the year: it began with a whirlwind, dust rising and swirling, making everyone disperse, and then the sky poured down on everything. A neighbor brought out buckets and lined them under the roof. Binyelum watched from the window. Did she not know not to fetch the first rain? he wondered.

He got a job washing bottles at a pharmaceutical company a few blocks away, stopped attending choir practice. You have to understand, he thought of saying to Dave, but instead stopped picking up his calls. Dave showed up on his street for the first time ever, breaking an unspoken agreement. Wetin? he asked, putting on his harsh voice, aware of the guys' eyes on him. Nnamdi stood up. You hear the guy, he said, Who you dey find? Binyelum saw Dave's eyes, darting toward him, confused and a little brave, and looked away. Just go, he thought, just go. Binyelum, Dave said, but Binyelum simply glared at him—all those eyes, he thought, all those suspicious eyes.

Nnamdi laughed, putting his arms around Dave's shoulders. I just dey play with you, he said. See as you dey shake. Why you dey find my guy?

Choir practice, Dave said.

A week later, outside Baba Ali's compound, Binyelum and Nnamdi argued over Messi and Ronaldo, and everyone who asked could not believe that a boy like Binyelum, quiet and unproblematic, would throw the first punch. Day after day, his heart ached more, and he often had an urge to cry that could not be tied to anything in particular.

III.   Nobody believed it would happen in Kano, Somadina's father said over the phone, and yet here they were, in the middle of a curfew, the entire city still and uneasy, waiting to see if there would be another bomb. Binyelum called his mother and asked her to give the phone to his sisters. Don't go outside Sabon Gari, he said. Be careful. Distance made him helpless. His presence would do nothing real for them, he knew, but he could not shake off the feeling that if he were close, somehow he could keep them safe.

He missed them, that was what it was, a homesickness made urgent by worry. For a whole year he'd been away from home, in Lagos, serving Oga Lawrence. He had balked at the idea at first: learning a trade was for dull students and village boys with no hope of another way. But after three years of waiting, his JAMB score getting lower with each try, his friends getting into small schools in Katsina and Kogi, he had begun to feel useless. In the company of his friends, he felt unreal, nonexistent, as though life were not happening to him, even though all he could feel was its force: his father always reeking of alcohol, the talk of the neighborhood; his angst about never getting into the Defence Academy and becoming a pilot; his worry about his sisters.

In many ways, the apprenticeship was like being in school: after four years, he would be given a shop, goods, and some money to start up his own business. He could always go back to school, he would tell himself at night, lying exhausted on the mattress with the other first-year, Innocent, assailed by his scent, his snore, both of them shirtless, both of them sprawled under the insistent whir of the fan, their shorts rumpled, their thighs golden in the soft light of the appliances. The job was hard, it involved lots of walking under the sun, unloading trucks, sweet-talking often surly customers; it involved, for him and Innocent, starting the generator every evening, going to the main house to help Lady B in the kitchen, sneaking into the living room, spacious and high ceilinged, to peek at episodes of *Grey's Anatomy* or whatever Oga Lawrence's children had decided to watch, Lady B's voice raised in scolding—*useless bush rat!*—or little Mary-Ann saying no she would not move her legs so the boys could sweep the floor. Do you know that my smallest sister is older than you? Innocent said to her often. Binyelum liked him, his nightly smell of bitter lemon and fresh bath; his limbs, of a boy who had spent his childhood weeding and tilling; his accent, the *l*'s that rolled into *r*'s, so that *rubber* became *lubba* and *love* became *ruv*. There was a softness about him, though, that made Binyelum wary, a gentleness in contrast to his hard face, a way of moving and being that was too familiar for comfort.

Innocent, having served a former oga who in the end did not settle him, was always ready with advice. Nothing we say or see among ourselves gets back to Oga, he once said, but you never can tell when a Judas might appear, so don't join the other umu-boy in openly bad-mouthing him. The last thing you need is for Oga to get it in his head that you're disloyal, life can get very hard then.

Binyelum wondered how much harder it could get, he felt already like someone walking among broken glass, his life dreary—a necessity, he believed, *Growth flourishes in stillness*, he'd written in his notebook where recently he'd begun leaving himself reminders, goals, motivations—sometimes he imagined breaking Oga Lawrence's curfew, imagined getting on one of those hookup apps and finding someone to sneak into the boys' quarters, the way the seniors did with their girlfriends. You don't have to do everything Oga says, Innocent told him. There are ways around these rules. Binyelum listened eagerly but told himself that he would break no rules, he had huge plans and narrow options: he could not afford the cost of recklessness.

The bombs were followed by shootings: a sixteen-year-old boy seeing his friend off after a visit was shot and killed as they both stood at the junction, chatting. The men were driving an okada, the gunman in the passenger seat behind, the driver speeding away, cries of *Allahu Akbar* lacerating the night as they zoomed off, as the spared boy froze and then fell on his knees beside his friend. They must leave Kano, Somadina's mother said to him every time she called, they simply had to—but his father, his father was stubborn, talking all the time about his job, could Somadina believe it! That boy could easily have been you, she said, and then what would a job mean? What would it mean?

This is the first major fight my parents are having, he told Kamara, holding her. It was dark in the room, there was no power; they had left the windows and door open to let in some breeze, the night crackling with the noises of crickets and toads and with the occasional caw of a nameless bird. He pressed his lips to Kamara's hair, wet and smelling of shea butter. Funny, he thought, how fond he now was of a scent that used to nauseate him.

My parents argued all the time, she said. This one time, my mother threw a plate at my dad and it missed him and hit my little brother on the head.

He placed one hand on her breast and the other on her stomach, twirling his finger around her navel. We will never fight, he said.

She backed into him and he held her tighter. His father had been furious when he chose to go to Nsukka: Who chooses Nsukka over NDA, gbọ? Do you know how many phone calls I had to make to ensure they didn't dash someone else your spot? But Somadina did not care for NDA nor anything else for that matter, did not know what he wanted to do with his life. He was good at many things but perfect at none, liked many things but was passionate about none; he could go wherever the wind blew him but why should he, when he felt, with Kamara, such profound happiness, when he could simply follow her wherever she went?

Was he not tying her down? her friends had argued when they moved in together. Men were already knocking on her door, her parents' door, prosperous men, some of them handsome and nice too. Her mother introduced most of the men to her and she talked to them merely to satisfy her. Lying in Somadina's arms, she read their text messages aloud, and they laughed together at these desperate men and their outmoded ways. God, you're an expert at nonchalance, he said to her, this man basically says he cannot live without you and all you say is *aww*. After a while, they became serious, and he told her he loved her and this was it, the two of them together until death. Here was the plan, he said, here was the plan, she agreed: they would both get a job in Enugu after graduation, find a room at Ninth Mile, and then a flat; they would save up, get married, have two or three children, ideally more girls but boys would also make them happy, wouldn't they?

Sundays were for church and football. Oga Lawrence and Lady B did not approve of girlfriends, because to have a woman was to need money—for dates, and Valentine's Day, and birthdays, and shoes and handbags, and shawarma—and to need money was to steal from Oga Lawrence's business. That was, however, not the speech they gave after morning devotion. *Don't get a girl pregnant and derail your life*, they said instead.

Don't get a girl pregnant and derail your life, Innocent said as they walked back groggily to the boys' quarters, rolling his eyes. As if they care about us.

Binyelum laughed. In their room, he picked up his phone to find his father's missed calls. He called home every other evening, to speak to the guys, or to his mother and sisters, rarely ever to his father. You never call your old man, gbo, he said when Binyelum called back. He laughed and maybe if he hadn't the hurt wouldn't have stuck out so much, like a bone jutting out of torn skin, it made Binyelum queasy. Haba, Daddy, he said, and laughed, too, and then they both waited in silence.

Did you hear about Nnamdi? his father asked.

Yes, Binyelum said. He'd heard, from his friends back home, from his sisters, from his mother: a nine-year-old girl had named Nnamdi as the reason she was injured down there, and her father, a retired army man, had stormed the street in a vanload of soldiers, dragged Nnamdi into the middle of the street, and beaten him until his eyes were onion purple, and then thrown him into the back of the van and driven away.

A shameful thing, his father said.

A shameful thing, Binyelum agreed.

They waited, again, in silence.

How is work? his father said finally.

Binyelum gazed out the window, at the milky harmattan haze hovering over the conspiratorial cluster of roofs, at the people, bright in their Sunday jeans and gele and agbada, trudging up and down streets and alleyways, vibrant even in the cold, their noises—of laughter and greetings—rising and merging with the rumble and clatter of drums, with the brash songs and prayers blasting out of the speakers of the Mountain of Fire church down the road. It was so much like home, the riot of everything, the splattering of crumbling, brown-roof bungalows around that one compound ringed by flowers, the compound in which he now stood, looking out at all these people: Iya Ibeji, whose tomato-grinding machine made so much noise; Baba Bolu the police officer, Bolu who always accosted Binyelum and the boys on their way from the shop, chanting Broda mi until Innocent handed him his PSP for the evening. Binyelum wanted to be the person looking down at everything from the house ringed by flowers. He wanted to be the person who, when his sister texted him saying there was nothing to eat at home, didn't immediately fall into a hole of depression and helplessness. He wanted to be the person who told others when they could date and when they could not. The plush couches in Oga Lawrence and Lady B's living room, the huge TV that started from the floor and rose nearly to the ceiling, the endless rows of Cerelac and Indomie noodles for the kids, the crates of eggs, the cornflakes: he wanted to have all that, a life of ease and plenty. Downstairs, Innocent was washing Oga's car, whistling to Osadebe, his arms, his bare back shining with sweat. Binyelum wished he could stay home, skip church today, but Service was compulsory. If he were in Kano, he'd be seated outside Mama Ayo's shop after football training, staring idly at the churchgoers. How he missed having nothing to do.

For Easter, Oga Lawrence took the family to visit his brother in Ibadan, and Binyelum went with Innocent to his first Lagos club. Walking in, he was frightened by the mass of people—everybody was beautiful, or had mastered ways of making themselves appear so. He felt self-conscious in the ordinariness of his black T-shirt and blue jeans, but a few bottles of Heineken later, he was in the middle of the dance floor, bodies pressed together, people floating from one dance partner to another, it made him think of folks trying on clothes at a boutique. A woman wrapped her arms around his neck, twisting into him. She smelled of sweat and perfume and looked into his eyes as though she'd known him all her life and loved him with a sad, quaking love. He wondered what her story was.

Outside the club later, he stumbled into the street with Innocent, arms around each other's shoulders. It was past midnight. A car sped past them, men sticking their heads out of its windows, spraying the street with champagne and yelling, Na we get Lagos!

Your papa! Binyelum yelled back, then turned to Innocent, laughing.

You're wasted, my man, Innocent said, laughing too.

They got on the same okada, Innocent seated behind, his body warm against Binyelum's back. In their room at the boys' quarters, Binyelum collapsed on his mattress, his shoes still on, he felt sleepy yet wide awake.

Next time we go out, Innocent said, sitting at Binyelum's feet, I'm going to take you somewhere different.

Binyelum looked up at him.

He smiled. It's not as big and flashy, but I'm sure you'll find what you need there. At least you'll dance with someone you actually want to fuck.

Binyelum hesitated. Perhaps it was a ploy: get him drunk, ruin his life in the presence of everybody. But the silence felt heavy with potential. He sat up; slowly, he took off his shirt. They were now seated side by side. He hugged Innocent. How terribly he'd missed it, the warmth and solidity of a man's body. Innocent sat there, letting himself be hugged. What am I doing? Binyelum muttered, chuckling into his shoulder.

You've been alone too long, Innocent said, guiding Binyelum's head onto his lap where he cradled it like he would a sleeping child.

IV.   There were birds on the trees outside the Enugu Premier Secondary School where Kamara broke up with Somadina over the phone, and on the trees under which Binyelum stood, months after his settlement, scrolling through Facebook as he waited for his bus to arrive. Somadina sat on the bench outside the ash-and-oxblood building, head bent, hands covering it. To a passerby, he would look like a man suffering from a terrible headache. One moment a city is still, he thought, the next there are bombs; one day his father was stamping tickets for independent oil contractors, building a house in Enugu, another at the village—and the next he was struggling to get his tickets signed, could not finish his house in the village, peace giving way to strife.

And one moment, he was telling Kamara he loved her and she was saying she loved him too, and the next they were graduates and she had a dream job in Abuja and he had a shabby one in Enugu, a graduate of physics teaching mathematics to junior students and physics to seniors, and soon she was telling him, over the phone, that she wanted to start a family, could no longer wait, It's complicated, you have to understand, you have to understand. All those years, eight years, had those promises meant nothing to her even as she lay beside him? How could she, he wondered, how could she. The voices of students at play drifted toward him; watching them at break time, the junior boys and girls running after one another, dirtying their school uniforms, the seniors standing in corners, whispering, plotting, being dignified, he remembered his own secondary school days. Suddenly, it was all over, his years of carefreeness, it made him pity them. He felt it in his palms, the wetness, and squeezed his eyes shut to force it back in—what a sight he would be, a twenty-three-year-old man crying publicly, in the glare of the sun.

Finally home, Binyelum collapsed on his bed, exhausted. Today had not been his day: he'd woken up much later than usual, run after several buses before finding a seat and, at the shop, had lost a major sale to his neighbor. The elation he felt after his settlement had long since faded, now when he took the bus to work, he thought of the day ahead with hope and apprehension—would customers flock to his shop, he worried, or would he sit idly all day?—and on his way back, he thought only of his bed.

It was raining, and his room was dark and cold. He'd pulled the drapes; something about the street soaked in water, the rust-colored roofs dripping, people clutching umbrellas as they skirted around puddles—something about all this made him terribly homesick. Perhaps it was the ordinariness of rain, the way it subdued people anywhere and everywhere, so that the woman clutching an umbrella down the road would remind him of his mother rushing home in the rain, clutching her old yellow umbrella that said The Taste of Goodness.

His phone tinkled with a notification: *Somadina Obi Accepted Your Friend Request.* Scrolling through Facebook earlier as he'd waited for the bus, he'd come across Somadina's profile in his People You May Know. He went back on, looking at pictures. The face, bearded and grown, smiling teeth white against a face so black and smooth, not the boy he had known all those years ago, but boyish still, and familiar. Binyelum scrolled through the page, more pictures: with a girl in front of a water-spitting lion, his arm around her waist, her head on his shoulder. *My world*, the caption said.

He imagined messaging Somadina. He would be effusively familiar, *longest time, my gee*, he would say, and Somadina would respond as enthusiastically. He imagined their friendliness evolving into flirtation, that on the loneliest of nights, such as this, Somadina would say to him, I have been thinking of you all my life.

He chuckled to himself, how wild, his imagination. He messaged Innocent about a party they were planning, then went on WhatsApp, where his fuckbuddies were. *Wyd*, he typed to Yomi and Ferdinand, who lived closest to him. It still surprised him, the leeway they allowed him. He rarely ever texted them back outside of sex, and he lied to them all the time—I am an only child, he once said—lies that he told not to make himself appear in a striking light but to avoid being known, because to be known was to be invested. Sometimes, after they'd fucked, they would cling to him, and the slightest moment would present itself in which he wanted to hold them, too—and then he would feel only encroachment, the air suddenly too soft with feelings. He would hurry into his jeans and say, E go be, like he always did, and leave. In his apartment, he would wash his face in the bathroom sink, looking in the mirror, his hair spiky and tangled, his beard trimmed into a funnel, his eyes, red from smoking, looking back at him, saying, *Who is this stranger, who is this man?* Twisting the faucet, he would lower his head again, cup his palms under his face, cold water hitting him. Every day he lived, he felt less like himself. Growth, people called it; he thought of it as estrangement.

WHERE THE HEART SLEEPS

Two weeks after her father's death, Nonye returned to the house in Lekki. The evening she arrived, Tochukwu met her at the gate and helped her with her bags. He was a slim man, and when he took off his glasses as he asked about her trip, his eyes looked dim. He plucked a hankie from the breast pocket of his blue shirt and began to wipe his glasses, his motions gentle, almost like petting. His fingers were too slender for a man. She told him her trip was fine.

In the living room, she stood and stared at the high ceiling. It was the same gleaming white, the ceiling, and the chandelier shone softly golden. The curtains were drawn over the large arched windows, blocking out the waning sunlight. She remembered that the curtains used to be taupe, not this deep shade of gold, but could not remember, although she tried hard to, whether the changes had already been made when she last visited two years ago, whether she'd simply failed to notice.

"I prepared your old room," Tochukwu said. "I thought you'd like to stay in it?"

They walked upstairs. The paintings on the walls were the same, abstract, they looked childish to her. She used to marvel at how much her father spent on art. Only one of the paintings had any intimation of something real, the colors spiraling into the shape of a man. She remembered being absolutely terrified of walking down the stairs at night if she needed something from the refrigerator; in the dim light reflecting from the kitchen below, the man had seemed full of colorfully expanding eyes into which she could sink and never be found.

"It was Dubem's favorite," Tochukwu said, noticing her pause. "At first, I didn't understand it, didn't understand any of the paintings, to be honest."

He laughed. She could sense his discomfort, slight and well preserved—he was a man with his edges tucked in—but there nonetheless. She wanted to be kind, to laugh with him, but all she could think about was the stirring in her chest, an old and pulsing resentment.

He must have sensed it, because he said nothing else. In her room, he pulled her bags into the wardrobe. "Let me know if you need anything," he said, stepping out and easing the door closed.

She went to the window, parted the curtains. Something felt lost, missing, the space right outside too vacant, and it took her a moment to realize that the cashew tree was gone. It had been there the last time she visited; she was certain about this because, although she didn't sleep in the house, she'd always come into this room to smoke.

She pulled the curtain closed, sat on the bed. This was real, she thought. She would never sit with her father on the veranda, never brush a leaf off his hairy arm, and he would never again ask to smoke with her. She'd come here to feel him, to see his fingerprints scattered all over, in the decor and the paintings, in Tochukwu, and now that she was here, she was no longer certain feeling would be enough. When she had looked at Tochukwu earlier, she'd not seen her father, she'd seen a man helping her with her bags, a man with his own look and voice and walk. What she really needed was to see them together, to hear what her father's laughter sounded like with Tochukwu in the room, to experience the man he became when they were together. To do this without feeling like a peace offering, a compromise spread between this and the house in Ikoyi.

Tochukwu knocked to tell her that dinner was ready. In the dining room, the table felt long for two people. Even with the three of them, her mother across from her father, it had been too large. She used to wonder if her parents had planned to have more kids.

As they ate, she thought of things to say to him, hoped that he would say something. In the past, when she visited, she ate alone with her father. Tochukwu never joined them. He would return home from work in the evenings and sit briefly with them on the veranda, talking about current affairs, conversations that intentionally floated, never sinking deep.

Dinner was fried yam and egg sauce. She wanted to ask if her father had told him that it was her favorite food. He had cooked it well, the eggs clumpy like popcorn in the sauce.

"This is delicious," she said, raising her fork and nodding.

"Thank you." He sounded almost shrill, as though surprised that she had paid him a compliment. He had changed from the blue shirt, now wore a yellow open neck, his chest hair peeking out, dark and curly, his beard trimmed in a way that made him look younger, and she had to remind herself that he was several years her senior. Still, he was good looking, in the way that a well-tended lawn is beautiful, purposefully. She wondered if that was something her father had liked about him, wondered if they'd had parties, and if yes, who their friends had been, which of her father's old friends had remained, secretly, wondered if any had. Often, she had thought that more than anything else, her mother, alone in her house in Ikoyi, had missed playing hostess, wearing her most glittering earrings and waving off the compliments her father's friends gave on her cooking, Oh, this small thing, her father beaming with pride.

Did her father show him off? she wondered.

"Have you spoken to your mother yet?" Tochukwu said.

"We talked when I arrived at the airport. I'll go see her when she returns from the village."

He nodded, stared into his plate. "I don't have any idea what's happening. No one will tell me what the plans are. I didn't even know when he was moved from the mortuary at the Teaching Hospital. Nobody told me."

She put down her fork. *Mortuary.* Whenever her mother called, she'd talked only of plans for Nonye's travel, and it had been a gift, keeping her away from the practicalities of her father's death. Tochukwu had just snatched that away from her. Her father was lying somewhere, cold and alone.

She stood up. "Thank you for making dinner," she said.

The pain in his eyes, it was full and brimming. "Please finish your food."

"We're in the same boat, Tochukwu, I don't know anything either." She picked up her plates, took them to the kitchen, dumped them into the sink, the force, it was a miracle they did not crack. She stood by the sink until the water warmed up. Her hands shook as she held a plate under running water, and to steady herself, she returned the plate into the sink, clutching the countertop. She looked around, the walls white but no longer tiled. The last time she was in this kitchen, the tiles from her childhood had been intact, and her father had stood by the refrigerator while she washed the plates, and he'd said, "I miss your mother, I miss being on good terms with her."

"Daddy, why are you telling me this?" she said, looking up at him.

"It's just a thought." He shrugged. "Can't a man share things with his daughter anymore?"

He'd not always been that way, prone to bouts of sharing; he'd been sufficiently tender, asking, whenever she visited, what was going on in her life, teasing her about boyfriends she didn't have, asking if she was having a good time at her new school. But then she'd gone to Nebraska for university and he became the sort of father who told stories, reaching deep into his past for anecdotes about his parents, his childhood, his early days doing business in Lagos—to keep her on the phone, she'd concluded, now his stories felt to her like chronicles, told to be remembered. Sometimes she'd wake up in a panic, afraid she'd forgotten them all.

She stacked her plates in the cupboard, wiping her hands with a towel. Her anger had dissipated; in its place was sadness, wide and gaping. What would her father be doing were he here now, alone with Tochukwu? Would they have seen a movie together? If yes, would they have curled up on the couch, holding each other, or would they have sat separately, arms grazing occasionally as they reached for the remote control? Had they been happy until the very end?

Her phone was ringing. Sweet Mummy, the caller ID said. She let it ring. They'd talked for almost an hour earlier in the day, and Nonye knew what sorts of things her mother would say if she picked up. "Don't eat or drink anything he gives you," she'd said earlier.

They'd been quiet, and then her mother had laid it all out again, as though she hadn't repeated it like a favorite song even when Nonye had been in Nebraska: *I don't understand why you're going there, while you could stay in Ikoyi until I return.*

Her phone was ringing again, vibrating against the counter. She picked it up and slid it into her jeans pockets. In the dining room, Tochukwu was clearing the table, his back to her. She stood by the alcove, watching him, wondering what her father had seen in him the first time, wondering who made the first move. "I'll try and talk to my mother when she returns to Lagos," she said.

He turned, looking startled. "Thank you."

~

She was so obviously unlike Dubem, having inherited her mother's light skin and fiercely beautiful face, that when she'd stood up and thanked him for dinner, Tochukwu froze, petrified by how her anger eyes mirrored Dubem's, how her movements, terse and immediately aloof, were exactly like his. He'd spent years teasing Dubem about how his daughter had none of his features, and now, weeks after his death, she was looking at him with the same eyes that Dubem did whenever they quarreled.

He thought about this as he walked upstairs. It was the only quiet thought he'd had since he returned from the hospital two weeks earlier. That first night, he'd stood in the middle of the living room, hands on his head. He could not cry because he did not believe it, that a small complaint about a headache after a business trip would lead, by morning, to him speeding to the hospital because the headache had intensified, it was as though someone where knocking a nail into his skull, Dubem had complained; he did not believe that by late morning, the doctor would call him into the office and say, "I'm sorry, we did all that we could, but the aneurysm had ruptured," that he would laugh.

He'd slept on the couch that night. When he went upstairs into their bedroom, the bed had seemed endless with Dubem's absence, still he dreamed of Dubem's laughter, of Dubem's arms around his shoulders. And then he'd woken up to the sun pouring into the living room, Dubem gone forever, and he'd sat up on the couch and cried, loud and ugly.

It occurred to him that morning that it was up to him to tell everyone: their friends, Dubem's senior employees, Dubem's family. Prior to this, the biggest loss Tochukwu had experienced had been his grandmother's, in his first year of university. They had been close, relatives calling him her *little purse*. He'd fled to his mother's room during the funeral, he could not stand the thud of sand hitting her coffin, the sound so precisely lonely, so heartless. What he had not understood then was his privilege of flight, of grieving without obligations—his uncles had to stand there, stone faced and bleary eyed, until the priest said the final words, watching their mother disappear forever shovel after shovel of brown earth. Now he had to tell everyone that Dubem was dead.

The first person he called was Nkiru, Nonye's mother. "Onye?" she said when he told her who he was—it wasn't that she hadn't heard him the first time, he knew. "Tochukwu," he said, pacing the room. "Albert's friend." He'd never called Dubem by that name.

"Ehen?" she'd said, impatient.

He opened his mouth, but no words came out, instead he gulped air. He sat on the edge of the bed. "Dubem," he said, blinking, holding the trembling in his throat by pressing his mouth closed. "Dubem a-nwuọla." It was easier to say in Igbo, a language in which he'd heard that sentence said before.

"What? Ị sị ginị?" Her voice was low, and then it was shrill. "I did not hear you well, biko kwukene ya ọzọ."

"Dubem died," he said, this time in English. "Yesterday."

She asked what had happened, and he told her about the headache, and how fast he drove to the hospital—the roads were not yet cramped, he told her, it was early morning.

She cut the call suddenly. He would have to call Dubem's brothers, James and Maxwell. He would have to answer their questions, people who had long stopped talking to Dubem, except for the text messages from James's wife every Christmas, New Year's, and Easter, seasonal greetings laced heavily with small sermons about the impermanence of *earthly things* and the reality of *eternity*. She always signed off with *Jesus loves you.* Dubem would shake his head as he read the messages to Tochukwu, smiling sadly, and yet he always called her after, thanking her for her message, asking after his nephews and nieces, after his brother, telling her that he was thinking of them. "Why do you continue to entertain this?" Tochukwu had asked last Christmas. "I see how much it hurts you, I see how much it ruins your mood, and yet Christmas after Christmas, you call. Why?"

Dubem tapped the space on the bed beside him. Tochukwu hesitated, he was angry for Dubem and a little annoyed with him. Finally he sat on the bed. Dubem wrapped his arm around his waist. "I do not know how to be without my family," he said. "I was raised to need them. 'After you've trekked round the world and you're dirty and smelly,' our mother used to say, 'return home and your brother will bathe and feed you.'"

"It seems you alone listened to that lesson," Tochukwu said, laying his head on Dubem's shoulder.

Dubem squeezed his side, gently. "I have you, nnwa, so I count myself among the lucky." He looked at Tochukwu, smiled. "And one day, Nonye will come to understand fully."

He was lying in bed, reading a novel, when someone knocked. At first, he thought it was Musa, the gateman, but when the knock was not followed by a loud "Oga," he knew it had to be the only other person in the compound, Nonye.

He put on a shirt, shuffled into his slippers, and went to the door. She was already dressed for bed, in a white nightgown sprinkled with tiny pink flowers, her hair bunched in a black hairnet. She was barefoot, and the hallways were not carpeted, the tiles always cold. "Is everything okay in there?" he said, certain that she would ask if he had spare slippers.

"It's stupid," she said, shaking her head. "Sorry to disturb you." She turned around. She'd stood very briefly there in front of his door, yet he'd seen it in her eyes, the weariness, the far-flung look of someone lost. He called after her, asking if she was sure everything was okay. Did she need anything? Slippers? More blankets?

"I can't sleep," she said.

He stood there, saying nothing, the light in the hallway dull and yellow.

Her arms were wrapped in an X across her chest, like someone shielding herself from a terrible cold. They were multiplying, the little things that made her alike to Dubem, such as this X, the gentle rotating of her fingers around her shoulders.

"Can I come in for a while?" she said.

"Absolutely."

He moved out of the way, letting her in, shut the door behind him. She stood in the middle of the room, looking around, his eyes moving with hers, settling on the green couch by the wardrobe, the pencil portraits on the wall, one of Dubem in an Afro he hadn't had since he was thirty, having gone totally bald by the time they met, and the other of Tochukwu squinting at the sky, the huge table by one of the walls littered with papers and on which a lamp gave out golden light, the door beside it, shut, leading into Dubem's study—and, finally, the huge picture above the bed, the both of them in white, a coral necklace around Tochukwu's neck, the both of them laughing, Dubem's head thrown slightly back, teeth bared, Tochukwu leaning against him, and below, in cursive calligraphy: *Home is where the heart sleeps*. They'd taken the picture at a beach in Kigali. The photographer, a young man in his early twenties named Pius, had said, "Hold your husband," and they'd both been taken aback, in a good way, used already to people calling them brothers or calling Dubem Tochukwu's uncle. "We're not married," Dubem had said, smiling mischievously at Pius, to which he'd retorted, "Well, you should be, you're both beautiful." Was that the only reason people married one another? Dubem asked. "No," Pius said, fiddling with his camera. "But that's the most important reason. I know, what's in the head is important, but it will not give you fine children." That was when they'd laughed, the way he said it, his face serious and set. "Perfect!" he said, clicking his camera.

"I've not been in this room since I was seventeen," Nonye said. "I cannot believe how much it's changed and how much it has remained the same." She nodded toward the couch. "Can I sit?"

"Feel free," he said.

He sat on the bed opposite her, the space between them so wide, they wouldn't be able to touch fingertips even if they stretched their arms. He wondered why he simply did not sit at the other end of the couch—it would have implied a comfort that did not exist, but that would have been better than the feeling of exposure he had sitting on this high bed, doused in the light, totally seen. He laced and unlaced his fingers, and then, telling himself not to do that again, placed his hands under his lap, his palms pressed to the bed.

She looked at the picture hanging above the bed. "Did my father decide on the inscription?"

Tochukwu stared at the picture, so huge, so tall, it was like a kindly watchman. "You know it."

"It's just like him, always ready with his aphorisms." She shook her head, a tiny smile on her lips. "When I was little, he would summarize all his fatherly lectures with these. He called them *wisdom nuggets*." She chuckled to herself. "*Run fast, but only against your shadow from yesterday.* One time, I think I was in primary four, some mean boys taunted me and when my mum picked me up, I was in tears. She told my dad when he returned home from work that evening and he called me into this room. He said, 'Never let them see your tears, they are hungry for it and it will only make them more cruel.' Of course, he said my mum would go with me to school the next day to talk to my class teacher, but those words stayed with me. A bully never made me cry again."

"He loves that word, *cruel*," Tochukwu said. "Next to *sons of destruction and desolation.*"

"That one he reserves solely for every Lagos State governor that ever lived!" she said, laughing, her head thrown back and her teeth bared. The sound, so pure, so unlike Dubem's in its gentle highness, surprised him. It occurred to him that he'd never heard her laugh, that she'd never laughed in his presence.

He was laughing too now. "It's true, though," he said. "The inscription. Home really is wherever the heart sleeps, the things and people it retains and remembers fondly."

"You sound just like him," she said.

"Well, it rubs off." He felt freer, thawed, as though their laughter together had unstrung something between them, and he could finally be himself with her.

They were silent, but it was not the silence of before. It was not exactly comfortable, but it was nice. He was happy to be on her good side.

"Did you notice?" she said.

"Notice what?"

"We talked about him in the present, as though he were still here." She blinked, brought her fingers to her eyes. "It's still unbelievable to me, the thought that I will never see him again. My daddy, gone, just like that."

She sat there with her head bent into her palm. He wanted to tell her that she was right, he was grieving too, but who in the world cared for his grief? It was this that made the mortuary attendant release Dubem's body to his brothers without consulting him, the person listed officially as Dubem's emergency contact, who had signed the fatality papers. He wanted to tell her how he'd yelled at the man, saying repeatedly, "You don't know who I am," how those words, coming from a man like him, a man who had driven into the compound in a Chrysler, would have worked wonders in any Lagos office, how it only elicited in the attendant a snort-like chuckle and the words, "Orí ẹ dàrú. Oga, wait until I call the police, then you can explain to them what you're doing asking for the body of a man who is not your father or brother." He wanted to tell her how he hated the attendant, how he hated himself, that after all the years he'd been in the world, surviving men like that, outsmarting and outachieving them, they could still make him feel small.

He did not tell her any of this. He asked, instead, if she needed a tissue. She nodded, wiping her eye with the sleeve of her nightgown, then smiled up at him, the smile of someone caught doing something deeply private in public.

"Maybe it would help if you shared some memories." He paused. "It would help me, too, to be honest. I need to get my mind off some thoughts, onto something… *meaningful*."

"That's an interesting word to use in describing memories." She huffed out a smile. "Talk about no pressure."

"Nothing in this life is easy," he said.

"Well, what do I share?" She looked thoughtful and a little shy. "It feels artificial bringing up stuff after being cued. Plus, the memories in this house aren't exactly happy ones—don't get me wrong, there are many happy moments, but my cohesive memory of this place is one of strife, especially the last two years we all lived together as a family."

He knew what she was referring to and was immediately afraid. Yet, he thought, perhaps this was the conversation they needed to have, the conversation she should have had with Dubem all these years; perhaps they had needed to break things in order to rebuild them. That was probably the reason she'd come here, not just to this room, but to the house in Lekki, to dissect the demons of her past.

"Maybe you could start with the happy ones," he said, shrugging, trying to seem both curious and uninvested.

"Maybe," she said, smiling.

～

When she woke up, it was raining outside, and she had several missed calls from her uncle James. She went to the bathroom, then downstairs to make herself a bowl of cornflakes, standing briefly by the window overlooking the veranda and peering out into the rain, sheets of pouring silver. Musa was busy outside, squatting in front of his house by the gate scrubbing a rug, his bare back twitching. She imagined dashing out in the rain toward him, the way she sometimes did when she was a kid. She imagined that he would smile at her and say, "Small madam, you go catch cold o," that her mother would yell at her from a distance to leave the rain if she did not want to receive slaps for dinner. She closed her eyes. For a moment, everything was as it had been: her father was alive, and her mother still lived here, and she was in her room, near tears, unable to understand why she could not play in the rain when it was the most exhilarating thing to do.

When she'd knocked on Tochukwu's door, she'd told herself that what she wanted was to see her father's room, smell him in the air, and there had been some of that, but what she hadn't acknowledged was the feeling in her, like small persistent bites, of an unworthiness to grieve. The evening her mother had called to say that her father was dead, she'd felt, after shock and disbelief, a nebulous surge of contrition, as though she'd spent her entire life doing something wrong and his death was penance. She'd cried, not only because she would no longer see her father, she'd cried because she could no longer say to him the things that she knew she would have one day said, that she forgave and understood him. Before this, she'd never experienced a death up close, her mother's parents both still alive and her father's parents dead before she learned to walk, and so she didn't have in her what she now had, that feeling her friends who had lost a sibling or parent described often, of urgency and pervading dread. Her father, healthy and boisterous and always on a trip, had seemed durable, and it never occurred to her that something so casual as a headache would snatch him away.

She'd rebuffed all his attempts at drawing her into his life in recent years and, sitting in the room with Tochukwu, she realized that it had not been so much from resentment as it was loyalty—all the times she heard her parents scream at each other, there had been a pain in her mother's voice, a pain Nonye feared and responded to—and hearing him talk so intimately of her father, it sliced something in her open, and she'd burst out in both grief and gratitude.

She drew the curtains, the living room plunged into an even darker gold, ate a few spoonfuls of her cornflakes, disgustingly sodden, went back into the kitchen and rinsed off the bowl. As she ascended the stairs, she wondered if Tochukwu was up and what his plans for the day were. She wondered how he usually filled his days, since this happened but also before; she knew nothing about him, she realized.

Her uncle had called again. She called him back. "Nne, kee kwanụ?" he said, his tone the joyful peal of someone who was talking to a favorite niece. She hadn't spoken to him since he surprised her last New Year's. She'd taken the call from an unknown Nigerian number, thinking, since it was that time of year, it could be anyone she knew calling to say happy New Year, and it had been a little awkward, the first minute between them, when she had to pretend to be sorry that she didn't have his phone number saved.

"A dị m mma," she said, uninterested; she would not pretend, this time, to be excited by his call. She hated it, the falseness Nigerians forced upon themselves in the name of respect and politeness. If he was going to pretend that a relationship existed between the both of them, she would not.

He asked how her flight had been and why she didn't go to his house instead. "I know I'm not around and your cousins are in school," he said. "But you're just like a daughter to my wife. She would have made you correct ofe ora and kept you company."

Nonye dug her toes into the rug. "This is where I am supposed to be at this time, Uncle, in my father's house."

He laughed. "Ị bụ nwoke!" he said. "You're the son Albert never had."

She did not know what to do with his pride, so unexpected. If she held her phone any tighter, it would shatter in her palm, which was sweaty in the coolness of the room.

"What about that man?" he said, after some small talk. "Is he still there?"

"You mean Tochukwu?"

"Who else would I be talking about, nne?"

"He's here. This is his home, too."

"What kind of talk is that?" he said. "How is it his home? Biko don't say that kind of thing. He's very lucky we didn't storm that place with police immediately after we heard and demand an explanation. I thought he would have left by now, but he still has the audacity to stay, Ị fụkwaa!"

Nonye said nothing. She shifted farther into bed, pulling her legs together. It was like something from an old Nollywood movie, the oppressive brother tormenting the bereaved widow. It had not occurred to her that Tochukwu could be made to leave.

"Like I said, Uncle, this is his home."

"Stop talking nonsense," he said. "It belongs to you and your mother."

"I'm sure my mother doesn't want to live here."

"You are not your mother's mouthpiece, Nonye nnwa. I don't know what that man has given you to eat that you're suddenly dancing to his music, like your father did, but we will talk about this when we return from the village, ị nụgo?"

After the phone call, Nonye remained on her bed. The house was so quiet, she could hear the ticktock of the clock, the sound of rain reduced to a soft patter. It would be merely drizzling now, and soon the sun would be out. She picked up her phone and called her mother.

"Did you know that Uncle James and Uncle Maxwell moved Daddy's body without telling Tochukwu?"

"What kind of talk is that to wake me with this morning?" her mother said.

"It's not fair, Mummy."

"They're his brothers." In the background, the sound of the toilet flushing. "Don't tell me this is the reason you called me this morning. I have a flight back to Lagos in a few hours and I spent the whole of yesterday attending meetings, these umuada women giving me headache as if I'm some widow."

"He would have done the same for you," Nonye said.

"Well, guess who's not here—*him*. And guess who is leaving everything behind because of him, again—*me*. So please don't lecture me this morning about what he would have done because we will never know now."

Nonye's eyes burned. All she could think about was Tochukwu in the dining room after she went into the kitchen the night before, how he'd hidden his face away from her when she came back in to say she'd ask her mother, she suspected he must have been crying. Ghosts did not exist in her daily imagination of the world, yet she could not stop imagining her father watching him hurt.

"What has come over you?" her mother said.

What, indeed, had come over her? She knew now why she'd come here: to grieve together. Her mother was hurt by her father's death, she knew, but not in the same way that she was hurt. Her mother felt sad because she was a good person who had once loved someone and that someone was gone forever, but it wasn't grief. Her mother had experienced that grief years ago, when Nonye had returned from school and found her seated on her bedroom floor, crying. Nonye had stood briefly in the middle of the room, watching her; she'd never seen her mother looking so dejected. She'd known something was wrong when the driver picked her up from school that Friday; usually, her mother did, because she did not work on Fridays. Nonye enjoyed those drives with her mother, the songs they played, songs that belonged to Nonye's generation but which she loved sharing with her mother, the both of them singing along, *e get as e dey do me, do me*, how the inappropriate became delicious on her mother's lips, so that Nonye often burst out laughing. All her classmates said her mum was cool, which made her immensely proud, but also a little sad, because she sensed that there was, between the countless quarrels her parents had and the familiarity she shared with her mother, a precise thread. So, that afternoon, when the driver picked her up instead and she trudged straight to her parents' bedroom to find her mother seated on the floor, crying, Nonye took off her schoolbag, letting it drop onto the floor, and sat beside her.

"It is even worse than I suspected," her mother wept, almost incoherent. "It is worse."

"Is the woman pregnant?" Nonye said.

"Oh, ada m," her mother said, looking up at her with such pity in her eyes, Nonye's lips began to quiver, too. "You will not understand— you think you know a man and then one day he shows you his real face." Her mother sobbed even more loudly. Nonye lay her head on her mother's shoulder, between them was something intimate, a shared femaleness, a sense of the mistreated.

She said to her mother now, "I really do not understand why Uncle James and Uncle Maxwell are carrying Daddy's burial on their heads. They were not even on talking terms when he died."

"And me," her mother said, "was I on talking terms with him?"

"It's different," Nonye said.

There was quiet on the other end of the phone, soft breathing. "Nonye, nwa m," her mother said finally. "I understand that you're going through a lot but you're not unaware of how things are done here. And I am aware that, in your grieving, you are trying to bond with your father's friend. But that relationship has ended. It ended the day Dubem died. Your uncles are your family, regardless of what has happened in the past. Tochukwu will be an old story soon, a memory, something that happened. He will move on to the next man and this family will be a past and it will be as if nothing happened here. But you, Nonye nwa, you will be in this family for a long, long time. When you find a man, your uncles will have to step in for your father and give their blessings, and if your husband's people are bad, they will be the ones with whom I will go and confront them. Be wise, nne, and don't throw your family away." She paused, a thoughtful calm. "You are not your father."

"Don't say that," Nonye said. The tears surprised her, a rush, crowding her eyes, strangling her voice. "Call me before you board. I have to go now. Love you."

She ended the call before her mother could say anything, and then lay flat on the bed, her loud cries muffled by pillows. She'd thought that the worst thing to happen to her was her father's death, yet here she was, shattered at the realization that she had no power as to how he would be mourned. It was like being punched over and over while someone else cried on your behalf.

～

They were in the kitchen after dinner, Nonye leaning against the refrigerator, wineglass in hand, Tochukwu seated on the counter, between them a half-empty bottle of chardonnay he'd found in Dubem's study, when Nonye said there was something that had been eating at her all day. "My uncles are planning a meeting here, and they threatened to kick you out."

He slid off the counter, began to load the dishwasher, his hands shaking. He'd expected this, and yet his hands shook.

"I'm sorry about this," she said.

"I expected it," he said. He leaned back against the counter, breathing, steadying himself.

"What will you do?" she said, the way one does when they are saying that a problem is not theirs even though they care.

"I don't know," he said, reaching for the bottle. "Right now, though?" He refilled his glass, smiled at her, exhausted.

When Dubem's family members arrived, Tochukwu came downstairs, sat on a couch, and crossed his legs. He did not avoid their questioning, aggressive eyes. He recognized James from the wedding pictures in a photo album somewhere in Dubem's study, long nosed, like Dubem, and, in his eyes, a hint of something once beautiful, something fiery and boyish. But he was not like Dubem. He was sprawling in his posture, legs spread as though the house were his, arms flung across the backrest, his stomach a wobbling ball. Maxwell, lean and bespectacled, looked like a university lecturer who claimed to have high moral standards but secretly enjoyed the suffering of the students he failed. Their wives looked twenty years younger, coiffed and radiant even in their mourning whites.

There were two other people in their company, apart from Nonye's mother, Nkiru, who Tochukwu tried not to look at, not out of shame or guilt, but out of courtesy, because he knew that whatever happened in that living room eventually, she would be the only person who sincerely did not deserve the indignity. The other two people, young men, most likely cousins, were there, he sensed, to look burly and intimidating. He did not know and did not care.

"What is he doing here?" Maxwell said, his voice deep for someone so lean. He was looking at Nonye, who was seated beside her mother. Nonye looked away.

"Rapu Nonye nwa," James said, smiling, his face alight with the arrogance of a man who handled people. "It's not her fault. She's just a child, she cannot tell a grown man how to behave." He turned to

Tochukwu. "Nwoke, you are an Igbo man, and you are not a child. You know how this goes. Whatever thing my brother had with you is now in the past. You are not his son, neither are you his brother." He cleared his throat, his eyes glinting an evil light. "You also are not his wife, regardless of how hard that must be for you to grasp."

A chuckle rippled through the room, like a baton being passed around. Tochukwu did not want to, but he swallowed. He felt Nonye's eyes on him but avoided them, he did not want her pity. Pity made him weak, it assumed a helplessness, a powerlessness that he could not afford, not right now, when he needed to be strong. He thought of how much they had hurt Dubem, these same people who sat in his living room calling themselves his brothers.

"What I am saying, in essence," James said, after he'd left enough pause, "is that this gathering is for family alone, in case you did not understand."

"I hear you," Tochukwu said. "But this is my house"—their laughter came after shocked silence, like bad engines coughing awake— "and you came in here without my invitation, without even asking me, yet I let you in. I let you sit. I do not expect a *thank you* from you because I know how important what is going to be said here is. We all lost someone dear to us and, even though you abandoned your brother, I assume that you are grieving, but I spent his last years with him, and he called me family." His pause was intentional—they would expect him to complete his thought, stunned by his effrontery, and he would say instead, as he now did: "Can we proceed?"

"Nna, what kind of insult is this?" Maxwell said. He looked ready to stand up and leave.

"Wait, wait," James said. The smirk remained on his face, arrogant, knowing. He looked impressed and excited, as though he'd underestimated his enemy and, now that he knew that he was ready to put up a fight, was looking forward to the bloodbath. "We have been patient with you so far, letting you stay on in our brother's house, but it seems our patience is being misunderstood for foolishness." He looked around for affirmation, getting nods from the two strange men. "In the coming days, visitors will be coming to this house to condole with the family. We will be cleaning this place up in preparation on Tuesday. If you know what is best for you, you will have packed out of this place by tomorrow evening. For now, peacefully leave this meeting and stop causing a nuisance."

"Where did you move Dubem's body?" Tochukwu said.

Maxwell looked stunned. "Hah, what is wrong with this man?"

"Let him see the body," Nkiru said. All eyes turned to her. It was almost as if she had not been in the room at all. "Kedụ ife ọ dị? There's nothing wrong with that, James, if it will bring peace."

"What does he want to do with the corpse?" Maxwell said. "Will he fuck it?"

"What nonsense is this?" Nonye said, standing up. "It is my father we are talking about—*my father*. My father who is lying somewhere now, cold, and this is how you talk about him."

"Nonye, o zugo," Maxwell's wife said.

"Mba!" Nonye waved her arms at her in expressive arches, *no-no*. "Nobody should talk to me. In fact, I want everybody out. Leave this house, leave my father's funeral. I will bury him myself."

"Nonye nwa," her mother said, a plea in her eyes.

"Mummy, no!" She was like a thing erupting. "I have kept quiet for too long while these men, these people who abused *my father* decide what happens to him." She glared from James to Maxwell. "Why are you here? You hated him, so why are you here? Did you enjoy seeing him lie there, helpless? Is that what all this is about? Does it give you joy seeing the people he loved suffer?" She quieted, her breathing loud and rapid. "Please leave. Just go." She sank back into her chair and, face buried in her hands, began to wail, her body shaking. Nkiru stood up and pulled her into a hug, cradling and patting her head, whispering, "Nne, o zugo."

Tochukwu stood up, near tears himself but vowing not to cry in the presence of these people. "You have to go now," he said. He'd not expected Nonye's outburst, and watching her, he'd felt both protective and alone; everyone in the living room understood her pain, had become gentle in the face of its eruption, and even if they chose not to understand, they would have to tolerate it—she belonged to them.

"Nkiru," James said.

"You heard them," Nkiru said, still holding Nonye. "Just go, bikozienu."

"Nkiru, this is wrong. Ọ bụ ihe ọchị!"

"Ya dịba. She's all I have, the only reason I'm here in the first place. If she wants you to leave, you leave."

They stood up reluctantly, muttering among themselves. At the door, James turned around one last time, looking toward Nkiru and Nonye, it seemed he wanted to make one last appeal but changed his mind. He glared at Tochukwu. After he'd shut the door, Tochukwu stood with his back against it. His chest pounded, he felt like he might fall down, his legs without bones. He felt a wave of relief and gratitude, and yet he felt afraid, afraid of morning. Nonye would leave to be with Nkiru, and then he would be alone. His friends were scattered around the country, the few in Lagos working from dawn to dusk, commuting long hours to and from work, and he was thankful whenever they made the time to come be with him; but he did not, could not, feel entitled to their presence, their time, and they would never feel for him the same sense of responsibility and obligation that his mother or siblings would feel, and no one in his family knew about him. It hit him like a sudden shard of light at a precarious bend on a dark road, the extent of his powerlessness. He would have to move out eventually, he realized, in a year, two years—a few months. The house would not be the same without Dubem, would never feel warm and safe and welcoming: he would return home from work, he would open the fridge, turn on the microwave, expecting to hear the sound of Dubem's car a few minutes later as it drove into the compound, but all he would hear would be the sound of the clock ticking, the refrigerator droning on, loud in the emptiness. All he wanted was to see Dubem one last time, to say goodbye, truly say goodbye.

"Please can you get her some water?" Nkiru said, pulling him away from his thoughts. Nonye clung to her, letting out small intermittent sobs, the both of them now seated on the floor. "I'd do it myself but—" She tilted her head at Nonye, her eyes pleading, as if to say, *but as you can see.*

GOD'S CHILDREN ARE LITTLE BROKEN THINGS

I.   You met in your second year. At the stadium one cloudy June evening when you played against his department. He was not a player, he was too small to be, even though you knew that bigness wasn't the stuff anyway. But he was so small, so fragile, you were dead sure he had never kicked a football.

He reminded you of Dave.

You walked up to him at halftime and told him he reminded you of someone. The way he smiled, his eyes lingering briefly on your sweaty chest and then on the ground, made you certain that he was one of them. Dave was one of them too, and he had almost put you in trouble.

I wanted to tell you that you reminded me of someone, you said, and then you were gone.

You lost the game to his department. On your way home, you called Rachael and told her you loved her so much, did she know that? She giggled and you told yourself again that Dave had almost put you in trouble, Jesus!

You met him again. At Christ Church Chapel, where he played the organ so well on Mothering Sunday, the entire church was filled with a tender light, the women burst into tongues in the middle of hymns, and the chaplain for once didn't say, First and last verses only. He did not look fragile on the organ.

After the service, you lingered around the door of the choir room until he came out and said, Hey.

Hey, you said, scratching your head and glancing at the floor. That was great, what you did up there.

T-thanks, bro, he stuttered. I wasn't sure at first, b-but then…

You learned that day how well he could talk and not bore you. (Later, he would tell you that he had been afraid you would walk away again, so he'd talked and talked.) You exchanged numbers, and you whistled on your way home, skipped by the roadside like a little boy.

You did not call him. He called you, twice, first to know how your day had been. You said, Fine. The second time he called, he told you that his piano instructor was OCD, the man didn't give him any breathing space, and you said, Really?

Yes, he said.

After that, he stopped calling, and you did not call either. Not until the night Dumebi texted you that Mum and Dad were quarreling, could you please call them now? You were asleep when the text message came in, and when you woke up at midnight, you had eleven missed calls. You tried to call her back, but she wasn't answering. You started to dial Mum's number but then stopped. Then you dialed his number. His voice was rough: Hey, Lotanna.

You sat on the bed, running your fingers through your hair. Hey, Kamsi, you said. Didn't expect you to be awake.

I'm rehearsing my exam pieces.

I see.

You told him everything, how every time Mum and Dad quarreled, even though it was in low tones, the entire house seemed to reverberate with their bitterness. How it hurt you in the chest so badly you couldn't breathe. He was so quiet, you said, I'm not even sure why I'm telling you this. I hope I didn't disturb you.

No, no, he said. N-not at all.

Okay, you said, and asked how he was doing, and what were the pieces he was playing?

The girls from your department had a football match with the girls from his. The match was already on when you came, and you walked straight to him after shaking hands with your friends. He folded his arms across his chest, smiled so widely it made you happy simply to stand there, saying, How've you been, bro?

He was wearing three-quarter shorts and his Arsenal jersey, the hair on his legs and arms black and curly against the light brown of his skin.

You have nice legs, you said. Let's run.

He said no, weakly, but you pulled him up, called him lazy, and laughed at his pout. He had not run a hundred meters before he bent over, his hands on his knees. His classmates were laughing: Mozart, you dey fall hands o. He was panting. He collapsed on the track and lay on his back.

Lazy, you said, smiling down at him. Is this how you do your girlfriend?

He arched an eyebrow, stared at you.

You did not hold his gaze, merely chuckled. You sat on the ground beside where he lay.

II.   You told him Rachael was the best thing that ever happened to you. Told him she saved you.

From what? he asked.

You won't understand, you said.

You were seated on a step at the stadium, watching the sun, once white, fade into a calm yellow, and all you could think about were his hands, how they tapped rhythms on his knees as he tried to get the words out of his mouth.

Don't conclude so quickly, he said. But I understand if you don't want to tell me.

You stalked him on Facebook, squinted at every update ancient and modern, and told yourself that you found him interesting. Simple. Sometimes you would lie in bed trying to visualize Rachael from last time. Her lips, what did they taste like the last time? Lemon mint? Tom Tom? What would his lips taste like? Like Tom Tom too? Or like nothing.

You remember certain things about him. Little little things. How his stutter became obvious only when it was cold or when he was emotional. How when he told you about his hookups he looked you boldly in the eyes, teasing, Does my story make you horny? Though he tried to sound flippant and cool, the shyness billowed in his voice. He liked to sing when he was in the bathroom, you often heard him screaming *Ekuro la labaku ewa...* and it made you laugh because he sounded so much like Justin Bieber screaming *Baby, baby, baby, oh.* Nobody sang Davido with that kind of voice.

You were trying to make sense of your History of Nigeria lecture notes the morning he came to your house and flopped on the bed facedown. You watched him him for a while, and then you asked, What is it?

When he looked at you, his eyes were red. His lips quivered. I h-hate e-every. One o-of them. I've met, he said.

What happened? you asked.

He grabbed your bedsheet, bit his lips so hard, you thought he would draw blood. I. Told him. No, he said. I t-told him. No.

He covered his face with the bedsheet. He was shaking terribly.

You sat beside him on the bed and held his hand, rubbed it gently. He was still shaking. But as you rubbed and rubbed, he began to calm down. You rubbed and pressed, rubbed and pressed. Better? you asked. He nodded, sniffling.

Who was it?

Kent, he said.

All his friends had funny names: Kent, Klay, Vinny. Like names on body cream bottles—Kent: Light & Lovely. I thought you were just friends, you said.

He nodded, blew his nose. I want to bathe, he said.

He refused to dress in front of you, yelled Stop! when you teased him about acting like a girl, why couldn't he dress in front of you? As you sat on the veranda, waiting for him to be done, you thought of nothing but how hard you wanted to punch Kent.

You learned to handle him even more gently. He was delicate, always lying in bed, eating plantain chips. Sometimes, he woke up in the middle of the night kicking. You learned to hold him close, to press his head against your chest and whisper, It's okay, I'm here. It's okay.

You asked him to bring his keyboard to your house. He didn't want to be in his room, so you walked with him to Lemon Villa to get his things. No, you didn't mind the noise, you could cope. He smiled and said thank you.

You called Rachael often to say I miss you, I cannot wait to be home. Yet your heart beat too fast when he rested his head on your chest, and you wanted too much to bury your nose in his neck and sniff the talcum powder he wore to bed; and every time you saw the tears that made his eyes look silvery in the dark, you wanted too much to touch his chin, his lower lip, to kiss him hard and gentle.

It sometimes rained all night in July, and you had to wear a sweater and socks as you studied for exams. One night it rained so hard it sounded like pebbles hitting the roof, the wind filtering in through shut windows. You stopped reading and eased into bed beside him. You had to spoon against him, the blanket was small. Your nose brushed his neck. You whispered, Kamsi, are you awake?

Yeah, he said. I want to practice the Sam Ojukwu piece for my exam, but I'm feeling so lazy.

He adjusted slightly, his back warm on your stomach. You held his hand and pressed it, then pressed your nose so closely to his neck, you could smell him, clean as air, through the talcum powder. When your hand eased under his sweater and rubbed his stomach, he whispered, I thought you would never decide.

Decide what? you asked, moving your hand upward and upward, until you found his nipples, two tiny hard grains. He stifled a giggle (he did that often when he was turned on, stifle a giggle, so that it sounded like a snort). He tilted his head backward to look at you, and you pressed your lips, tentatively, on his. He tasted almost of nothing. You helped him out of his sweater and inner shirt, put your hand into his trousers. Your eyes closed. Your lips and tongues dancing. He had given himself up so easily, so gently, and then all of a sudden he was shaking.

You had his hands pinned down, and his legs were wrapped around your waist. You leaned forward. Just relax, you said. Relax.

No, he said. His legs slackened.

Come on.

No, he said, shaking his head.

For a while you towered over him. Then you rolled over and lay beside him, staring at the dark ceiling, your hand on your forehead.

Was this what happened with Kent?

No, he said quickly, like he had been expecting the question.

I see.

After your History of Nigeria exam, you said to your classmate Pascal, I have this babe who was hurt, and it's affecting her sex life badly.

Pascal nodded. She no wan' give you, eh?

Something like that, you said. Pascal was the perpetual lover boy in class, he had to know some stuff.

Give it some time, he said. Keep trying, small small. No force am o.

God forbid! you said. I no fit try that one na.

You searched on Google. You wished there was someone else you could ask, someone to whom you could say the words. Someone who would certainly understand.

II.   The first time you quarreled, it was because he did not tidy the room after he returned from school. You came home that evening to the sound of Beethoven's "Für Elise." (You were beginning to know the names of his favorite pieces.) The room was dim, the only light coming from the dying sun. The bed was unmade, your clothes scattered on it just like you both had left them in the heat of the previous night. The room still had the air of morning rush—two empty cups sat unwashed on the cupboard. His schoolbag lay open on the floor. You picked it up and hung it, together with yours, on the wall beside your clothes rack.

Normally, when he was on the keyboard, you did not talk to him. But today had been bad, and the sound of the keyboard felt like someone sticking pins into your ears. You returned since afternoon, you said. How could you have left this room like this?

He played two more notes of the music, and then there was utter silence. Lotanna, he said. Good evening.

Why didn't you tidy the room?

I was rehearsing for my recital, as you can see, he said. He sounded rebuked, confused. But there was a hint of testiness, too. He fiddled with the collar of his polo shirt like a child.

You began to pick things up. He stood to help you, but you said, No, please, and took the rag from him. He stood there, watching you. Then he took his schoolbag and left the room.

You wanted to tell him about the phone call. How Dumebi had sounded like she had been crying all morning. Mum was going mad, she had said. Mum was hurling things at Dad, the television was on the floor now, broken, and Chisom was crying, but Mum wouldn't stop. You wanted to tell him how when you called Mum and she did not pick up, you felt all these tiny insects crawling in your head.

All through the evening, you stood on the veranda waiting for him to return. The evening turned from orange to blue and then to gray blue. When your lodge mate put on his generator, you rushed next door to charge your phone and call Kamsi. The voice came through, soft and sweet: *The number you're calling is currently not available....*

You boarded an okada to his house. He wasn't there. You returned home and sat on the veranda, waiting.

When Mum called back, it was night, and she did not sound mad at all. It's your father again, she said. This time it's with my friend, Mama Ejima's daughter. Her voice sounded nasal and tired. You wanted to tell him you'd had a bad day. He did not return that night, nor the next day, nor the day after. And you did not tell him.

The next time you quarreled, you flung words at each other. Quietly, so that the neighbors wouldn't hear. He wanted you to end it with Rachael, and you called him selfish. He said, No, it's you who is a liar, stop fooling the girl. You told him, See who's talking, you knew I had a girl, and you still came to me. He snorted. I didn't come to you, dude, stop lying to yourself. You bit your lip hard and called him a fucking child, and he looked at you with tears in his eyes and yelled, I am not a child! He flung a pillow at you and stormed out of the room.

You lay in bed. The ceiling spun so fast it was about to fall on you.

IV.   He liked to pray. On mornings when there was no lecture rush, he sat on the chair in front of his keyboard, his hymnbook open before him, his Bible closed, hands clasped in a praying posture against his chest. He muttered the words softly softly. Sometimes the sun drew fine lines on his face, and his lips became redder, his skin brighter, his aura more childlike.

V.   It was on the day of your last exam that Mum fell in her restaurant and had to be carried home by some of her customers. On your way to Peace Park, you called Kamsi. I won't make it to your piano recital this evening, you said. My mum fell sick.

Where are you now? he asked. I'm c-coming.

He met you at the motor park. What happened? he asked.

They said it's hepatitis B, you said. My sister said she's not been well for a while. She went to a chemist, got treated for malaria, said she was fine. She does this all the time.

He sat beside you on a bench. You both watched the hawkers and agboro. Most departments were through with their exams, and the park teemed with students. You'll still travel tomorrow, right? you asked.

Yes, he said. My b-brother will meet me at the airport.

Okay, you said, moved closer and held his hand, you were trembling so badly.

You need a sweater, he said. It's going to get cold by the time you approach Kano.

I have a sweater in my bag, you said. He had his hand in yours, hidden from view by the way you both sat so closely.

You had never said it to anyone before, but now you told him, how you were afraid that Mum would die suddenly, just like her mother, and you wouldn't be able to buy her all the cars and clothes she didn't have now. It's like mourning someone many years before their death, you said.

Everything will be fine, all right?

All right, you said.

As your bus ambled out of Peace Park, the girl seated beside you wouldn't stop giving you the eye. Nsukka glided past, rusty roofs and red dust, the evening turning gray blue so quickly. You blocked your ears with earphones. The song was Aṣa's "So Beautiful."

VI.   Only three months, and Kano looked changed and new. You opened the window and devoured the sight. The sun shone remorselessly bright. Houses, tall and short, ugly and beautiful, stood side by side. And people. So many people. People who didn't care whether you said good morning to them. People who were I don't care like that. *Ba komai.* That was the word. Nsukka had reminded you of good behavior, with the town's dusty red roads and old houses scattered between farms and bushes, and people who took offense if you did not say good morning. But Kano, big ancient Kano, Kano of merciless sunniness, Kano of wide-road and coffee-smelling Bompai, Kano of slang-and-decay Sabon Gari. Kano reminded you of the word *be*.

In Sabon Gari, the air smelled of decaying refuse, the roads had holes, the houses like discolored matchboxes strewn around by adventurous children. And so many people speaking Igbo and Yoruba and pidgin. You closed your eyes, breathing deep, absorbing the sounds, all the tongues; everything felt like huge arms spread out to welcome you home.

There was no okada in the streets, you noticed.

Yes, army pursue okada, Chisom said, searching your bag for the toy car you had bought him when your bus stopped briefly in Lokoja.

Why? you asked.

Boko Haram, he said. Boko Haram use okada to bomb.

You noticed, like a newcomer, the smallness of the living room, so square, so artless, the fading blue walls covered with pictures bearing everybody's stories, from Mum and Dad's wedding to Chisom's first birthday. The dimness, how the neighboring house blocked much of the light.

At the hospital, Mum could barely talk. She lay in bed, too bony to be Mum, Mum who had always been described as *full*. The room smelled of cleanness. Dumebi sat on a mat spread on the floor, her legs stretched out in front of her. Four people from church sat on plastic chairs, looking prayerful. Their leader, an evangelist in a too-ironed ankara, stood up and said, Brothers and sisters, the devil came to steal, to kill, and to destroy. He waved a huge black Bible in the air, spoke with an authority like he could kick open locked doors and storm dark rooms and make them super bright. As he spoke, his prayer warriors hummed, it was like he was pulling them with an invisible string. When he said Rise, *rise*, let us pray, *pray*, the room filled with voices high and mighty, and you stood reluctantly, worried that a nurse would storm into the room and yell at everybody to fucking shut up, they were too damn loud.

———

Later it was just you and Dumebi and Mum. When she said How is school, in a voice so thin and cracked, something inside you broke.

Dad came in with Chisom. He shook your hand and asked, Nwoke, a na-eme kwa? You left the bed and sat in a chair. Dad sat on the bed beside Mum, saying something softly to her. She nodded now and again, and once you caught a smile on her face, and the broken thing in your chest began to collect itself.

Leave that thing, now! Dumebi said to Chisom, who was trying to get the bottle of Lucozade Boost on the medium-size refrigerator.

I want to bring it for Mummy, he said in his three-year-old voice. The way he stood on tiptoes, struggling to get the bottle, was comical. You made to help him, but he'd already grabbed the bottle. He held it up, hands shaky with its weight, face brilliant and proud as he turned to you all.

Oya, go and give it to Mummy, Dumebi said, but he rushed to you, screaming, Lota, open for me!

You all began to laugh, Chisom standing there thinking he had fooled everybody. When you described this scene to Kamsi, you told him how it had made you feel hopeful, how briefly the world had seemed capable of tenderness.

VII. You emerged from Rachael's bathroom and found her curled on a sofa in the living room, crying.

She tossed your phone to you. You picked it up, confused, and flicked it on. You'd forgotten to delete Kamsi's text message. It glared at you now: *I'm listening to Davido right now, and I'm thinking of that night we went to Flat and the Klin promo car was playing "Ekuro" and you said you'd kiss me behind the old buildings if I dared. Miss you, man.*

When Kamsi had sent the message, you had read it over and over, had searched for hidden meaning. And you'd forgotten to delete it like you did the others.

Who is Kamsi? she asked, sniffling. Who is she?

She's my course mate, you said, then added quickly you'd stop seeing her.

You sat beside her, held her, letting her struggle until she relaxed.

Kamsi called to say that he had finally arrived in Kano, could you come to his house at Bompai? You said no, you were a little sick and needed to rest.

Who was that? Dumebi asked.

My friend, you said.

Kamsi?

Yeah.

She nodded, patted Chisom on the bum—Stay one place, let me wash your armpit—and said to you, You lied to him. You'd told her about Kamsi, your wonderful new friend who was king of church organs.

You shrugged. Well, sometimes it's necessary.

She hoisted Chisom out of the plastic bath and proceeded to wipe his body with a towel. I can't lie to Obika, she said. He'll not talk to me for weeks if I did.

Digressing, you asked, What's up with you and Obika, sef? I've not seen him since I returned.

Oh, he traveled to China, she said. He should be back next week. She paused, helping Chisom into his pajamas, then, without changing the color of her voice: He wants to bring wine to Dad, I agreed.

You laughed. But she wasn't laughing. She meant it.

Do I look like I'm playing? She patted Chisom's head and sent him off to watch TV with his friends—If you dirty your body you'll enter the bedroom and sleep. He ran off, his gait shaky, like the breeze would carry him away.

What about school? you asked. No more JAMB?

JAMB, kwa? Exam that I have passed how many times. Where is the admission? I cannot continue to wait for university, biko.

You didn't get her. You had waited three years before you got into the university, changed your course choice from law to political science and then finally to history and international relations. She had waited just two years, and there she was, complaining.

She scoffed. Biko, don't forget that I am a girl. My time is short.

But you're just nineteen.

She shook her head. Me, I have decided, she said, turned her face away from you. Besides, I'm tired of all the quarrels in this house.

II.   It wasn't that you couldn't have kept quiet. Wasn't that you couldn't have swallowed the phlegm. But as he stepped into the living room the night before you returned to Nsukka, laughing at something Chisom had said, you looked up at him and simply could not understand.

At the hospital, you'd been playing a game on your phone when Mum said, You see how heartless your father can be, eh?

Her cheeks looked sunken, her cheekbones jutting out. Just look at me, she said, lying here like this, and he can't even show some respect. Small respect.

You placed your hand on hers. Mum, what is it?

Where did your father sleep last night?

I thought he slept here?

Here, kwa? Your father, your father left me here and said he was going home to you and Chisom. Only for me to hear this morning that he was seen coming out of that useless girl's house. Does he have to do it on the street we live in? With girls who say "good morning" to me?

Who told you? you asked—you did not know what else to say— but Mum had already shut her eyes and was shaking her head slowly.

Your anger swung like a loose-hinged door. You weren't sure if you were angry that Dad had slept at the girl's house, or because someone had brought the news to your sick mother. So when he stepped into the living room that night, laughing, you said, You're heartless.

He looked around the living room, behind him, above him. What?

How could you do this to Mum? How?

He stood there, mouth open like he was going to say something.

You wanted to stop, to apologize—but your heart burned, like you had hot charcoal on it, and your tongue was bitter. The words poured out. Nwoke, he said, looking struck and confused. Nwoke.

You had almost forgotten how tall he was, how you looked so much alike, with the same broad shoulders and the same sleepy eyes and well-kept goatee. It stared you in the face like a child's taunting, this resemblance, sticking out its pinkish tongue at you.

You walked out into the looming darkness. Through Abedie and Sanyaolu Streets where the sound of Hausa music filled the night, the street cramped with so many keke napeps, and you remembered your days in secondary school when one night, on your way to Dave's house, a lady stopped you on Abedie Street, speaking florid Hausa, and when you gaped at her, she tugged impatiently at your arm and asked, You wan' poke? You wan' poke?

I no wan' fuck, you had said to her, dragged your arm away, and ran.

You walked to France Road. France Road with the streetlights beaming orange light. France Road with locked-up shops at night and with rushing cars during the day. France Road with Dave in a room of his own, chatting on 2go all day and hooking up with hunky guys, short guys, fat guys, married guys. France Road that led to Bompai and Airport Road, to Kamsi and Rachael.

You turned around and began to return home.

IX.   He had texted every day. Called every day. Had wanted to see your mother and your siblings. Had wanted you to meet his twin brother, Kosi, and his parents if possible. But every day after Rachael cried you had bounced his calls, deleted his text messages mostly unread. And now you were back to school, and he was standing at your door, and you were staring at each other.

How is your mother? he asked finally.

She's getting better, you said.

Okay, he said. I returned yesterday. Couldn't get to you. I c-came to get my keyboard.

You watched him throw his music books into his bag. Clothes he had left behind before traveling. Watched him lift the keyboard. Watched him walk out of the door. We'll see later? you asked, and he shrugged and walked away.

X.   Every evening you sat on the veranda and stared into the street, hens and people ambling by, and hoped that something would fall from the sky and break the silence in the house. Sometimes you walked down to Flat because it wasn't so quiet there. Not once, not twice, you'd picked up your phone to call Kamsi. But not once, not twice, you'd stopped yourself.

Then, one evening after football training, you came home to some students and a lecturer from your town's union at your door. You hadn't attended their meetings since eternity. You opened the door and let them in. The light from your rechargeable lamp cast tall shadows on the wall. The union secretary, a lanky guy in sociology, spoke like a character from *Things Fall Apart*, and you wanted to tell him that your heart was beating too fast, you could have a heart attack, that proverbs were cliché, and that this generation, your generation, spoke in monosyllables: She. Died.

And then he said the words: Your mother died this evening.

You watched the shadows and nodded like an agama lizard. Everybody was saying sorry, and it was like something was killing you slowly.

When everyone left, the lecturer took you in his car and drove you to Jives. You sat at a table for two. He ordered two bottles of Hero, said, That's the new drink for men.

Jives was open air, students and lecturers lounging around tables. The speakers were blaring out some fast song, and a handful of people were dancing.

The lecturer said, When my mother died twelve years ago, I was twenty. My father was already dead four years.

He had a flat nose and small lips and dirty eyes. He drank from the bottle and said, And all I could think about was how much she had suffered. And also how I was going to take care of my younger siblings, all four of them.

He drank again. But somehow, God helped me, he said. Our last born will be doing her convocation next month.

He paused. You glanced away, at the people dancing.

Where do you worship? he asked.

Christ Church, you said.

Do you have a relationship with God?

Church had always been routine, something to do on Sunday mornings. You did not attend any fellowship meetings, no midweek Bible studies. No revival hours for you, either. And God was simply there: at Holy Communion on Sundays when the choir sang your favorite hymn, "Abide with Me." And "relationship" was what you had with Rachael, with Kamsi, with your teammates.

I don't know, you said.

He chuckled, shaking his head. You don't know, he said, leaning in. I think it's God you can talk to now, really. It will help. And, you haven't touched that bottle.

You raised the bottle, and the image that never left your eyes was of Mum lying there, shaking her head slowly.

On your way home you asked him to drive you to Lemon Villa. A few minutes, and you were standing in front of Kamsi's door, listening to muffled strains of guitar music.

You knocked. Once, then twice. Tentatively. Who's there? he asked.

It's me, Lotanna, you said.

There was the clicking of bolts, and then he stood in front of you, a near silhouette in green shorts and a white singlet. Mum died, you said, swinging your arms like you were in Sunday school and he was your Bible recitation instructor.

He covered his mouth with his palm, eyes bulging. Stood aside to let you in. He shut the door. When was it?

Today, you said. This evening.

For a while you were both quiet. His wall clock ticked, the walls more green than lemon in the whiteness of the electric bulb, the rug red and soft under your feet. The room smelled of him, that mix of talcum powder and nothing. You told him how you had called Dumebi and wished you had not because her grief inflamed your own, how you had ignored your father's calls until the lecturer asked you why, and how Rachael had called to say God cares. Does God really care?

I hope he does, Kamsi said. Otherwise what's the use of everything?

You touched his face, tilted his head up and kissed him hard and gentle. You heard the grunt at the back of his throat. You were a little tipsy from drinking Hero. But not too tipsy to feel all the things that you felt at that moment: relief and love and that heavy, drumming sensation in your chest that always exploded in tears.

I.   They said they would beat the gay out of me, he said. But that I was so cute they'll have a little fun raping it out of me.

He laughed, like that sounded funny. Like he was unfazed. He was on the bed, his chin on his knees, which were drawn to his chest.

It had been going on for about a month. He hadn't told you.

Since October, around the time you traveled for the burial, he said.

But how did they find out about you? You don't even look gay, for Christ's sake.

How does one look gay, Lota? They even said what's the size of your macho boyfriend's thing.

You grabbed your phone and began dialing a friend's number.

What are you doing? Kamsi asked.

Calling some of my teammates. They'll deal with this.

And what will you tell them? Please forget it.

You cut the call, flopped on the bed, and covered your face with your hands.

XII. You would not be returning to Kano for the holidays, you told him. Enugu made sense, you had relatives there. He said, It's about your dad, right?

At Mum's funeral, Dad had tried to tell you how it felt like sinking and sinking, and you had told him, coldly, that you never knew he was a poet. He had called you into his room and told you a long story about how all that time your mother had been his number one, how even though he couldn't help it, seeing some other women, she had been the one he truly loved. He'd said, I'm telling you this because you're becoming a man, and that evening, you went to Rachael's house and told her you had to end it.

I think you should let it go, Kamsi said. He's your father, after all, and I can tell you miss him.

You continued folding your clothes into a travel bag.

He held your hands, gently pressed them to his cheeks. Then he began to blow on them, in circles, like you usually did to help him relax, his eyes fixed on yours. The room was suddenly still, the air calm and waiting. You felt like a child stealing milk.

Wait here, he said, his eyes lighting up. He rushed into the bathroom, returned to the room with a new razor blade.

Let's have a blood covenant, he said.

Don't be silly, you said, laughing.

Yes, I'm silly. Let's be silly together.

XIII. You watched Enugu from Aunt Oge's balcony, its calm, orderliness, the gray hovering over the faraway houses. November. The air in the mornings was cool, a little wet, not wet wet like in Nsukka, and not dry and brittle like in Kano. You were on the balcony in your singlet and boxers when the yellow taxi pulled up by the gate. The passengers alighted—Dad in jeans and a baseball cap, Chisom looking bigger, and Dumebi carrying two small bags, her stomach the shape and size of a football. At first they looked a little clueless, and then Chisom looked up and started shouting, Lota! Lota!

You did not tell me! you shot at your cousin.

Mum said it was a secret, he said.

At the door, Dad said, Since the mountain has refused to come to Muḥammad, and smiled.

Welcome, you said, after a slight pause, and took Dumebi's bags.

Somadina drove everyone around Enugu—Dumebi, Chisom, and you. There was something vainly ambitious about Enugu. A tidy city if you drove or walked through the right places; Enugu with the wide roads and do-not-litter policy, and pretty housing estates, and Shoprite, young people watching their villages transform into something big and glittering.

Enugu glided past you. You nodded when they asked a question. You could not pull out of the dark hole into which you were sinking. Chisom tugged at your arm.

Leave him alone! Dumebi snapped. He's not happy to see us.

You whipped out your phone and sent a WhatsApp message to Kamsi: *Hey love.*

You were not sad or anything. You just didn't feel right.

Dad had not left his business in Kano to simply visit Mum's sister in Enugu. He came for something, and seated alone with him and Aunt Oge in the living room, you felt trapped.

Aunt Oge said, You must forget all that has happened, life must go on.

But how can I forget? you wanted to ask. Like, maybe I should press a button in my head and say Delete?

Lotanna, Dad said. You cannot continue to run like this. You have to return home.

He said, We can start afresh.

He said, I'm sure your mother is in a better place now, and she'll want us to forgive, so that we can all meet her again at that place someday.

All this in Igbo, which you could not speak in a situation like that.

Because you had very few Igbo words. You kept mute, kpịm, tapping your bare feet on the floor.

Later, you called Kamsi.

    Someone else picked up. Lotanna, right?

    Yes, you said. Good evening.

    Now listen, young man. Don't ever call this number again. Our son is a good boy—

    You cut the call while he was still talking.

Dumebi wanted to know what was wrong. Was it Dad? Were you sure it was just Dad?

    Yes, you said. I'm sure.

    Then you have to sort it out, she said. Sharp sharp.

    I'll do that in my own time, you said. He should respect that.

    But every night, you slept with that heavy thing in your chest that rose up and up, until it choked you, until it strangled out a sob from your throat.

XIV.   In Nsukka everything looks worn, fading. You walk to the stadium, still incomplete one year after everything, and sit on a step on what should be the spectators' stand. It is getting late, and the bodybuilders are packing and leaving. A flock of herons have descended on the football field.

    You used to return here often, both of you, watching the herons and the late evening joggers. He used to tease you about checking out the bodybuilders, which made you laugh.

    It reminds you of Dumebi in Enugu, asking how long you had known.

    You sure this Kamsi guy didn't convert you? Because, from his pictures, I'm sure he can convert even the pope.

    So you don't think I'm handsome enough to have been the one.

    Vanity, she'd said, rolling her eyes. Was that why you broke up with Rachael?

On the street below, cars flooding the night with yellow lights.
I don't get this, she kept saying. What will people say? What
would God say?

Since when did you start caring about God, Dumebi? you asked,
and she chuckled and said, I be God pikin, abeg.

You still expect him to show up at your door at any moment.

After his friends came to your place, someone having heard from his
twin brother, Kosi, you called Dumebi and told her. I kept waiting for
him to return to school, you said. I even dared it and called his number,
but it was switched off. I didn't know, Dumebi. I didn't know.

You walk out of the stadium. It is getting too dark, and soon bad guys
will come here to smoke, and you don't want to be there when they
arrive. You put your hands in your sweater's pockets to keep the cold
away. The harmattan haze is so low, you can't see the world ahead of
you. You walk and walk and walk. Slowly, like you are walking with
someone. Listening to their footfalls.

You create dreams in which he comes and talks with you. You
talk and talk and laugh and laugh, and it feels like you are stretching
a fractured arm, testing it. When you wake up, the room is cold.

You want to ask him, Why?

And, Did you think about me?

And, Why didn't you just endure like everyone else?

There is no power. You light a candle, and everything else becomes
shadows.

You call Dad. He sounds surprised: Lotanna?

A sị m ka m malụ otu ị dị, you say.

Oh, thank you, he says. A na-emekwa?

Ee, a na-eme.

Tonight, you dream that he walks into this room. He is wearing
his Arsenal jersey and green shorts. He lies beside you and says, What
happened to you, Lotanna? You look so broken.

ALỌBAM

It was past ten when Obum finally called back. By then, the club was packed, and Ralu had stopped telling anyone who asked that he was waiting for someone, and so had allowed a couple to settle in the private booth with him. The girl in her Christmas hat had glanced at him shyly, almost apologetically, before they'd begun making out. He'd let his eyes settle on them for a second, and then looked away, at the dance floor that was dim between the sparkle of lights. The DJ had been on fire all night long, giving them jam after jam; now he was playing Olamide, and if he were here, Obum would have been on the dance floor. Ralu loved to watch him, his joy and his freedom that pulled people in, women who turned around to hug him through bouts of laughter between songs, the occasional guy grabbing his waist in a way so brief and loud as to be humorous, but underneath which Ralu saw desire or curiosity.

Things had been different recently. Ralu had tried to make him talk whenever he was at the house, each attempt met with stoicism, which had made Ralu all the more worried because Obum liked to talk, his Instagram bio said *in this house, we are vulnerable and radically honest*, and so he had decided that perhaps what Obum needed was a distraction, this, a wild Friday night at the Element. But two hours after he was supposed to show up, having said he'd take a keke after hanging out with his friends, he was only just returning Ralu's calls.

Ralu watched the phone buzz on the table. He poured himself another shot of Hennessey, which he'd opened after the first hour of waiting. Now that his phone was ringing, Obum's name flickering on the screen, all that anger and uncertainty had vaporized, replaced with relief. It was loud in the club, Teni blasting out of the speakers. He downed his shot, reaching for the phone just as it stopped ringing. He could feel the couple's presence, the girl in her Christmas hat, now that they were no longer kissing, now that they were whispering earnestly to each other. They were young, probably Obum's age-mates, twenty. He caught their eyes on him. "Feel free," he said, loud and smiling, nodding at the bottle, still half-full, on the table between them, and the guy smiled and said, "Manchi!" Ralu's phone buzzed again, stopped, and then flickered with a text notification. *I'm so sorry*, the text said, *I'm high af and seated alone outside a store on M.M. Way. Please come get me.*

∿

All the cars, all the lights on the road. It was as though he had water in his eyes, he saw everything first through a glaze, and then extra bright. When a car approached, he felt both hopeful and afraid, hopeful that it would be Ralu's dark-blue Honda pulling up to the curb, afraid, when it wasn't, that the quizzical glint of the headlamps would linger for too long and that the car would stop suddenly and a stranger would emerge and march toward him. He plugged in his earphones. Before the store owner, Inusa, locked up for the night, he'd said, handing Obum a blanket, "You fit sit down for here, I go leave the bench outside for you, and the security light go dey on," and Obum thought he would cry. He'd nodded and said thank you and watched the man walk down the street, his white jallabiya so long, it almost grazed the pavement.

If the evening had gone well, it most likely would have ended at Inusa's store, as it usually did, Ibrahim chatting with him while he made their Indomie and fried eggs, Obum practicing his Hausa by interjecting every other minute, which pleased and amused Inusa.

But the evening had not gone well.

He reached into his pocket for his phone, opened Instagram. The cold nibbled at his fingers. Top on his feed was Ralu, who in several pictures was wearing a red Christmas hat ringed with blinking stars, his colleagues, all in almost uniform suits and ties, smiling around a Christmas cake.

Obum wondered what was taking him so long. He eased his hand under the blanket, warming it, and then returned to his phone. He found himself on Ibrahim's page. His fingers seemed to move of their own will, scrolling through high-resolution pictures until they got to the grainy ones in which Ibrahim was not yet so inked, not yet ripped. He was lanky in these pictures, all arms and legs, a gangly boy. In one of the pictures, he was holding a chair above his head, facing a classmate who was also holding a chair above his own head. Obum remembered that day, the sun, the roughness of their play. They'd just written their final exams in their final term as juniors and were heady with joy (if they knew then what they knew now, would they have looked forward to adulthood?). He remembered Mr. Jackson walking into the classroom and barking at everyone to kneel down, they were making so much noise. He remembered that he got his first note from Ibrahim that afternoon, slid expertly into the *New General Mathematics* textbook he'd borrowed, or pretended to borrow, earlier that day. *Every time I look at you*, the note said, *I feel confused but I don't hate it.*

Obum sifted through his texts, rereading Ibrahim's recent messages. The earliest, sent a week before, said, simply, *Hey ;)*; the second, a few days later, *Baby, how are you? Sorry, I was going through shit with my elder brother, that's why I disappeared like that.* The third, sent before daylight this morning, was a nude pic, lean body covered in tattoos from V-line to chest: wings above the chest, a snake here, a cherub aiming an arrow at a heart there, a prayer in Arabic, "and from dust shall We raise you again," the prayer said—Ibrahim had translated, lying beside Obum years ago after their first hookup. He'd taken the picture lying on his bed of gray sheets, arm extended in front of him, pointing down at the spread of his body, at the lofty obscenity of his hard dick. Under the picture: *Why aren't you answering your messages?*

You come here full of promises & good times, ghost me and then return like nothing happened, Obum had typed hours after that. *I am a human being, Ibrahim. I feel things.* He deleted it. Openness made him weak, he told himself, lying on his friends' couch, listening to their playful singing, their guitar strumming—"That progression, very tricky," Tomi said, chuckling to himself after missing a note—and he was done being weak. *I just want to fuck bro*, he typed instead, *send your keke driver.*

He looked up from his phone now, sensing a car's approach. Ralu's Honda stopped in front of the store, headlights blinking. The road remained washed in all those lights. How the evening had turned, Obum thought, blinking to prevent tears, he did not want Ralu to see him crying. Billie Eilish's voice shivered in his ears, aching, and the world felt bloated with the sadness.

~

"Are you okay?" Ralu asked as Obum put on his seat belt. He did it with religious care whenever he got into the car, something people rarely did in Kano. He sat with stillness, his back pressed firmly against the chair.

"Yes," he said. "I'm sorry I stood you up."

Ralu said nothing. Obum was that way, even in his apologies, always naming things as they were. Ralu had found it endearing in the past; now, it annoyed him, even if slightly, that sentence, "I stood you up," signifying an awareness that had not deterred him from doing it anyway.

"Were you with Ibrahim?" he asked.

"Yes," Obum said.

Ralu nodded, engaged the gear, easing the car onto the main road, which was wide and smooth in this part of town. He loved to drive here. Unlike in Sabon Gari, where the roads made his car bounce, forcing him to drive slowly, here he could accelerate, fling the car into all that wideness, wind rushing in or, as it did now, beating against the rolled-up windows. He wanted to ask more, wanted to know why Obum had chosen this particular day, when they had a date, to go see that boy, but something in Obum's demeanor, something both stricken and ready to strike, made him pause. They had been fighting more about Ibrahim recently. You do not own me, Obum had said the last time, and Ralu had retorted, I let you see whomever you choose, I'm just worried about you. You "let me," Obum said, *Let!* For two days, they did not speak to each other. Two days in which Ralu moved around feeling confused; he had done nothing wrong, he knew, and yet he felt he had to apologize. He'd never felt that way with Obum, confused, not in the two years since they'd begun doing this, not in all the years since they'd known each other. On the third day, before Ralu could send the apology he'd crafted in his head, Obum messaged. *I was being unfair,* he said, *I'm sorry.*

Ralu kept one eye on the road, another on Obum, who was now fully relaxed into his seat, eyes closed. Perhaps he was asleep and dreaming something wild. At New Road, cars and keke jammed for as far as the eyes could see, the air had changed, tainted by all that honking and all that smoke. The windows were rolled up, and yet the harmattan cold seeped into the car; he turned up the heat, then rested his eyes fully on Obum. The car's dimly gold light poured across his face, his clenched jaws, lower lips, pouted as though in sadness and anger, so pink they were almost red, skin a lustrous black. Ralu had long since ceased to be startled by the resemblance, but right now it jolted him afresh, how keenly Obum had grown to look like his brother, Makuo, even down to the spread of his shoulders, the way they took up the whole width of a seat, so that it reminded him of Makuo sitting beside him in secondary school. He was wearing the polka-dot shirt Ralu had bought him last Christmas, had left the first three buttons undone, and Ralu could see the coy sprinkle of hair across his chest; it would have traveled down his body, that sparse hair becoming wild, were Obum not obsessed with smoothness. Ralu thought of the tubes of Veet lying in his bathroom cabinet; he, too, had begun using them when he noticed that Obum loved to play with his balls when they were smooth. How he loved this boy, he thought, sometimes it terrified him.

Driving to M.M. Way, he'd felt a rush of jealousy, he knew who lived on M.M. Way, knew that Obum had gone to see him before he admitted it, his flame from secondary school. And yet, seated beside him in the car now, all he felt was worry, his anger and jealousy blunted until it was an imperceptible spark in his chest. He reached his hand behind Obum's seat, letting his fingers graze his ear. The traffic moved and then stopped at the next intersection; he turned off the light in the car, so that people would not see, and then let his fingers travel to the back of Obum's head, caressing his neck, toying with his coarse hair, returning to his ear, the softness of his earlobe. Exactly like Makuo's, Ralu thought, and then cautioned himself against the endless comparisons, Makuo was gone and Obum was here, and yet he could not stop thinking of Makuo.

The warden standing in the middle of the intersection waved Ralu's side of the road forward. Suddenly, vehicles blinked on, the entire road going ballistic with the sound of stirring engines, of honking. Ralu made to withdraw his hand and place it on the steering wheel, but Obum grabbed it and held it there, eyes still closed, rubbed his right cheek against it. Ralu left his arm there, maneuvering the car with just one hand. Soon, they were hurtling toward Airport Road. A song had begun playing on 95.1 Cool FM, where, earlier, there'd been a talk show. Obum stretched his hand in the same carefree way that he reached for Ralu's balls and turned up the volume, Nonso Amadi's voice swelling in the car.

Makuo used to say, "You see my brother, Obum? He will go places," before regaling Ralu with all of Obum's recent exploits at school: a statewide spelling competition that he had won first place at, a televised debate competition that he'd participated in, the youngest participant, at the age of eight, his report card with first and second positions only. Makuo brought Obum to almost all their football trainings. In the beginning, after their mother closed her shop to become an evangelist, and Ralu and Makuo began watching Obum almost full-time, the other boys had resisted. First, they teased Makuo, "Your brother be like MTN—*Everywhere you go*," they said, or cautioned him, "You no go get girlfriend fa," and then they resisted outright, "Guy, na everywhere you go you dey bring am?" Finally, they got used to his quiet presence, which was every so often broken by a funny quip, even came to expect it, so that, when he missed a training or two, they wondered, "Where our small man dey?"

When Ralu thought back to those times, their teenage years, one of the recurring images was of eight-, nine-, ten-year-old Obum seated on the sideline, calm in his faded jeans shorts, in the relentless sun that left his forehead shiny with sweat. But it was not everywhere Makuo went that he brought Obum, just as he did not bring the other boys everywhere he and Ralu went. Sometimes, it was just the two of them, Ralu and Makuo, when they went to the uncompleted building that would become, twelve years later now, the resplendent Saint Rita's Multipurpose Hall. It was four stories; they would climb to the last floor and stand by the window, gazing at the farm behind the church's fence, at the stream that ran across it, black and thin in dry season, clear and gushing when it rained. Makuo liked to make up elaborate stories about the men who were bent over, tilling the earth or pulling vegetables out of it: in daylight, he would say, these were ordinary men, but at night, their true natures revealed themselves, their spirit natures, eyes glowing green or deep white; they walked among the crops, watching over the city, making sure everyone got a good sleep, but if you walked onto the farm after midnight and saw one of them as they truly were, that would be the end of you—not death, exactly, but a permanent absence from the presence and memories of the ones who loved you: it would be almost as though you never existed.

He would pause, letting the birds and frogs and the singing from the parish fill in the silence. "Once, there was a boy."

Ralu loved stories, and nobody told them as well as Makuo. "You know," he would say to Makuo, "you fit become writer like Chinua Achebe, my mother get all him books." The light, fading across the farm, signaling the closing of day.

"I know am," Makuo would say. "But, him be billionaire?"

"I no know o, I no think so."

"See, I wan' be billionaire when I grow. Like Dangote or Bill Gates, so that I fit buy duplex for me and my brother, then live very far from our parents."

Ralu knew what Makuo's parents did to him, had seen the welts on his legs and back, red and black and placed as though with intention, like patterns in a work of art. "You must to take me with you," he'd say. Lying on his bed later that night, he would imagine Makuo and Obum traveling far away from him, and the thought would fill him with sadness.

"You know why I no get any sibling?" he said to Makuo one evening. "Because my mother almost die when she dey born me. My father tell me so I go stop to dey ask her when she go born another pikin."

Makuo looked sad listening to him. "I be your brother," he said, and then, sliding an arm around Ralu's shoulder, said, "me and Obum." Their sides pressed together, Makuo warm and smelling of sweat and soap, of *him*, Ralu knew that he wanted to be more than a brother, that he wanted Makuo to hold his face and look in his eyes, the way men and women did on television, but that was a weird feeling to have for a friend, a terrible thing to feel for a brother.

~

Obum was starting to feel better. His heart no longer raced, and his head no longer ballooned, making the world seem endlessly confounding; he was still worried that Ralu was angry with him, and that the moment they got home, he would grab his shoulders, pin him against the wall, and yell in his face. He reminded himself that it was Ibrahim's edibles speaking, he'd never seen Ralu raise his voice at anyone before, and then he worried that he was muttering his reassurances out loud, and that Ralu was hearing everything and silently judging him.

They were closer to home now: the road had become bumpy, the streets darker, electric poles looming in the darkness, no streetlights around. He tilted his head and gazed at Ralu who, both hands maneuvering the steering wheel to turn at a corner, glanced at him and said, "You're awake." His face remained unchanged after all these years, light skin, pink lips, eyes smoky and dull, like someone who was always high: that was the feature that Obum loved the most, those eyes.

By the time they arrived, the bell was ringing at Saint Rita's for Christmas Eve, and the road leading into his street had been blocked off. The security men, in their orange and lemon vests, looked like squares of light in the darkness. Ralu would have honked and shouted at them in jest as he often did, and one of them, a parishioner volunteering, would have hailed him, "Ralu the man!" and lifted the barricade—but there were soldiers around tonight, seated in their vans, looking hungry and ready, and so he waited quietly until one of the volunteers walked up to him.

"Una go soon start to pay for the inconvenience," Ralu said, driving through. The man, Echezona, said nothing as, unsmiling, he waved at his colleague to lift the barricade.

Echezona was not really a man, he was a boy, could not have been more than twenty-one, but already he wore the grimness of a person who had seen it all, his shirt, oversize, tucked into trousers that swayed as he moved, indifferent, uncaring, as though he were declaring to himself, and to everyone around, that this world was not his home. He had not always been this way, pious and dour. His was a story of divine transformation: the women liked to talk about it in storefronts, or in their living rooms, or on balconies overlooking the

street, the remarkable story of the street boy who went to the Blessed
Sacrament every day, promising to change his life if God healed his
mother's breast cancer.

They said, "Oh, see am, perfect example of how God can send a
difficult situation just to save your soul."

They used him as a whip for their strongheaded children: "Do you
want God to make me suffer like Echezona's mother before you change?"

They turned him into a love epic, reminding one another that
no matter how errant a son was, no matter how impenetrable the
walls of his heart, deep down was a well of love for his mother, that
at the slightest glimpse of her suffering, a new person would emerge,
hurting with goodness.

To Obum, however, he was merely another young person lost to
the streets, to the lack, violent and unrelenting, that clung like algae
to the discolored walls and the bumpy roads and the tainted air. It
did not matter to him that it was not a knife stab at a street fight or
an abortion gone wrong, didn't matter that it was only a consuming
spirituality that left no room for joy: a loss was a loss.

Driving into the compound, Obum tried to banish the thoughts
of Echezona from his mind, they made him think of Makuo. As they
stepped out of the car, the compound kids rushed at them, tiny hands
hugging Ralu's legs, his waist, his hands, sparkling voices chanting,
Brother, oyoyo, Brother, oyoyo. Ralu lifted them up one after the other,
the littler ones—the older kids stood on the fringes, waiting for the
end of the *spectacle*, when he would walk them to Papa Ebuka's shop—
throwing them into the dark night and catching them midair. Their
screams, terror curdled into delight, made Obum happy, so that he
almost forgot everything that had happened at Ibrahim's.

Obum walked ahead of Ralu, who would spend a few more minutes
with the kids, buying them biscuits and Capri Suns at Papa Ebuka's
shop. As he trudged upstairs, he said good evening and happy Christmas
Eve to the women making their hair under the golden beam of Papa
Ebuka's outside lights, and to those who weren't so lucky, who, in dark

corners, had to hold kerosene and bush lamps over heads that would look, by morning, either like intricate artworks or gaudy portraits, depending on the chosen hairstyle or the chosen hairdresser. On some Christmas nights past, a woman's hair had caught fire, and the compound had reverberated with the commotion, screams and rushing and, eventually, laughter. He wondered if it had happened tonight. He said his hellos quickly, so that the women would not engage him in banter and, in so doing, see that he was high. He should be above caring, and if he were sober, he wouldn't have cared—but right now, he cared about everything in the world, sad things and happy things, everything vibrated at the tips of his fingers.

Ralu lived at the end of a long corridor. His was the biggest flat in the entire compound and was the only house with its own bathroom and kitchen inside. Standing by the door on which a sticker said My Year of Enduring Joy, Obum struggled a little, sliding his key into the keyhole, but eventually he was able to steady himself.

It was dark inside. He took off his sneakers but left his socks on, yet he still felt the coldness of the tiles on his feet. The floor used to be covered in a brown rug, soft to the feet but itchy if you lay on it too long, as Obum liked to do. Ralu had removed it after taking over the flat from his parents, replacing it with cream tiles that reflected the ceiling lights, beautiful but too cold in this weather. Lying on the couch, Obum came to the conclusion that a warm rug was better than aesthetically pleasing tiles any day. He slid out his phone. Two missed calls from Ibrahim. A text from Tomi saying, *Go on Twitter!! Beyoncé is that imperialist, capitalist queen I stan!* And, from Ibrahim, *I'm so sorry, I don't know what came over me.* And: *Please let me know you got home safe. I shouldn't have gotten so high.* Finally: *My brother just called to ask me all sorts of useless questions, I'm so tired of his wahala. Please talk to me.*

Obum put his phone away. He wanted to cry, not because of what had happened, but because he feared that he still cared in spite of it, still wanted to hold Ibrahim's sad head, stretch forth his arm and heal his pain. He was not okay, he was not okay—and he was afraid that he would not be okay for a long time to come. He wondered where Ralu had gone to, why he wasn't here yet, upstairs; being alone made him think, and thinking made him cry. He could still hear the women talking, but his mind registered only the ripples of their voices, just as it registered the street from a distance: music blaring, men laughing, drunk and happy and celebratory, children singing and playing, glad to be out and about this late. He should not have left his friends to go see Ibrahim; he'd been doing well. His head was full of memories, of their early days. The notes they wrote each other. The meat pies and buns Ibrahim bought him at break time. Their heads huddled together as Obum showed him how to solve an equation or conjugate a French verb, Ibrahim distracted and distracting, sneaking a kiss when he was sure no one was looking. Those memories, now tangled with recent, painful ones.

At his place earlier that evening, Ibrahim had answered the door shirtless, a smirk on his face. "My sexy troublemaker," he'd said. Obum said nothing as he walked into the living room. It had been years since he stepped foot in the house, before Ibrahim's father got the ministerial appointment in Abuja, before his brother, Hassan, found them together. All the other times Ibrahim had returned to Kano, he stayed in a hotel close by, said he was trying to avoid his brother's "spies." Obum wondered how Ibrahim could sleep alone in that one-story duplex in a compound covered in trees, a compound that was too dark at night, wondered if he was bored, or lonely, and then cautioned himself against feeling. He marveled afresh at the ordinary fact of space, the wide verandas with their polished terrazzo floors, the living room with its high ceiling from which dangled chandeliers, its spacious floor covered partly in a soft red rug around which black leather cushions were arranged in a semicircle and partly in gleaming white tiles in which Obum could see his face.

It was different now, unlike those times Ibrahim had brought him home under the guise of doing homework when the house would bustle with the movement of servants and cousins, the air sweet with the aroma of cooking, Ibrahim's mother doting on Obum, asking the cook to bring him snacks, asking about his comics. "Ibrahim has told me so much about your drawings," she would say, "I'd love to read." How infatuated he'd been with her, her olive skin without blemish, her slender face, the regality of her motions, the grace, as though anything she touched would combust in a flare of colorful dust. Sometimes, when Ibrahim finally got him alone in his bedroom, Obum would clamp up under his touch, unable to relax with the thought of that floating presence somewhere close by.

"I'm glad you came," Ibrahim said, handing Obum a video game controller.

Obum waved his hand, no. "I need to get clean," he said.

"What's the hurry?" Ibrahim said, punching his controller. "We have all night. We can relax and watch *Home Alone* or something."

Obum took a deep breath. It was like listening to an old song on repeat, Ibrahim seated there, face made mildly blue by the television, controller in hand. He'd barely glanced up from his video game as he spoke, that casualness, it had to be intentional. You left me on read for a month, Obum wanted to say, but there was nothing new about that and perhaps Ibrahim was right in acting nonchalant, this was, after all, the status quo and yet here they were, together again. Obum thought of all the times Ibrahim had shown up in Kano, lodging in hotels for days, sometimes weeks, rekindling what they had, and then disappearing without a word. Last month's had been the most brutal. Ibrahim had said, out of the blue, I wish things weren't so complicated, I really miss you, and Obum had shown up at the hotel carrying a hastily packed bag, cuddling and fucking and holding his sad head. Then Ibrahim said his brother was at it again, surveilling him, threatening to freeze his bank accounts, and he'd left.

Ralu had not liked it. "That boy is a distraction," he said one evening when Obum came to spend the night.

"You don't understand," Obum said. "You don't know him, he's going through a lot."

"What about me? What do I do while you go take care of him?"

"We agreed to keep this open, Ralu."

"Because I wanted you to enjoy yourself. This does not look like enjoyment."

They had been cuddling in bed after fucking, and their playlist was still on, 6LACK's voice sifting through the speakers. The ceiling fan ruffled the curtains.

"Is this how you want to spend the evening?" Obum said. "Arguing?"

Watching the shirtless boy who was now seated on the floor, video game controller in hand, it was difficult to reconcile the tornness Obum felt inside with the love, perfect and wild, he'd felt in their teenage years. He remembered, clearly, one morning during Ramadan. They were both sixteen. He had slept over, having lied to his parents and told them that he was attending a night vigil, and Ibrahim, too sick to go to the mosque, had spread a prayer mat on the floor of his bedroom. As he prayed, his pink lips moving silently, Obum had watched him from the bed. At that moment, he'd felt a fierce possessiveness. My man, he'd thought.

Now, he said, "I'm going to shower."

Ibrahim paused his video game. "Okay, babe," he said. He dropped the controller, crawled on his knees to where Obum sat, wrapping his arms around Obum's waist, his head on Obum's lap. He said, "You always smell so good," breathed deeply. Obum resisted the urge to caress his hair, jet black and mildly curly, resisted the urge to pull him close and bury his nose in the crook of his neck. Inside him, immense love wrestled with immense distrust. He would fuck and he would feel nothing, that was his mission here today, to use and be used: afterward, he would not text to say good morning, would not send memes he knew Ibrahim would find funny, would not respond to Ibrahim's memes either. He would be a wall, unfeeling and impregnable.

He left his arms hanging awkwardly at his sides until Ibrahim looked up and asked if he was okay. "Yes," he said. Ibrahim reached up and took his face in his hands, Look at me, he said, and Obum let Ibrahim gently pull their faces close, Ibrahim's warm breath on his face. Letting him go, Ibrahim caressed his arm, his neck, looking all over his body with a quiet attention, the absentmindedness of it, like someone checking a prized possession for wear. Obum eased him away from his body. It had to be a moral weakness, his inability to choose his own serenity no matter how hard he tried.

"Do you have edibles?" he said.

Ibrahim looked up at him, and then he smiled. "Someone wants to have a wild evening," he said. "There are a few left in my bathroom cabinet. I think I might have one myself." He stood up, his dick print sideways in his red Man-U shorts; he pinched the shorts between his legs, adjusting it, a small, careless act: it filled Obum with lust, after all these years they still responded to each other's bodies with thirst. Obum wished they could return to a time when it was not yet complicated, a time before Ibrahim's eldest brother, Hassan, suspicious and bossy Hassan, had dressed up and pretended to go out so that he could walk in on them, as he did, ten minutes later. Obum wished he could go back to a time before Ibrahim's mother asked him never to show his face at their house again, hate and disappointment on her face as she glowered at this boy who had come to corrupt her precious son, a time before Hassan slapped Ibrahim, reached out to slap him too until Ibrahim stood between them, pleading, saying You can't beat someone else's child, you can't beat someone else's child.

He missed the times before confusion, when Ibrahim did not show warmth one day, coldness the next. At first, around the time they began their final exams, the coldness had been absolute: they would pass each other in the corridors at school and Ibrahim would look away, or harden his face, and it had felt, each time, like fingers digging into a wound. And then Makuo had died in that street fight, and everyone at school had gathered around Obum's table to say sorry, which had made him cry even worse. Ibrahim there later, in front of his desk at break time when the class was empty, just the two of them. He pulled up a chair and sat in it, silent. He held Obum's hands. Obum began to cry again, for Makuo and for himself. Ibrahim sat there, saying nothing, holding his hands and saying nothing.

~

Two years after they graduated from secondary school, after Ralu entered his second year in Nnamdi Azikiwe University and Makuo didn't even gain admission, Makuo started going to Weather Head with Crazy Man, who was about ten years his senior. He returned to Aminu Road one evening, Ralu was told, high like there was no tomorrow, found his father beating Obum, and punched him. Nobody liked the way the man beat his children, they told Ralu. After all, he and his wife weren't the only evangelists in Sabon Gari and others didn't beat their children like that. But nobody supported Makuo for fighting his father, for standing in the doorway after letting Obum run off and saying, "If you ever touch am again, I swear, you go regret my next action." Nobody liked that he turned on his mother and said, "And you, too, if you didn't want us, why did you bring us into this world?" After his real death at twenty-three, people began to say he had died on the day he'd punched his father and insulted his mother.

Obum had once shown Ralu the ladle with which his parents beat him, brown, smooth, sturdy wood, the same ladle with which his mother turned garri. "If I don't teach you," Makuo's mother would say, "then I don't love you." By the time they entered secondary school, Makuo had learned and mastered ways of manufacturing other experiences he'd had with his parents—they had gone to the zoo on Christmas Day, they had gone to the amusement park on his birthday—each experience lacking, at first, in specificity, and then becoming outlandish. One day, in JSS3, he came to school with a camera phone. "My father bought it for me," he said, his classmates clustering around his table, touching the phone, taking pictures. The next day, the principal called him out on assembly ground. There was a song the students sang to taunt people who had stolen. That day, they sang it to Makuo, clapping their hands, stomping their feet. "Mai thief! Mai thief!" they chanted.

That night, someone knocked loudly on Ralu's door. It was late, the compound had gone to sleep, and the sound of Baba Tosin's snoring could be heard from next door, a constant fixture of night. Ralu's father came into the living room, where Ralu slept on the sofa. "Who's there?" he barked, his machete clasped firmly in his hands, as though wielding it against darkness itself.

Makuo simply wept.

Ralu's father opened the door. In the room, Makuo continued to cry, head bowed. It was shame, Ralu would realize years later after the knife fight that killed him, to be seen that way, helpless, always helpless, it made Makuo ashamed. Obum stumbled into the room, holding his brother's hand. In the soft moonlight that cut the room conically, he looked lost. Ralu's mother rushed to them, ushering them in.

Long after Obum had slept off, on a blanket spread for him on the living room floor, Ralu and Makuo stayed awake, watching WrestleMania. They sat closely, their arms brushing. The television was muted, so that even as images flickered in the living room, the night still lent its sounds to them.

"Them no go try this rubbish with Obum," Makuo said, so quietly it seemed he was telling himself. "They should wait and see."

"Let me see," Ralu said.

Makuo took off his shirt silently, turned his back to Ralu. Ralu touched Makuo's back, tentatively at first, then gently. The welts were too red and too many, even though his mother had massaged Makuo's back with a towel soaked in hot water. Makuo turned around and leaned backward, so that he rested on his arms, his stomach exposed. Ralu touched his stomach. It was hard and rough. The marks were smaller there, thinner, purplish. Ralu touched his navel, drew circles on it. Makuo chuckled. Tickles, he said. The night was so quiet. Even Baba Tosin's snoring had diminished.

"Sorry," Ralu said, looking away. He wasn't sure if he was sorry for what had happened to Makuo or for what he was feeling in that moment, what he had felt so many times before, but more intensely at that moment: a need to be closer to Makuo than mere arms grazing, than mere playing football together, than mere sitting together in the same uncompleted building.

When Ralu insisted on returning to Kano after university, his parents having relocated to Enugu by then, his mother said, "It's because of Obum, okwia?" and he looked out of the window and said nothing, and she returned to reading her Bible and said nothing else about the matter.

Ralu sat on the armrest, watching Obum sleep on the couch, running his fingers in slow circles through his hair. Walking into the house earlier, he'd moved the curtains aside, the darkness softened by the light from the street. The way Obum lay on the couch, in a fetal position, it reminded him of their first time together, a Friday night two years earlier, almost one year after Makuo passed. Obum had rushed into the house, waving a newspaper, bubbly with joy. He'd just been admitted to study fine arts at ABU, Zaria. They hugged, Ralu opened a bottle of moscato, and they clinked glasses. It was April, the air soft with impending rain. By then, Obum was already spending half his nights at Ralu's flat. His parents gave him money for upkeep, promised to pay his university fees, and in return, he did not totally disappear from their lives, spending every other night at theirs, accompanying them to church every other Sunday, he was eighteen, which, for a boy, especially one who had somewhere else to lay his head and fill his stomach, was grown, he could not stand them, and Makuo's death, the gruesomeness of it, had changed them: they had become meek and more agreeable, perhaps out of guilt, or fear, or a mix of both.

Obum shared Ralu's bed, choosing always to sleep by the wall, it made him feel safe, he said.

And so, that night, as Ralu felt Obum's hands on his body, he could have jumped out of bed, but he did not. The room, dark, was occasionally brightened by a slash of lightning: it illuminated the billowing blue curtains, the wardrobe, the portrait on the wall, of his mum, dad, and himself in their Sunday best. Obum's fingers caressing his hair had surprised him, and when they paused, he held his breath. The fingers flicked across his arm, a single tame motion. And then, with a sudden boldness, they reached around his waist, caressing his thigh. Obum, Ralu said, grabbing the boy's hand, and then letting go. You're like a brother to me, he said, and thought of Makuo saying, I be your brother, me and Obum. Yet, there he was, hard as iron. Maybe it was because he hadn't felt a strong attraction for anybody other than Makuo. What was he? he used to wonder. He liked girls and he liked boys, but it manifested as a general curiosity, roving and aimless, without fire. He'd had to know Makuo before he loved, or even desired him, for his storytelling and for his face, but especially for the way he looked like he needed to be held, and though Ralu had learned to control that feeling for the sake of their friendship, it never went away.

His first time with a guy, and it was Obum, Makuo's little brother. Between them, the sound of rain, the coolness of air, desire charged with sadness and hope. Obum gripped and stroked him with such possessiveness; he simply lay there, letting himself be kissed. When he came, he shuddered, wailing into Obum's mouth, the ugliest wailing. Obum's lips parted in a sweet, low chuckle, Yeah, he muttered, fuck yeah. They clung to each other. Ralu said, Your turn to come, unsure what to do to make that happen, but Obum shook his head, Just hold me, he said, that is all I want.

Ralu remembered how he stayed awake long after Obum had rolled away, deep in sleep. How he'd stared at the ceiling, at the fan that stood motionless in the gentle morning light. How he'd gone to stand by the window, listening to the lone tenor chanting "Allahu Akbar!" A few seconds later, Saint Rita's bell started tolling, sonorous and majestic in the gaping silence of early morning. The muezzin's voice continued, almost sad in its abundant tremolos. Ralu's face was cool with the after-rain breeze. The years he had spent going to university in Awka, he had risen on many mornings, longing for that duet, of man and bell. It was what he'd missed the most about Kano, after the people, and yet he knew that when he returned, they would be there, the minaret and the belfry, the streets, the convoluted interconnections of main roads and alleyways, shortcuts he knew like rhymes from childhood, intimately. The people, not so much, at least not Makuo. He'd been away, tidying his MSc thesis, when he heard the news of Makuo's death. He thought how unfair it was, the impermanence of people and the permanence of things. Obum muttered something, still asleep, turned and faced the ceiling, his hands spread, his left leg swaying. In that moment, he was exactly as Makuo would have been.

~

Obum had not felt himself fall asleep, but now he woke up to Ralu's fingers in his hair. At first he remembered nothing, only the sadness that had lulled him to sleep, and then he remembered everything. He remembered Ibrahim's bathroom, the white tiles on the wall, the white towels on the rack, the mirror that was clean and clear, making him think that a cleaning person must have come around recently. He remembered that he was still seated on the toilet, that the water he'd been shooting up his ass had finally come out clear, when the edible kicked in, his head light and awake, his heart palpitating, his toes, dick, asshole awash in a sweetness. Remembered that he stood up, flushed the toilet, and then got in the bathtub, under the shower that was already spraying hot water. Almost immediately, Ibrahim rapped on the bathroom door before gently pushing it open. He got in the bath behind Obum, wrapping his arms around Obum's body, his hard dick pressed against the cleft of Obum's ass. His arms, sturdy and inked and veined, Obum caressed them with his fingers, throwing his head back, allowing Ibrahim to grip his neck, to pull his head back, staring into his eyes and forcing him into an impossible arch. The spank on his ass, it was shockingly rough, too rough, too early; Obum gasped, whimpered, and Ibrahim gripped his neck even tighter. Whose are you? he asked, and Obum whispered, Yours.

I can't hear you.

Yours.

Always remember that.

Obum remembered that he only heard the sound of the shower when Ibrahim reached around and turned it off, the silence awaking him to the gushing sound it had replaced. He remembered Ibrahim kneeling behind him, prying his cheeks open and burying his tongue in him. He remembered the clarity of his pleasure, his feet lifting until he was on the tip of his toes. He remembered, also, the clarity of his pain as Ibrahim stood up and pushed in, searing pain that split his body in two, from head to toe. Fuck, he said, beating on the wet walls, pull out, I need lube. Ibrahim holding him there, saying, I ate it, you can take it. He remembered that he did take it, and that for almost an hour, as they moved from bathroom to bedroom, the pleasure he felt morphed into dread as Ibrahim became rougher and rougher, saying, Thought you only wanted to fuck, well get fucked, anger in his strokes, real anger, not the playful kind, punctuated with laughter and smiles, that they both liked to toy with when they got high like this. There was no smiling, no laughing, and when Ibrahim put him on his back and looked in his eyes, all Obum saw was that anger: in the whites of his eyes, now red, and in his sweating, laboring body, muscles taut from his aggressive movements. Perhaps it was a culmination of the high and everything that he'd been feeling lately, but in that moment, all Obum could think was Why? The question gripping his body, making him clench up, filling his head, every pore; he thought Why are you doing me like this? and said, Ibrahim, stop, grabbing Ibrahim's arms to push him off, but Ibrahim did not budge until he came, an eternity later, shuddering and muttering, Fuck, fuck, his eyes closed, his body shiny with sweat, a bead of sweat falling from his forehead onto Obum's face. When he pulled out, Obum felt a sharp, slender pain inside; he clutched his legs, his body tingling with the pain. He'd been crying all along and had not even realized it, real crying, tears streaming down his face. Ibrahim had fucked him through his tears. He felt such pity for himself, and such rage. He got up, silently, and began picking up his clothes from the floor. Throughout, Ibrahim said nothing; he sat at the other end of the bed, his back to the wall, knees drawn up to his chest, head bowed. Occasionally, he glanced up, but Obum could not bear to look at him, confused and ashamed and enraged as he felt, and so did not see the expression on his face. They said nothing to each other, even as Obum dressed and left the house, easing the door closed behind him, as though afraid to disturb the peace.

～

One moment, Obum was asleep, and the next he was awake and crying. Ralu immediately slid beside him on the couch, holding his head against his shoulder. Obum wrapped his arms around him. His body was warm and trembly. "Am I a terrible person, Ralu?" he said, between sobs. "Do I deserve terrible things?"

The question pierced something inside Ralu and then shattered it. He hated to see his baby so beaten, hated that boy for doing this to him, as though he'd not had enough beatings to last a lifetime; and he hated his powerlessness, that he could not end it all with the right words, the right actions. He looked into Obum's face, his eyes glossy with tears. "What would make you think that? You're one of the kindest people I know. And you're so beautiful. You deserve everything good." He paused. "Did something happen at your friend's house?"

Obum's voice increasingly steadied as he spoke, each mounting second of his story making Ralu quake with anger. Halfway through his story, the siren went off on the street, and a roar went up, "Up NEPA!" The appliances beeped awake, blinking blue and red lights all around the living room, as did the Christmas lights that Obum had hung up the previous day, twinkling like multicolored stars in the darkness. A neighbor's speakers came on, a band was singing a carol.

"How are you not angry with me?" Obum said. "I don't understand it."

"Why would I be?" Ralu said. "I've said it before that you can see whomever you please, as long as you're safe." He smiled at Obum, hoping that it would calm him. "And as long as you bring your beautiful self back to me."

He kissed the side of Obum's head. Of what use would it be, telling him that waiting in the booth of that club tonight, he'd come close, for the first time, to feeling disappointment? The boy was clearly hurting. There was always tomorrow to talk about what *he* needed. All he wanted right now, holding Obum's head against his chest, was for Obum's life to be easy, for him to return again to that boy who would walk into a room, talking excitedly about comic books and TV shows, the boy in whose presence everyone felt at ease to be themselves. That was what made him happy, seeing all that light, and knowing that, in some small or big way, he was responsible for it.

He thought of the last time he saw Makuo, an evening before traveling back to Awka. They had taken a walk, chatting, aimless in their ambling. Finally, they arrived at Saint Rita's Hall, climbing the staircase with its gold-plated banisters. Already, Ralu could sense something different in Makuo, a remoteness; he talked about life in a defeated tone, dropping unsolicited advice like an old man who had been through it. "See," he said, when they got to the last, and only—at the time—uncompleted floor, "you're so lucky that you're bright, please don't lose focus. This country eats people alive, and only the strong and sharp can make it." Ralu had watched him, his worry mellowed by Makuo's earnestness, his use, completely, of English instead of pidgin, his baggy trousers that were a faded blue, his white shirt with the green letters that said My Money Grows like Grass, his eyes with their look of sad resignation. "You see Obum? He has that brightness, too, I think he can even get a scholarship anywhere he wants, he has brains and talent." He paused, looking out the window. Ralu followed his gaze. Below, a group of women had gathered on benches, singing in Urhobo, and beyond the fence encircling the parish compound, the farm loomed, green and brown, the stream running through it a thinning black. "But there's something about him, he doesn't want to tell me, but I know. I know he likes boys. I know that he is doing something with one of his classmates, one Hausa boy like that. He will not tell me, but I know. I accept it, it is his life and I want him to be happy." Another pause, this time he looked straight into Ralu's eyes, and Ralu knew that he was speaking to him, not merely about Obum, but also about him. His legs felt weak, and his heart pounded. "I am telling you because you are my person, aloba m, and I know you will understand when I say that I'm worried that his life will be very hard here because of it."

Ralu thought of that evening all the time, how the sky had become a canvas of warm colors, yellow, orange, red, all the bats fluttering against it. He thought of it now as he held Obum. "I love you," he whispered, kissing Obum's ear, "never forget that."

Obum held him tighter. Outside, Papa Ebuka was yelling Happy, happy, his voice thick with laughter. He must be closing shop. He never closed quietly, even on nights when the street was not bright and loud; he would yell out words, or burst into song, *for this life, I can't kill myself o*, his voice, bright and cheery, multiplied by the deep quiet. Tonight, his words did not come back to him in echoes, but as the responses of passersby, Saint Rita's parishioners on their way home from Mass, neighbors out in the street, drinking or making their hair. Happy Christmas! they yelled at him. Banging through all that noise, Saint Rita's bell tolling the end of Christ's Mass.

GOOD INTENTIONS

You could end it at dawn. It would shatter him, for how long, you do not know. But first, you take a walk.

It is not yet daybreak, the full moon is receding, the pavement glowing with its borrowed light. It is a perfect morning for this. It has rained all night and the air is quiet and smells of kneaded earth. Tall trees flank the tarred road, long branches reaching out like desolate lovers, and when the breeze rushes through them, they shake the water off their bodies and it falls on you, a blessing.

You're walking past the tall brown building where your office is housed on the last floor. Trapped light beams behind most windows, tender white light, but not behind yours, you do not leave things unresolved. Right now, you wish you did—to see the fan twirling behind your empty office, to glimpse, from this distance, the swollen bookshelves, to be part of something that's yours without being present, your life from a distance.

He'll be gone when you return. If any of your students run into him in the corridor as he walks from his department, they'll ask What's up, where is your guy, and he will shrug and say he does not know, it's not like you two sleep in the same room or anything; he will be defensive today because of the stories, the whisperings.

"Will you tell me how it went?" he'd said yesterday, after you returned from the preliminary hearing and went straight to your study, saying little of consequence to him, and then as you prepared for bed later, "You don't have to go through this alone."

At forty, you were almost twice his age. You had grown up under two military dictatorships, you teased him, and this was nothing in comparison.

You remember now your first night together, how, after you rolled off his back, panting, he turned toward you, as though he'd forgotten something, and touched your face, lifted your chin, *wow*; how he looked at your face, searching, until, overcome by shyness, you shut your eyes and kissed him.

In those early days, his attentiveness had flattered yet terrified you. You feared that if he looked hard enough, he'd see how troubled you truly were, see the ghosts from your past lurking behind curtains of accomplishment, and leave. But for over a year he had stayed and loved you. You had spent so many years running from yourself, when you finally stepped into the light, years had passed you by, the men your age had loved and lost to exhaustion. And the younger men, the big boys, they lay beside you for what they could get: access, money, meals in sanitized spaces off campus, the comfort of a big bed in an air-conditioned room. You let them stay for a while, waking up to their snoring, their scent, sometimes all you wanted was to touch and to hold, nothing more. And then you let them go. It was easy: give less and less of the things you used to until, frustrated, they disappear.

You wonder who the other boys are, faces rising now in your memory. Many faces. How easy it had been, moving through those younger bodies, their wants precise, your needs nebulous and wild, until you met him. Walking up to him after Poetry Friday months ago, you hadn't imagined that he would follow you home that very night and strip you of all other curiosities. You'd found him beautiful, especially when he stood in the spotlight and dramatized "Invocation," the rich baritone of his voice, the ruggedness of his towering stance, the force that he was, the hall drowning in manifold applause. Okigbo would be proud, you'd said to him, and he'd smiled and told you he'd heard so many wonderful stories from your students, that you were fair and respectful, and how much he loved your book, *Reflections on Loneliness*, how he'd looked up all your essays afterward and fallen in love with your mind, the way you were, unlike most literary critics, profound without sacrificing clarity. You'd thanked him, surprised and pleased, by the honest audacity of his compliment. "Fell in love with your mind"—it seemed like something a colleague would say, even though you hadn't heard many nice words from your colleagues, who had sent a letter to the dean asking why you, a single lecturer, got a bungalow on campus while they, family people, had to manage flats in neighborhoods off campus swarmed by loud, rich students.

"Let's have a drink sometime," you'd said to him, and he'd replied, "Whenever you want," and smiled.

"How about now?" you'd said.

You walk now past engineering, past the faculty of biological sciences, away from the conspiracy of trees and into unburdened air, onto the road leading, on your left, toward Chitis and, on the right, to the stadium and male hostels. A figure hurtles toward you, it is a man and his face is hidden beneath a hood. He is a tall tree and a rock, possibly one of those students who skip classes to go to the gym. You expect him to stop and ask for your phone, nicely at first.

He dashes past you, saying nothing. His motion brushes against you. You smell him, too, the stench of exertion, and you turn to glance at him, to see what he looks like from behind. Your eyes meet, but briefly, because you snatch yours away. You glance back again and, again, he too has turned to look at you, his speed retarded to a trot.

It is the sort of thing you would mention to him at bedtime, fluffing your pillow, to light a certain fire in him. Consider the variables, he would say. That man is either checking you out or luring you to make the first move so he can have a reason to be violent. A violent man on a dark, lonely path with someone three times smaller does not need a reason to be violent, you would respond. His elbow pressed on the bed, he would look at you and ask what would you have done had the man propositioned you, and you would pretend to think about it, and say, I'd invite him home for a threesome, and he would laugh and say, As if you can handle the both of us.

You will miss this joy made possible by his laughter, the beauty that it is, at once hesitant and shy, at once free.

"You can talk to me, you know," he'd said, when the boys first came forward with their stories.

"About what?" you'd said, pretending not to know.

"You know what." He was seated on the bed in his favorite red briefs, his ankles pulled together, knees in a V, clutching a pillow against his chest. You did not look at him, could not remember what it was you'd been looking for in your cabinet, but you began to pull out drawers, fingers dancing over files.

"Doc," he said, his voice soft as a sigh. For the first time in over a year, there was nothing tender about the way the name sounded in his mouth; it reminded you instead of the things you were trying to hide from.

"What did you hear?" you said.

"Things." He shrugged, he looked unsure. "The stories are many but I find it difficult to believe any of them. But, again, we've never talked much about the guys you used to date."

"This is about the article, I hope you know that," you said.

His shoulders moved a little, and he frowned, a very boyish frown. "Why does that sound like an accusation?"

"It's not. It's simply the fact of the matter."

"I didn't ask you to write it," he said. "I was proud that you did, but I didn't ask you to."

You frowned, returned to the drawer. You were angry, and it made the feeling return, the exposure that opened into darkness, and it made your heart thump.

"I am proud that you did," he said, breaking the silence. "It was very brave, and very, very foolish."

"*Very you*, you mean," you said, you chuckled and he chuckled.

"Those boys." You turned to look at him. "I was never their teacher. The men you and your friends have been protesting against, who threaten girls with failure, those are the men sitting in judgment against me."

He was quiet, as though waiting for you to say more, and you wondered if he felt it, too, your fear. You'd been trying to imagine what had been done to those other boys to make them surrender their shadows and appear before a bench of men who would look at them with disgust. What would they do to him, your wise, beautiful boy who did not yet know the heartlessness of powerful men?

You had always thought of painless ways to do it—you have always been afflicted.

You are fifteen, the neighbor's son is sixteen, and your mother has returned home unexpectedly to find the both of you entangled on the sofa; her scream, piercing like jagged glass; the indignity of your naked fumbling, of his trousers pooled around his knees; the days that followed, your mother's eyes looking everywhere but at you, the shame clouding them; the smell of incense in dark rooms; the phone calls she made, to your brothers and aunties, phone calls that led to more dark rooms, to strange men prancing around you, pastors and prophets whipping your naked back with palm fronds, whipping so hard you still have scars, which he caresses.

Your mother cried every time you came out of those dark rooms. At first her tears had shredded you, your dear mother hurting because of you. Months later, when you came out of the dark rooms feeling nothing, when her tears made you angry but also indifferent, you imagined how long it would take after a knife sliced your wrist, you'd seen it done in movies, and you wondered if it would be painless.

"I can't have sex with a woman," he said weeks after he moved in with you. "Like, I'm totally gay, not even bi-curious, where does the erection come from?"

What would he do, you asked, if someone pointed a gun at his head and asked him to fuck with a girl?

"Of course I'll do it," he said. "Have you ever thought of getting fucked? Like, just to see if you'll like it?"

You'd both been lying on your living room floor where earlier, you'd walked in to him doing his evening sit-ups and, taking off only your shoes, knelt astride his chest, counting and teasing him, saying, "One more, soldier," the both of you laughing, and then kissing and taking off your clothes.

The rug scratched your naked back now. You rolled onto your side, facing him. "Are you asking to fuck me?"

"Maybe," he said. He smiled shyly, looked briefly away. "I promise I'll be gentle. Soon you might even be begging for it."

It wasn't as if you didn't think of it every time he came out of the bathroom, his body wet, but hearing him say it, that he wanted this, it spread a shadow over you.

"I cannot see myself getting fucked," you said, standing up. "I can't." You were surprised by how angry you sounded.

"We're only talking, Doc," he said, sitting up. "Why are you getting angry?"

"Please, let's free this talk," you said, hoping it would dispel the tension. Under different circumstances, he would have laughed and asked if it didn't feel good, speaking like a true Nigerian.

"Why do we have to free the matter?" he asked. "This is the first time I'm bringing it up, you don't have to agree, but you cannot simply shut the conversation down. I stopped making pro-gay posts on Facebook because of you. You said they put you in a precarious situation and I agreed, even though I don't agree. I quit volunteering at the NGO because there were 'too many fem and open guys working there.' What have you given up for me?"

You stared at him. How could you explain to him that it was absolutely necessary for you to demand certain things of him?

"I understand what you're saying," you said, calmly. "But I'm simply not that kind of man. I don't get fucked."

There was a split moment when his face showed nothing, and then his expression erupted. "You're not that kind of man?" he asked. "What kind of man am I, then?"

He stood up, shaking his head as he slipped into his shorts. He headed for the bedroom door.

"No, no." You followed him into the bedroom. "I didn't mean it like that, nna."

"You know exactly what you meant," he said. "You have to control everything. Sha don't expect me to call off the protests, because it's happening."

"So that's what this is about?" you said.

"It's about the fact that you think only of yourself. Perhaps moving in was a bad idea, if it means I have to only make choices that make you comfortable."

He'd been aggressively straightening the bedsheet and patting the pillows as he spoke, now he stood straight, facing you.

"That is an unfair conclusion," you said. "I'm not perfect, I know that, but when it comes to this protest, all I am is worried about you. It has nothing to do with me. There will be backlash." You paused, you needed him to understand. "And the way you're going about this, it will be easy to single you out."

He stood there, shaking his head. "You talk as if I don't know what we're up against."

"Do you, really?" you said.

He was quiet, one hand on his waist. Then he walked to the wardrobe and began to pack his things.

Walking past the female hostels, you remember your undergrad girlfriend, Ndidi, who'd stayed in one of the halls down the hill from Hilltop. You can't remember which exactly, it must have been Akinola Hall. You lived in Hilltop at the time.

Her name, now that you think of it, was sadly prophetic, because of how infinitely patient she was, forgiving your mood swings, your philandering—you were like heating glass in those days, you exploded without warning. Your mother had introduced her to you, "My friend's daughter," she'd said, with an earnestness that made you feel sorry. "Take her like a sister." Every weekend Ndidi showed up in front of your door, carrying food flasks and stories about her week. At night, your roommate ostensibly disappearing for "night class," you turned off the light before feeling in the darkness for her breasts, before kissing down her belly. You'd learned, by then, to listen to a woman's body for what brought her pleasure. You'd also learned that by stripping your mind of thought, your body could will itself into an uncertain firmness. On Sunday evenings you walked her to her hostel, holding her hand, sitting in her room and chatting with her roommates, until it was late and the bell went off and you walked back home, while all around, boys and girls stood in dark corners, stealing final kisses before the final bell.

On these same streets.

The evening after he left, you drove to Franco, parked in the postgraduate compound, and called him. He came out of Alvan Hall, holding a bucket, his shorts too big, his singlet too thin for the weather. It was one of those deathly cold harmattan nights.

"Pneumonia does not know you're angry with me," you said as he stood beside you, resting his back against the car. He shrugged, folded his arms, still holding his bucket. "Let's sit in the car. It's warmer inside."

"I have to go fetch water for tomorrow." He remained standing, unmoved. "You know how long the queues are in the morning, and we have Dance Drama at seven."

"You don't have to be here, queuing up for water. We can go back to the house and talk about this like two adults."

"There's nothing to talk about." He'd dropped the bucket on the ground, now he rubbed his palms together and touched his face with them. There was a slender darkness in his eyes. You had not imagined how much this meant to him—and why should it mean so much? He was not a girl, nobody had failed him for refusing to have sex with them. "I just wish you'd understand this time." He chuckled, a small, sad chuckle. "I actually thought you'd understand."

A sudden breeze sliced through the compound. He shivered. You took off your sweater, offered it to him; he stared at your hand for a while, and then he took the sweater. "Thank you," he muttered, pulling it on. You both stood there, saying nothing, your palms freezing. Every battle had a price, you wanted to say to him, hoping he'd choose not to fight this one. What else could a person want from life other than a private serenity?

"How are you doing?" you asked instead, giving up this particular battle yourself. "I hear they pack you all in here like sardines. Anybody tried to eat you yet?"

He tilted his head to the side, and then smiled. "You talk as if you did not briefly live in Franco in your days."

"It was different," you said. "It smelled nicer then, and we had water in the toilets. The students who came before Babangida had meal cards and didn't have to buy food, so they had it even better than us."

"It only gets worse," he said, shaking his head. "Naija."

He did not come back home with you that night. He'd move back in after the protests, he said. You thought of him as you drove home, how he could, by his very restless nature, obliterate you, and you realized, with a little dread, that you did not care.

Let's walk together, he used to say, you'll love it. Until he stopped asking. Mornings have always been for poetry, actual four-dimensional poetry, not contemplative loitering. Some have morning prayers, you'd told him, I have poetry, and he'd laughed, Such blasphemy, he'd said, must be the reason poets die tragically lonely deaths—because the Lord our God is a jealous god. You are not a poet and you had not told him about how you used to dream of a painless way to go. When he touched the scars on your back, you told him, eventually, where they came from. You'd never talked about this before, you told him. Never. When he touched your wrist, you moved his hand away, casually, and placed it on your groin.

These days, when you open a page of Rilke, it doesn't feel like prayer, you feel instead a fiercely corporeal despair, a premonition in your body of something gathering, roving, something both unsettled and unsettling.

Your mother found you. Poor woman, always walking into hopeless situations. "God, you were gone already," she said later, wiping tears from her eyes. "It's a miracle you're here, even the doctor said so. Chukwu arụka!" How are you, my baby? she said at the hospital, and you turned your head away, your body was a well in dry season, deep and empty and full of cavernous echoes. The hospital smelled nice, and *nice* meant clinical, the minimal whiff of medicine and antiseptics and quiet, until the people from church came and crowded your bed with their human scents, and their singing and praying, all of which felt like one huge pillow pressed to your face. Death by suffocation. Only if they could do away with all the feeling.

You yelled—rather, a yell rang out of you, you were incapable of *doing*, it felt as though you were standing apart from the boy on the bed, watching him scream.

They continued to pray and sing, their voices climbing into a crescendo, you wondered why the boy's yelling made them pray harder and surer, and so he screamed again, a keen and endless sound full of wrath. A nurse rushed in, followed by the doctor who came every evening to ask how you were doing. "Everybody, out!" she said. "Nurse, usher these people out." Movements, murmurs: the separate part of you observed all these while your body raged. Hands touching you. Hey there, it's okay, it's okay. Something piercing your skin, a warm palm on your head. Recede. The last thing you hear, the doctor scolding your mother: "What do you mean, *possessed*, eh? O dị ka ị chọrọ i gbu nnwa gị? You want to kill your child?" Your mother crying.

When you woke up, your mother was there, your father seated

beside her. "Mma," you said, and she rushed to your side. There was a drought in your throat. "Water." She whirled around, but already your father had snatched the bottle of Swan water from the refrigerator. He handed the bottle to her, sat beside your head and propped you up. She brought the bottle to your lips and you guzzled it, almost choking from eagerness, it seemed, only that morning, you hadn't wanted to die. The body, how incapable of fidelity. They chuckled, softly, and your father caressed your head. You had never been in such physical proximity with him, not since you started secondary school. You looked at their faces, their smiles so wide, it would rip the corners of their lips if God wasn't so great.

"Odogwu," your father said, a fierce happiness in his voice. "Į sị ka ị bata?"

You nodded, shy, you weren't sure if returning was a choice you'd made, but there you were, not gone, and all you could think about was how sure you were of your love for them, love that made forgiveness wash over you like a breeze. Your mother sniffled, took your hand and pressed, lightly. Her eyes were the reds of fallen dabino. The pastors and prophets she dragged you to, each slashing and whipping away at your innocence, until the final one snatched it all, on the hard floor of his huge church placed among affluent mansions. Three days and two nights of praying and singing and Bible study, your parents present, his prayer warriors present. And one night alone with the Lord. And his servant.

You thought, watching your mother, of the song that went like this: *What the Lord has done for me / I cannot tell it all.*

What the lord did to you, you will never tell for all eternity.

The protests yielded nothing—the dean did not step down, a female teaching assistant was made welfare officer of the panel, which meant all she did was make sure there were snacks and minerals during every hearing, and one man, out of the eight accused by over twenty female students, was found guilty of insensitive behavior and sentenced to a two-week course at the Centre for Gender Studies.

He came home early that day, skipping his remaining classes, and you expected him to seethe. "Insensitive behavior," you expected him to say. "So that's what they're calling it." You were thinking it, and so you expected him to say it, because before him, none of this would have lingered in your mind for long.

"God, I'm exhausted," was all he said, falling onto the sofa, closing his eyes, and you wondered if it was mere physical exhaustion. The enemies he'd made, and for nothing. You watched him walk around the house in atypical silence, opening and closing the refrigerator so many times, and you became convinced that what he felt was not so much exhaustion as that sadness that upsets the body, sending one into prolonged loitering. At night, you rolled over in bed and found, where his warm body should be, space. You shuffled to the living room, rubbing your eyes, and turned on the light.

He was seated on the couch, his legs covered in a blanket, his arms folded. He looked up at you, wide awake. "Jesus. Why are you sitting alone in the dark, nna?"

"I can't sleep," he said.

You went to the refrigerator and got two cans of Sprite, offered him one as you sat beside him. "Thank you," he muttered and placed it on a stool without opening it. You popped yours open and took a sip. "You have a right to be angry about what happened today," you said. "And it is healthier to show it. That's why I'm here, to be the ears into which you pour out your frustration."

He remained quiet for a while. "I'm not angry," he said, finally. "I wish I could be angry, you know, it would have been easier. But I can't stop thinking of Nneka and Anita and all the girls who exposed themselves because of this." He stood up abruptly and, his face buried in his palms, went to stand by the window.

You went to him. "It's okay, let it out," you said, placing your hand on his shoulder, you were unsure of the right words to say, if there were any right words.

"I'm stepping down as student union secretary." His voice, still tremulous, was trying to take on a brave resolve. "I don't see the use doing anything when the people who are supposed to look after us constantly ruin everything."

"I'm so sorry," you said, and began to rub his shoulders. He spun round and hugged you, his body shaking with low sobs.

Toward morning, you woke up to watch him sleep, his face peaceful yet sad, his words in your head. You turned on your laptop and searched for the email address of a former classmate who was now a top editor at *This Day*.

In this country, you began, we crush the hopeful spirits of our young, and then wonder why we have no future. Recently, some of my students came together to fight for something real…

There is a poet none of your colleagues know, probably because he was Scottish, probably because he loved men. He has a poem titled "Absence." "My shadow—," it begins.

At your preliminary hearing the day before, the dean said to you, "Do you know this boy?"

Yes, you said, and sat up in your chair. How could you forget him, the first man with whom you had been naked, years after your mother walked in on you and the neighbor's son? You have the feeling again, of being walked in on. He had been good, a boy with a pretty face and a graceful masculinity, but like the others after him, he'd not been what you were looking for, even though at the moment you'd not even known that you were looking. Now he stood there by the lectern, as though he were the accused, his head slightly bowed, his fingers dancing with one another.

"Was he your student?"

No, he was not your student, you said.

"So how did you get to know him so well, he now accuses you of these disgusting things?" You looked up, surprised; this, from a man who did not have his PhD yet. The panel comprised six men and two women. Apart from the dean, who was a professor, the others were your peers, people with whom you attended conferences in Ife and Ibadan and Accra, people of whom the dean had said to you months ago, "They rarely publish any papers and have no groundbreaking books and yet feel entitled to the privileges of people who do," before picking up the letter they'd written about you and shredding it.

This hearing, dubbed grandiosely as *preliminary*, was a prelude to what they had already decided for you. If shame and disgrace were what they wanted, you'd give them dignity instead.

"You heard the man," the dean said. "How did you know this boy?"

The boy looked up at you, briefly, and you saw something slip through his eyes, a tiny grin or flickering despair, you were not sure. How long had the both of you lasted? A month? You wondered, again, what they had done to him to bring him here. Wondered if they'd promised him something, instead.

You stared at the dean. In the article, you'd written simply that his handling of the protests and accusations had been deeply flawed, that you, too, had failed by not confronting him about it. You could have been harder on him, you thought now, but you'd felt a tenderness toward him, this man whose books and lectures on African histories and literatures had inspired you in your undergraduate days, and so had allowed yourself to think of him as an old man who did not understand.

"I know the seriousness of these accusations," you said, calmly, even though your heart was beating fast. "Which is why I'm treating this respectfully, unlike some of the people in this room who, months ago, used verbally and mentally abusive tactics to stop their accusers from coming forward. I am here to see my accusers, and I have seen just one, and I agree that I know him. I want to hear what his accusations are. I have never molested nor threatened any student, and I have never, in all my adult years, had relations with anybody less than the age of twenty. Does this student, or anyone, for that matter, accuse me of rape or assault? Do any of *my* students accuse me of improper relations? Anything beyond that, I will prefer not to answer to this panel."

The silence that followed drowned even the nearby gargling of generators. The man who'd spoken earlier turned to the boy. "So? Did he not molest you?"

"No," the boy said.

"Then what do you call what he did to you? Didn't you say that he fucked you in the ass? What's that called?"

The boy winced. *Fucked you in the ass* must have unsettled him like it would have unsettled you had you not come prepared. He looked from the man to you, then to the dean. "He—fucked me, yes," he said, staring back down at his fingers.

"So? What do you have to say to that?" the dean said to you.

"Nothing."

"Nothing?"

You shuffled in your seat, exasperated, exhausted. All you wanted was to be home, in your bed, away from all this. "Like I said earlier, unless I am being accused of assault, rape, or molestation, I will not answer."

"And what is that that he just said, eh? You sodomized him, a young man. What is that called?" It was that man again, the one who'd spent an eternity writing his dissertation and still wasn't anywhere close to completion. It was almost as if every other person on the panel was there to merely hear the gossip.

"You *did* complete a master's degree in European languages, Onochie," you said. "Certainly, you must know what that word, *molestation*, means."

"That's enough," the dean said, taking off his glasses, rubbing his eyes with his fingers. "It's your right to be silent, but by and large, this panel has to reach a conclusion and pass judgment. We will end it here today, but tomorrow, in the spirit of transparency—we learn from our past mistakes, you see—the hearing will be held in the New Lecture Hall, and all student excos from every department in the faculty will be present. Two other boys have accused you. All three will be there tomorrow."

You stood up. It was rude, to leave before the dean, but the look in that boy's eyes, of pure, crystal pain, had shredded you, even though you'd remained cold, for your own sake; and now you had to sit before hundreds of students, most of whom would be there with their phones, and witness the humiliation, not just of yourself, but also of three young men. On a campus so compact, the lights between trees kiss, humiliation is a murder weapon. You could see the headlines already, on blogs and newspapers: "Homosexual Lecturer Sodomizes Male Students"; "40-Year-Old Homosexual Lecturer Converts Boys to Homosexualism."

"Yes, one more thing," someone said, as you placed your hand on the doorknob. You turned around. It was one of the two women; she wrote poems with lines like "the iroko tree has fallen" and made her students buy and review her books. You knew, because he wouldn't stop talking about her last semester, how much he hated her poetry, even though he enjoyed the classes where she talked about other poets. "The student union boy," she was saying now. "The one who stepped down as secretary... "

"What about him?"

"Shouldn't we question him?" She turned to the dean, who was arranging a sheaf of paper on the table, and then back to you. "I learned you live together."

"And so?"

"Well, if what these boys are saying is true, and I'm not saying they are or not, shouldn't we be worried for his moral well-being?"

You stared at her. The color on her face, in her voice, of concern, the ostentatious falseness of it. She was passing a message they'd all agreed upon. You turned around and left the room, shutting the door behind you.

The trees that stretch over the road leading homeward, how beautiful, even in sunlight.

It was a conversation about cups, why they had to leave the dining table after use, why they had to leave the sink, too, clean and dried of water. It was also a conversation about fans and light bulbs, why they had to be turned off when leaving the house. You were standing by the sink, running water over the dishes from the morning, when you both had hurried out of the house, and he was leaning against the kitchen table, saying he wished you wouldn't rush to do the dishes every time they stayed a minute longer in the sink, it made him feel lazy. Not lazy, you said, just young, post-military-dictatorship young, and he laughed and said, What? You learned to cover your tracks in those days, you told him, to never leave anything unresolved.

Is this still a conversation about chores? he asked, and you said, Maybe, maybe not, and asked if he'd ever thought of leaving the country, studying abroad. He looked at you strangely. Everybody thinks about leaving Nigeria, he said. You shook your head and said, Not like that, what you meant, you said, was if he'd thought about it seriously, like, what would he do if someone left him enough money to leave and go to school?

Nobody would say no to that, he said, and then: Why? Do you have cancer? Are you about to leave me a bunch of money?

Thief, you said, and he laughed. You laughed. You felt happiness like a spring, clear and sparkling, standing there with him, talking mundane things. An ordinary evening. You could decide to end it at dawn.

I know you don't want to talk about it, he said, but I hope the preliminary hearing wasn't awfully terrible.

It went well, you said. I was ready.

Are you afraid for tomorrow?

Wiping your hands with a towel, you said, I'm not afraid, and then you kissed him. There would not be a reason to be afraid if there would be no second hearing, no need for him to be interviewed, no crowd of people around you, once again, chanting and yelling and praying.

Sweetheart,

For you, everything and anything.

Love,

Doc

———

Home, finally. You turn the key in the keyhole, push the door open. A lone cup sits on the dining table but the bedroom light is off. You smile. Baby steps.

You take the cup to the sink, turn the faucet; the sound and feeling of warm water, how calming. Opening the cupboard to return the cup, you find a small gift wrapped in purple and yellow; in front of it, in his boxy handwriting: "The cup was bait," a wink, and then, "a little something to say you are not alone." You clutch the small wrapped box as though to crush it—but it is you who are crushed, by gratitude and by sorrow. You will not open it, not right now with your hands shaking. You will open it later, when he is here, so he can watch your anticipation. You lean against the table, steadying yourself.

It's just you and I now, the Lord's servant had said that night before he did the thing you have never told, his breath piquant against your face. Afterward, he said, Will you tell?

No, you said, sniffling, wiping your eyes.

Why? he said.

And you repeated his words: Because no one will believe.

You see now the church's arched ceilings, the gentle majesty of the altar on which you lay, the moon seeping through stained glass windows, making the chancel glow. Your mother's sunny smile as she picked you up in the morning, her hopeful tone as she said, It is well. The warmth of her body as she hugged you, her chest thumping with good intentions.

You reach for your phone.

WHAT THE SINGERS SAY ABOUT LOVE

I. I'd seen Kayode once before, in first year, having a bath downstairs, his wet body an assemblage of small perfect muscles, his ass firm and flawless, his dick, *my God*. I noticed him in the way that one notices something beautiful but unattainable and did not see him again until second year, when I went with my friend Ekene to a campus celebrities' bash. He was going from group to group, talking, swaying to the music, and I only recognized him as someone I'd seen before but did not know, until I heard someone say his name. Ekene had talked about him a few times in the past, this handsome boy who made beautiful music. I sat in a corner of the room, watching people dancing, thinking how happy their lives were in that moment, how tomorrow this senseless joy would be absent. His eyes caught mine watching him. He looked puzzled, a look that, with most boys, usually turned into aggression. I glanced away.

When I looked back up, he was staring at me. I smiled, unsure of how to read and return that brazen stare. He smiled back, whispered something to a girl who was deep in conversation with Ekene, and she nodded, a quick, distracted nod. He strode toward me, holding a can of Star, which he placed on the table as he sat opposite me. I noticed, for the first time, the tiny gleaming silver stud in his right ear.

You seem to be having so much fun, he said, smiling. He had the whitest teeth.

You're teasing me, I said.

Oh no, I'm not, he said, lifting his arms innocently, and for a moment I believed him, but then he smiled widely and asked, Why aren't you dancing?

I can't dance, I said, shrugged.

He arched his eyebrow. The song playing now was loud, was full of clanging metal, of booming drums, and the dancers had gone completely mad, jumping and shaking their heads like people about to burst into incantations. When he spoke, he had to shout: Everybody can dance.

Not me, I said. I dance like a girl.

You what?

He leaned in and I leaned in, my lips to his ear. His hair had a distant scent, of something sweet and fruity. I imagined him in the bathroom, his head crowned in lather. Then I remembered his body, the muscles moving across his back and arms as he washed himself vigorously, and I felt a little guilty; it had been different seeing him down there among a dozen other boys having their baths outside as I brushed my teeth, each person a feature of morning, now it seemed like a small violation.

I dance like a girl, I said into his ear.

He looked at me weird. You dance like a girl, and so? he said, squeezed his face thoughtfully. Standing up, he held out his hand. What, I said, confused and a little excited, and he said, Trust me, smiling a playful-wicked smile. He led me to the middle of the room where he started swaying his shoulders. God, Kayode, I said, covering my face with my hands. *Love me, love me, love me*, the speakers boomed, and he sang along, holding out his hands toward me, *so ma fi mi si le / Oh I like it here.*

A girl laughed, yelled, Dance!

Dance, someone else responded, and soon it was a chant, Dance! Dance! Dance!

You see? Kayode said, taking my hands and twirling me round. God, kill me now, I thought, and moved my hips. Yes, people cheered, and if not for these shouts of affirmation, I might have collapsed from the exposure. Closing my eyes, I let the music take hold of my body, waves of pleasure rippling through me. This was what people meant when they said dancing was fun, I thought, this absolute surrender. When the music stopped, I opened my eyes, and there was Kayode beaming, Ekene cheering, the dance floor drowned by laughter and applause. I shook Kayode's hand and he pulled me into a manly hug, our shoulders clashing.

I need some air, I said, as the next song began.

God, me too, he said.

He followed me to the balcony, where a few people had carved a space for themselves to smoke and talk. The street below was dark, electric poles watching over the closed shops, and there was some breeze, and the music blasting inside was muffled, Kayode having shut the door behind us. I took a dramatic breath, saying how good the air was on my face. I felt happy yet anxious and exposed, a confusing meld: I'd noticed a few guys leave when Kayode led me to the dance floor, now I was sure that they'd left in disgust and anger, those had to be the only reasons.

I have to go home, I said.

He looked puzzled, concerned. Are you okay?

Yes, I said. I'm just not a party person. I'm exhausted already, but I'm glad you made me dance.

It made my night, he said, eyes alight, and then looked at me serious. I should probably see you off. You don't want to jam bad guys walking alone, this is their time.

I texted Ekene: *Walking home with Kayode. See you tomorrow, hun.* We walked downstairs and out the gate together, down the dusty road, the houses gray and forlorn.

So how come you know my name? he said. I was a bit surprised when you said it on the dance floor.

I glanced at him; walking side by side, I noticed I was taller. You're kind of famous, mister.

He laughed. You know, I used to see you in the hostel. I would think to myself, Who is that guy, I have to know his name.

I felt a small, sweet stirring in my chest. Why didn't you talk to me? I asked.

Because you always had this unfriendly look on your face, and you walk really fast.

He looked serious; I laughed, slowing down my steps. He laughed, too. At Hilltop Gate, a group of guys were seated on the corridor of a closed shop, smoking weed, and I reminded myself to put on my manly walk and my manly face. He called out to them, My manchi, and they called back, Baba, and I felt terribly grateful for his presence. We walked out of the gate, making small talk, little rocks crunching under our sneakers, onto Cartwright, the tarred roads illuminated by lights beaming from hostel windows. We walked toward the senior staff quarters, took the thin path leading to the boys' quarters, the ground a carpet of dead leaves. At my door, I said, Thank you, and he said, Yeah, sure, and looked at his feet and then at my face, a peculiar shyness rising into his eyes.

He was naked in my bed the next morning and almost every morning until the end of semester. For the first week, we stayed indoors all evening and fucked like two freshers newly discovering the joys of having a room away from home, stepping out only to buy food or get a change of clothes for him or more condoms from the chemist at Hilltop Gate.

Little things made him happy, such as my neighbor's singing, which was horrible (it sounded like a billy goat in heat, he said) but joyful, or the fact that I snored after a long day (or a long night, he added). We would be quiet one minute and the next he would shatter in laughter, flashing his phone, This is fucking hilarious, and it would be the most mundane thing.

When he was away at his lectures, or playing the occasional weekend gig in Enugu, and I was alone, I pressed his clothes to my face, thinking, This is a dream.

The holidays came and went—I traveled to Kano while Kayode returned to Ibadan, and we texted during the day and talked all night on the phone, his voice husky with need as he said, I cannot wait to hold you again, I go die on top your body—and soon it was November and the harmattan wind began to blow, ripping off rusty-old roofs, covering windows and furniture in dust. At first the trees were bare, their branches spread out and dry; later, they caught pink and purple fire, abloom. Kayode bought a big mattress, and we threw out my old one, which was slim and almost flat. He wore the thickest sweaters, the cold made him sick, and if he could miss a class, he did, so that I returned home many afternoons to find him curled under the blanket, either asleep or typing into his phone. When he was well enough to attend classes, he went with two or three handkerchiefs, because he was that sort of person: his clothes (jeans, T-shirts, ankara, whatever, really) were crisply ironed and spotless. Who are you kitting for? I teased him often.

For you na, he'd say. Abi you don't like me looking good?

And he would spread his arms and turn around, putting on such a show, I'd fall back on the bed, weakened by laughter.

I spent most of my evenings bent over my table, at war with quantum chemistry, which I loathed, and he spent his with his headphones on, hunched over his laptop, bopping his head. One evening, he let out a triumphant yelp, and I knew he'd cooked a beat he liked. I looked up from my book to stare at him. Sorry, he said.

Let me hear it.

I eased into bed beside him. He placed the headphones over my head, his arm wrapped around my shoulders. The beats filled my ears, bass strong and booming, drums understated but with a distinct, swinging movement, guitar lines joyful yet sad; it made me think of lovers at a beach, of the sun setting, of warmth and tranquillity. This was a love song, no doubt.

I've never heard anything like this, Kayo.

You like it? His face was bright with optimism, with expectation.

How could one ever say no to that face, to those tenderly childlike eyes?

Of course, I do, I said. It's like you found a new, more mature voice and yet retained the best parts of you.

He stared at me, as though unbelieving. Somto, he said, and then he grabbed my face and kissed me. He hugged me so tight, it almost hurt. I love you. God, I love you so much.

There had been other boys before Kayode. There had been Basil in first year, terribly cute Basil who had a girlfriend and said he wasn't gay but loved getting his dick sucked by me but would never suck dick himself because, hey, he wasn't gay. Before Basil, there had been Uzo, a customer at the warehouse where I worked after graduating secondary school, Uzo with his *I love you* and *I use to drive Toyota Corolla*, Uzo who was thirty-two and said he loved me, even though I was just seventeen, who said No need for condom, you're my only one and I am your only one, except, *he* was *my* only one, the other half was utter bullshit, a truth I learned the hard way trying to explain to my parents why I had sores *there*. Two trips to the police station, a fine, doctors' bills, and Uzo was gone. And before him there had been others, too, boys with whom I shared a dormitory in secondary school, who were gay and not gay, some who called me *homo* and *boy-girl* in daytime, their voices singeing with hate, only to become Nicodemuses in my bed or in the bathroom at night; boys who came and went out of my body because they needed a place to dump their fantasies and their frustrations and their anger.

Before Kayode, there had been all these other people, as well as a constant feeling of loss after most hookups, a loneliness that all the fucks in the world could not fill. Before him, I walked around campus with my body alert, that is what the body does when it has become a recipient of frequent violence, it perks up, an antelope, ready to flee, or a guard dog, ready to pounce. Guys walking past me would turn their heads to hiss and mutter, Guy, you be homo? Why man go dey do like woman? Sometimes, girls would burst out laughing as I approached, their laughter shrill with aggression.

One evening, as we walked to Chitis, a group of guys walked past us and muttered, Homo. Hold this thing for me, Kayode said, handing me his phone and wallet. He marched up to them. Talk that thing again, he said, his voice hard. They stared at him, silent. Kayode was not tall, he was short, in fact, and they towered over him, but there was something in his bearing, a readiness to defy consequences, that must have stilled them, so that they faced me and muttered, Sorry, guy, no vex.

That night, when Kayode kissed my lips, my nipples, my stomach, when he turned me around and spread me open and buried his tongue in me, I did not remember the boys who had dumped their anguish in my body, nor the boys on the streets with their aggressively puzzled questions; and when he kissed his way up my back, muttering as he bit and licked my ears, Are you ready, babe? I knew, finally, I had come home.

The only girl in our lodge, her name was Eunice, she started coming over to hang out in our room. First, she wanted to know if I had salt, later she wanted to know what movies I had on my laptop. Finally, she wanted to join us on the bed as we watched the movies. One afternoon, I returned from class and found her lying beside Kayode in a short burgundy nightdress, her arm around his shoulder. They were watching the latest season of *How to Get Away with Murder*. I had spent the whole of Saturday seated outside PAA where the school's Wi-Fi connection was strongest, downloading episodes, fighting the hunger that soon began swirling in my stomach, so that Kayode and I could watch it together that night; he'd stopped at Shoprite after his show in Enugu and bought two big sacks of popcorn. One sack stood on the floor before them now, beside my laptop, half-empty.

Hey, Som, he said. How was the tutorial?

I shrugged, sat in a chair, taking off my socks. It was really hot, like being in a room full of steam. I opened the windows, rolled up the curtains, sunlight pouring in. Took off my shirt, climbed on the bed to get a hanger from the clothes rack.

Please close one of the windows, Eunice said. The light is too much.

I turned and stared at her. Are you talking to me?

Yes, please, can you be a darling? She'd paused the show, had turned to look at me. She still had her arm around Kayode's shoulders.

I opened my mouth to say something, and then shut it. I put on a T-shirt, wanted to change into shorts, but my jeans trousers were so tight, I needed to sit in a chair and have Kayode drag them off. Whenever he did this, he would tease me about my calves, he would say, See your yam legs, Mister I Hate to Jog. I imagined stretching my legs now and saying Baby? in that innocent voice, and with that childlike pout, that he loved so much, imagined their faces contorting with shock and discomfort; she must know already—she suspected, at least, of this I was sure—what the deal was between Kayode and me, but had chosen to come in here anyway, touching him with abandon, flirting with him, simply because she could. I disliked her and what her presence meant, that whatever Kayode and I had was not real and so could be violated, specifically by her, the real deal. And I was angry at Kayode for allowing it, but not so much as to put him in a terrifying situation.

I stood up and closed one of the windows. Kayode glanced up at me, pleading and apologizing with his eyes. I ignored him as I returned to my seat, as I joined them in watching the show. Our lodge mate, Eji, began to play a song, *if I tell you say I love you, o, my money, my body, na your own, o baby,* the entire lodge reverberating with the force of bass. My skin itched with annoyance: the song was too loud, and Eunice had her head close to Kayode's ear, and the room was hot, and I hated myself for closing the window, for succumbing to her.

That's a great song, she said.

It's too loud, I said.

Kayode immediately moved her arm from his shoulder, looking relieved. He stood up, said, I'll ask him to lower the volume. Eunice paused the show and began scrolling through her phone, her back to me; I, too, brought out my phone, but my eyes stayed on her, her legs long and smooth and moving up and down with such comfort, it was almost as if I was not in the room. When Kayode returned, he sat beside her with his back to the wall, legs pulled in. I watched as she glanced repeatedly at him, her questioning look turning cold, watched him pretend not to notice, his eyes fixed a little too decidedly on the laptop screen, his face squeezed in forced concentration. I knew, right away, that something had happened here.

She stood up. Going to my room, she announced in a slightly irritated tone.

You fucked her, I said after she left.

Excuse me?

I leaped out of the chair. Don't you dare add lying to the list of indignities I've had to endure this evening, I said. I'd raised my voice without meaning to; Please don't shout, he pleaded. There was a stillness in the quarters now that Eji had lowered the volume of his speakers, now that John Legend had come on, cooing, *Love your curves and all your edges / all your perfect imperfections.* A stillness of walls listening.

I cannot believe this—you actually fucked her. And then you brought her into our room.

No, no, he said, standing up and holding out his hands to touch or hold me. I recoiled. We didn't fuck, you have to believe me. We made out only once, Som, and now she thinks we're in love. I wouldn't disrespect you like that.

You sound as though you need a trophy for not going all the way, I said, sitting back down, a little relieved but still full of rage and hurt. I wanted so much to cry.

I don't mean it that way. I'm sorry. I just didn't know how to refuse her without seeming—

I waited for him to complete the sentence; instead, he looked away. Without seeming what, Kayode? I said. Soft? Like a homo? You can say it.

Som, he said. He looked scared, a little boy unsure of himself. I felt a rush of tenderness in spite of myself, a powerful urge to hug him: it sickened me.

Do you still want this, Kayode? I said, calmly. Because I will not be your bi-guy's side chick.

There is nothing I want more than this, he said. Believe me.

Then you have to let her know the boundaries.

He nodded.

Promise me, I said. I want to hear you say it.

I will, I promise, he said, moving uncertainly toward me.

Ekene's room was always dimly lit, and there were always at least three other gay boys, often more, lying on the mattress, on the floor, laptops open to one TV show or another. We called it the Nsukka Gay Cathedral, though he preferred the Gay Capital. I see myself as the gaysident, he was saying now, strutting into the room with a tray of rice. I am no bishop. Ndị ahụ bụ amosu. They suck dick in their seminaries and then condemn us on the pulpit.

He set the tray on the floor, hot steam billowing; the aroma of spices filled my mouth with water.

Has a priest sucked your dick before? JJ said, looking up from his laptop.

We know you're nwa father, JJ. Ekene rolled his eyes. Food is ready o. He turned to me. Nwa, there's only one spoon here, you can have it. These ones eat like they're wolves, they can have the forks.

We sat around the tray, Ekene, JJ, Kenneth, and I. Who serves food without water? JJ said, getting up. His glasses made him look older and serious, or maybe it was simply his face, the way his mouth was shaped in a permanent scowl. He went outside, the door creaking behind him.

Kenneth dug his fork into the tray. Ekene smacked it. Wait for your boyfriend.

He's not my boyfriend, Kenneth said, frowning. He was a first year but I liked how mature he was and wished often that he would talk more.

What do you call what you've been doing with him? Ekene asked.

It's called fucking, Ekene, I said. Two friends can have sex without it meaning something bigger.

Tell him! Kenneth clapped his hands, and Ekene cocked his head sideways, his lips pursed, eyebrows raised, like, gurrrl. The door cawed open.

Are you faggots gossiping about me? JJ said, tearing open a bag of water, passing us each a sachet.

Bitch, don't flatter yourself, Ekene said.

The rice was good, as always, peppery without being impossible to eat. JJ took off his shirt, sweat beads dotted his nose, his chest, ran down the small folds of his stomach. I took off mine, too, the room had been warm, now it was hot, the white light from the rechargeable lamp shrinking, so that our shadows on the walls grew bigger and closer, converging together. Ekene took off his shirt, fanning himself with it. I felt my phone vibrate in my pocket before the song came on, Michael Jackson crooning *your love is magical*: my ringtone for Kayode.

Are you home, babe? he said when I answered. I told him I was at Ekene's, and he exhaled, Good, because I'm at Hilltop now about to head home and I think I left my key inside.

Come toward Green Lodge, that's where Ekene lives. I'll come outside with the key.

Ekene's eyes shot up, and he mouthed, Outside? He pursed his lips, playing judgment.

What are you guys doing? Kayode asked.

I stood up, headed toward the door. Are you far from Green Lodge? I said. I knew already that he would keep on talking until he got here if I let him.

I'm actually close. Was at a classmate's to get material for a group project. He lives close to Green Lodge.

Awesome.

This your bobo that no one ever sees, JJ said as I ended the call and opened the door, the rattle of generators assaulting my ears. Is he afraid he'll be contaminated by the fags of Gay Cathedral?

Capital, Ekene said. Gay Capital.

JJ waved him off. Bitch, please.

Kayode is not like that, I said.

Walking into the hallway, the walls dark and crowded with sounds—people talking in their rooms, movies and songs playing from laptops—I thought of what JJ had said. I knew that Kayode was not like that, and yet I never asked him to accompany me to Ekene's, even though they'd known each other longer than I had, and he'd never asked to join me.

At the gate, I hugged him, but briefly, the way guys did it on the streets: a handshake and a brief clapping of our right shoulders. He smelled of cologne and sweat. You look tired, I said, handing him my key.

I've been walking all day. He shook his head, making a sad face. These lecturers are always the first to go on rants about corrupt and despotic politicians while oppressing their students.

Fools and hypocrites, I said. I'm sorry, babe.

What are you guys doing? Let's go home.

A plea, his were eyes imploring, lips turned down. It was dark by the gate, though beyond the tiny path leading to it, students milled around, buying things from the shops in whose corridors beamed white or yellow lights, others heading into campus or home from it, and I could easily place my hand on his lips and nobody would see. He chuckled when I did, holding my fingers there, biting them, his tired eyes lighting up.

I have to hang out with my friends tonight, sorry, I said. Ekene accused me recently of abandoning him, and he's right, the bitch. Plus, we're watching *Orange Is the New Black* together, just one episode, and then I'll be home. I paused. Do you want to come inside? You can lie down for a bit.

To be honest, I don't even want to walk home alone, he said. He put his arms around my neck, leaning heavily against my back.

Don't break me, I said, trudging forward, carrying his weight.

Two boys talking as they approached us, I heard them before they appeared around the corner, and Kayode must have heard too, because he let me go. They barely glanced at us as they walked past, engrossed in their conversation, their white singlets stark against the darkness. Inside, Ekene said, Finally, the great Kayode steps into my house.

Dramatic as always, Kayode said, shaking his head. He shook hands with JJ, who muttered something, eyes slightly averted, and then with Kenneth. Ekene, he hugged. So what are you guys up to? Somto tells me you're watching *Orange Is the New Black*.

He sat on the bed. Ekene offered to get him some rice. He ate quickly, watching the show, and then he fell asleep lying on his back, hands on his stomach like a person lying in state, legs on the floor.

He's so hot, Kenneth said, pulling me out of the show. You're so lucky, Som.

Stop tripping for another person's man, Ekene said. Your man is right here, ho.

God, shut up, JJ said.

When he talked, my friends listened. The other boys watched him with something close to adoration, laughing too heartily at his jokes, agreeing with everything he said, and it occurred to me gradually that I did not like him with my friends. With Ekene and JJ, yes, but whenever the house was crowded with the other boys with whom I was not particularly close, I resented the very things for which I had fallen: his brimming confidence and the way he was able to make people comfortable around him, and so I stopped inviting him over.

———

We were at a recording studio somewhere along Oba Road. The huge signpost above the one-story building read MC Fleeky's Studio. What sort of name is that? I said to Kayode as we entered the building. The studio was located on the ground floor, upstairs was a lawyers' chamber, another signpost reading Ugo & Associates: Barristers at Law, everything printed in plain black. The building itself was humorless, old and peeling and crumbling, the railings brown from rust. Inside the studio, the walls painted the dullest blue, I had the feeling of being in my grandfather's living room, complete with faded pictures hanging on the walls and a ceiling fan that cawed, like a plummeting bird. Kayode and I sat on a sofa after the secretary, a curt girl whose face glistened with Vaseline, went into one of the rooms.

You cannot record here, I said, turning to him.

I don't know, Som, he said, eyes scanning the room. Ekene told me it's old. This is *ancient*. Are you even sure they have a boom mic?

He stood up and strode toward the secretary's table, as though to check for a boom mic. Flipped through books and sheets of paper piled on the table, many brown with age. I watched him, his back turned to me, watched his boots, brown and heavy looking (I could never understand his obsession with huge boots), his hand as he flipped through the books, the calm, unruffled tempo of his movement.

What are you doing?

He turned around, gestured at a typewriter that had been covered with a blue cloth. Who still uses a typewriter? he said, shaking his head. He returned to his seat beside me, his face crumbling with despondence.

We should go to Enugu instead, I said.

Ah, I cannot afford it o. Twenty K for one demo.

How much did they say it would cost here?

Twelve thousand, he said. But that if I price it well, nine K. I need this demo to be perfect.

I glanced up at the ceiling, the brown smudges almost elegant in the way they circled the fan, the way they ringed the electric bulb.

What if you pay for the sessions in Enugu, I said, and I handle everything regarding upkeep until the end of the semester?

Haba! No na, that's too much. See, don't worry about me, Som, I'll try and convince my dad to send me the money.

You've been trying to convince him all semester.

Maybe we'll go to Christ Church and sow a seed, eh, he said, smiled. Perhaps God will touch his heart then.

Stop playing. We're doing it. You'll go to Enugu next week.

Yes, Daddy, he said, his face breaking into an amused smile.

I elbowed him. Your head is not correct.

The secretary returned, sank into her seat without as much as a glance at us. Oga said no vex, she said, moving items on the table. They're repairing the mixer, but it will soon ready.

Kayode stood up, adjusted his trousers. Me and my friend want to take a walk, he said. We'll come back.

She shrugged.

Outside, I said, We will come back?

Keep moving, he said, taking my hand. And don't look back, or you'll become a pillar of salt.

Final year beginning, the entire campus stretching and yawning, roused from the slumber that had been the long vac, Kayode bought forms to contest for the post of director of socials of the Student Union. Every evening, his team congregated in our room, discussing strategy. They were boys like him, masculine, their laughter and their postures robust and uninhibited. They sat on the plastic chair, on the floor, on the bed, talking in impassioned voices about alliances and loyalty and mandates, stuff that meant nothing to me. Whenever I came home, I said hello, changed my clothes, and left the room. Sometimes, I'd lie on the bed, headphones on, immersed in Facebook or in a movie.

What faculty are you in? one of the boys asked one evening as I lay on the bed, watching *Scandal*. It was Anayo. Anayo with the voice like an explosion and loud gestures like a boxer circling to lunge.

Physical sciences, I said, taking off my headphones.

I am surprised, he said.

How?

Physical sciences guys don't usually do like women, he said. That's more like a faculty of arts something.

I looked around the room, five unfamiliar pairs of eyes staring back at me, Kayode nowhere to be found. That is such a weird thing to say to me, I said.

Guy, no be fight na, someone else said, laughed, and like robots they all laughed too. And you and this your English sef, every time, supree-supree. Guy, you be babe?

I felt my body recoil, it was as though someone had grabbed my neck and was going to start pummeling me. It is not my fault that you are barely educated, I thought of saying, consumed by a need to reduce them, make them feel equally small, but I thought of Kayode, he needed this win for his cred and for potential networks, he'd said, and he needed these guys, some of the most popular in their various faculties, to win.

I don't know what you're talking about, I said.

Are you and Kayode brothers? Anayo asked. Is that why you're roommates?

No, we're not. I plugged back my headphones. The images on my laptop screen blurred, the sound of the show pricking my ears like pins. I could hear them mumbling, did not need to hear what they were saying to know that they were talking about me. I thought of leaving the room, but what sort of person would I be, fleeing my own home? I was so angry, I could detonate: angry that they could come into *my* house and do to me what they did on the streets, angry that I had to hold back the many clapbacks boiling in my stomach.

When Kayode returned, bearing bunches of bananas and a bottle of groundnuts and laughing at something Anayo said, my anger transformed into a throbbing resentment toward him. Won't you eat? he said, tapping me and nodding at the bunches of bananas on the floor. I shook my head, turned up the volume on my laptop. In that moment, I could not stand the sound of his voice, the carelessness of his laugh, the ease with which he became one of them, throwing *guy* and *manchi* around, words with which they peppered their sentences, as though to remind one another that they were indeed men, Lord, wasn't that awesome?

Why are you angry with him? Ekene said when I went to see him that night. It's not his fault that the guys are assholes.

I said that Kayode should have known better than to bring those kinds of guys into our house. They could always have their meetings at Marlima or Chitis, no? And what was that shit he did, laughing with them when they talked about the girls they fucked, as if it hadn't been two years since he last saw pussy?

Ekene looked at me, uncomprehending. That is the kind of boy he is, Som, he said. You don't expect him to suddenly become a different person.

I started staying away from the lodge in the evenings, started taking long walks around school, visiting friends at Hilltop and Odenigwe, only returning home when darkness had swallowed the buildings and the trees, wrapping them in a black frock. Sometimes, Kayode called to know where I was, if I was fine and if he needed to get me anything on his way back from seeing the guys off. We'd then often meet at Hilltop Gate, so we could walk home together. I know all that talk about politics bores you, he'd say, and I'd nod, yes, that was it.

I helped him select the pictures to use on his flyers and posters, sat with him all night as he wrote his manifesto. Nah, I would say from the bed, too cliché, and he would look at me with exhausted eyes and say, I think I should fire you, sadist, which made me laugh. All right, I would say, how about this? And I would give him a different sentence. It gave me such joy, watching him do things, early many mornings, he'd wake me with his hushed humming, and I'd watch him seated at the desk with his laptop open, headphones on, listening to his demo, pausing to take notes. Turning and seeing me awake sometimes, he'd smile and mutter Sorry, or wave me over to sit on his lap while he worked.

The evening he called and asked where I was, and could I please come home, I assumed the guys had left early and he wanted to hash out the last points of his manifesto before bedtime. When I got home, there was no power, the rechargeable lamp on the table slashing the room into half light, half shadow. His flyers and posters were scattered all over the floor. He was lying on the bed in the jeans and long-sleeve shirt he'd worn to class, lying perfectly still on his back with his hands behind his head. I sat on the bed, placed my hands on his socked feet.

Are you okay?

He nodded, grunted, Yes, but did not move. I sat beside him, quiet. I could sense his sadness, it rose out of him, a wretched offering.

Talk to me, babe, I said, rolling off his socks, massaging his feet.

I'm pulling out of the elections, he said.

The room was quiet, the clock going tick-tick-tick, a conductor beating the time to a silent song. I waited for him to say more, there had to be more, but he said nothing, merely lay there, staring at the ceiling.

Why? I said, finally.

He remained quiet at first, and I thought he'd slipped into a mood, but then he began to talk, his quivering voice walled with anger. Could I imagine, he said, that Anayo went behind his back to campaign for the guy from theater arts? Did I know that when he confronted Anayo, the fool did not even feel any shame or remorse? They ended up shouting at each other, he said, right there under the staircase in public admin, in front of first years.

I'm so sorry, I said. I've never liked nor trusted that guy. Did he say why he did it?

Maybe you should ask Eunice, he said, shutting his eyes. When he opened them, they were full of anger.

Easy, I said, rubbing his feet.

God, I will fuck that girl up. She doesn't know me o, lai lai. Maybe because I'm always smiling, she does not know that she should be afraid of me.

Kayode.

He stood up, began pacing the room. Do you know that that girl is going around telling everyone I'm gay? That bitch does not know the market she's buying.

I stared at him, my tongue feeling like stone. I'd always found it wonderfully contradictory that he was cool with some of the most fearsome guys on campus and yet had only gentle bones in his body, now I felt a twinge of discomfort listening to him.

That night, we woke up to loud moaning. It was the same name as always, Eji, our neighbor with the short dreads who played loud music. Oh, Eji, fuck me, a girl cried. Someone banged a pan or a pot, something metal, against the wall, yelling, No kill the babe o! Laughter erupted in the lodge, the voices of boys snatched out of sleep, of masturbating, and of studying. Eji said nothing, the girl was quiet for a second, and I could hear in the stillness the rising tempo of their bed's creaking, and then she was at it again: Eji, oh, Eji!

I can make you scream like that, Kayode said beside me. I hadn't known that he was awake.

I chuckled, burrowing deeper into the blanket. I felt the heat of his body against my back, his hand around my bare chest, his lips on my neck.

You doubt me?

You're not fucking me to their soundtrack, I said, but did not move his hand away from my nipple, did not shrug his tickling tongue away from my neck. I was hard and he was hard, his dick straining against his boxers and poking my lower back. The security light from the corridor trickled into the room, soft and timid. I turned my head to look at the window, suddenly thinking of Eunice spreading stories about us: I imagined the face of a suspicious boy pressed against our mosquito netting, imagined curious ears pressed against our door.

Kayode squeezed me into himself, grinding against my ass, and I thought he'd pull down my boxers, tilt my head around and kiss me.

Instead, he let me go, put his hands behind his head, face toward the ceiling. They don't even fucking care who hears them, he said, his voice harsh in the darkness, in the sexual chorus that had now faded into a throaty diminuendo. I looked at him, his chest rising and falling, his body a silhouette in the dark. We'd heard Eji fuck many times in the past, and not once had Kayode reacted to it. I knew it had something to do with everything that had happened earlier. I lay my head on his chest. It was calm and measured, his heartbeat: he was alive, my breathing, palpitating boy.

There was a tension in his jaw where the corridor's light bruised his profile, a trace of violence in his silence, in the way he'd said, I can make you scream like that. I wanted to take it all away, to make him feel good, see him feel good. I nuzzled against him, making him turn around so that I wrapped my arm around him. We stayed that way, saying nothing, listening to the moans and the bed creaks until they were no more, until we both fell asleep.

We went to Enugu the week of the elections, spent six days in a cheap motel with windows overlooking a plantain grove—a window Kayode stood by most evenings, looking out into God-knows-what. On our last night there, he stood by that window and said, Now I know how you feel.

I paused the movie I'd been watching on my laptop (the motel's TV only showed Nollywood movies in which people wept disconsolately in every scene) and stared at him. What's wrong, baby?

All my life, he said, still looking out the window, hands in his pockets, nobody has treated me like this, like I am a leper or something disgusting.

I left the bed and went to him. Stood behind him. Wound my arms around his stomach and buried my nose in his neck, breathed deep. He placed his hands on my arms, twirling his fingers lazily. Outside, the sunset was something to behold: it had splintered into varying currents of the same ocean, yellow, orange, red, an ocean into which bats plummeted, like seabirds, fluttered, then soared.

You get better at tuning it out, I said.

Kayode let out a long breath.

I wished his sadness were a living thing, so that I could place my hand on his body and yank it off.

Every year, his favorite songs changed, but mine remained the same. He called one morning, saying, You have to ditch your next class and come home. When I got home, he was playing "Mad Over You" so loud over the speakers it seemed the roof would explode. He lay on the bed in blue polka-dot boxers, hands behind his head. It was the song on everybody's lips, "Mad Over You": *Baby girl I say, I say your body na killer o.*

Don't tell me you called me home because you're horny, I said, taking off my sneakers.

He stared at me, a smile struggling to break out of his quivering lips.

Jesus, Kayode! I'm missing Chem 422.

Guess what, he said.

Stop playing around, Oga.

Guess na. He smiled, the brightest, happiest smile.

You made an A in Pol 306?

He playful frowned. Seriously? I'll ask you to run home because of that?

Ngwanu, I cannot guess, I said. Just tell me.

I got a call from Kennis, he said. They loved my demo!

Oh my God, Kayo, I said.

We did it, Som, he said, pulling me onto his body, arms wrapped around me, his voice breaking. We finally got there. We got there.

And I kissed him, holding his face, I kissed him. He kissed me back, holding my face, too, and muttering into my lips how so fucking happy he was.

II.   Lagos, charming yet disorienting, bubbled with uncontainable life. Two months taking the bus to work, two months going to the cinema and to the school where I taught and to the NYSC office in Surulere, two months drinking in the city like a person drowning, and I still felt lost in the noise, in the ever-surging feeling of anonymity. Too many faces, Lord, and the speed, the jostling, the peevishness of strangers, the brutal sense of one's invisibility.

You cannot hate Lagos, Kayode teased me. You'd be like the weird kid at school.

Whatever, I said.

But I came to like Lagos eventually, the way one becomes fond of the annoying class clown, and though I dreaded taking the bus to work in the mornings, the racket that it was, I came to look forward to the evenings when, snug in the back seat of a taxi, I was able to look out into the glittering prism that was Lagos's night, Ikoyi Bridge twinkling as if riddled with stars of Technicolor. The parties we attended were wild, but nobody bothered me, so I often sat at the bar sipping my Smirnoff, nodding to Kiss Daniel and Omawumi and Phyno, watching the bodies twisting on the dance floor while Kayode talked with his producer.

He's a great guy, Kayode said often, his eyes bright with surprise, it was almost as if he had not expected the people at Kennis Records to be nice. Lanre was very tall, he towered over me; next to Kayode he was a palm tree. He had an incredible bass when he talked, his entire body resonated with it, and it was with that bass that he said to Kayode, Don't worry about Youth Service, and now Kayode spent all day at the studio, lounging at home when he didn't, partying weekend nights. I teased him, saying, Maybe I should dump you and elope with Miracle Worker Lanre; grinning cockily, he said, Does he have this? He took off his shirt, his trousers, slipping his thumbs into his boxers, his body taking on the slant of performance. *God*, I said, both of us bursting into laughter. When there was no power and the low ceiling seemed to descend, we spread a blanket on the balcony and lay there, talking about Nsukka, watching YouTube videos of celebrity houses, dreaming aloud.

The morning I woke up to something sweet wafting from the kitchen, his voice bright and soft as he sang *I love the way you move / Shape like Rihanna, heart like crystal*, I knew something good had happened. I went into the kitchen where he stood with his back to the door, flipping plantains in a frying pan, and wrapped my arms around him.

The single is dropping tomorrow, he said, turning around to kiss me.

Finally!

That's not even the good news, he said, his eyes like perfectly round plates, his lips stretched in a rubber-band smile.

I looked at him, excited, waiting.

Almost every big name we asked agreed to share it on their Instagram pages, he said, counting the big names off on his fingers, his face and comportment a picture of pure joy. I screamed, and he screamed, and soon we were singing out loud, *Make I love you like say I go die tomorrow*, singing in that tiny, sweltering kitchen soaked in the aroma of fried plantains.

Lanre was planning a party to celebrate the success of the song. Who would have imagined it, he said, the way it had rocked the entire country, every major club in Lagos was grooving to it, Twitter and Facebook and Instagram were on fire, too, and the blogs were going crazy—who could have fucking imagined it? We were in the living room of a flat in Lekki, his voice reverberating over the empty space. I stood by the window, looking out into the estate. I had never seen trees arranged so delicately, ornate palms and whistling pines flanking somnolent streets, the swimming pool a deep blue. Kayode was saying it really was crazy, he was wondering what would happen when the album dropped. I was thinking that our lives were changing really fast.

You like the place? Lanre said.

It's huge! Kayode said, and they both laughed.

Is your friend moving in with you?

Yes.

There was silence. A black SUV was slowly rolling down one of the streets.

So, the party tomorrow, are you bringing any chick?

I don't think so, Kayode said.

I was talking to your friend, Som—, Somto, right? He turned to Kayode: As for you, babes will be all over you.

He laughed, Kayode joining in. I wanted to laugh, too, it was what I was supposed to do, but my lips refused to move. Between them, there was a shared language that I did not speak.

But, seriously, don't you know any girls? Lanre said. Fine guy like you. No dey fall my hands fa.

I stared at him. Give me your sister, I wanted to say. He was saying more words to me now than he had all month.

Why you dey hassle my guy na? Kayode said, nudging him playfully. Lanre threw his hands in the air, saying, No be hassle o. His phone began to ring. He stepped out to answer the call.

Isn't this great? Kayode said, spreading his arms. He stood beside me, resting his back on the wall. I let my eyes travel round the room. It was great, the large sliding doors leading to a balcony in which potted aloes yawned in the evening light, the impeccably white walls, the floor of polished wood. Closing my eyes earlier, I'd seen the apartment furnished, all three rooms: the portraits on the walls would be pencil drawn, hyperrealist, the carpet in the middle of the living room plush and soft.

So what time are you meeting the decor guy tomorrow?

I shrugged. Who knows? I have to find a girl to take to the party, remember?

He looked confused, and then he chuckled. You're not serious, he said, nudging me with his shoulder. Come on, babe. He wrapped his arm around my shoulders. Don't be mad, it's Lanre, he's always playing.

I'm not mad, I said. What I really wanted was to ask if he truly did not see it, Lanre's quiet aggression toward me, his delicately placed acts of disrespect, but he'd been so happy lately, I did not want to sabotage his joy. Perhaps it's better if I don't attend.

You're going with me to that party, he said, looking at me like I had said the silliest thing. And if any girl disturbs me too much, I'll tell her *my babe* read chemistry o.

A small, intimate party, Lanre had said, and yet there were a little over a hundred people on the hotel's rooftop, faces and voices I knew from television and radio, and some others I did not know, girls in gowns so tight and stilettos so high, they seemed to hover and float. They sipped champagne, hung around in small circles, laughing at funny and unfunny jokes, the whole place electric with ambition and ego. After a few minutes of mingling, I retreated to the bar, where I sat alone.

I watched as Lanre took Kayode from clique to clique, introducing him to people who mattered. Watched as Kayode shook hands, laughed, said things that made them laugh; he was like a solvent, he dissolved metal. I felt a wave of pride watching him: this boy with whom everyone was enamored would come home with me tonight and every other night and take off his clothes for me and do ridiculous dance moves that made me laugh.

Twice, he'd walked up to the bar to sit with me, his voice alive with excitement. Are you okay here? he'd asked, and was I sure I didn't want him to introduce me to so-and-so?

No, go have fun, I said, smirking. I love to watch.

That his song na fire, the barman said now, startling me. How long have you two known each other?

I glanced at him, light skin with chubby cheeks covered in a carpet of hair, muscular biceps stretching the sleeves of his black shirt. Since university, I said.

You guys seem very close.

I murmured, Uh-huh, sipped my Smirnoff and looked away, partly to signal the end of the conversation, but also to scan all the faces for Kayode's. He was standing alone with a young woman who I'd seen in a Nollywood movie but whose name I could not remember.

She flicked something off his shoulder, her hand, lingering, slowly running down his arm. He leaned in and said something in her ear that made her laugh, head thrown back. I felt a sharp discomfort. All the years we had been together, I had never felt as vulnerable as I felt now, Kayode surrounded by the most beautiful people in the city. I wanted desperately to be a girl, so that I could place my arm in the crook of his arm and walk around with him all evening, and it would be okay; people would whisper *She's so possessive, so insecure,* and it would still be okay.

I'm Anthony, by the way, the barman was saying. What's your name?

Somto, I said, took out my phone to check Instagram. I wanted to sit in silence and listen to the band, which had been playing quietly in the background, and hoped he'd stop trying to make small talk.

I knew it!

I turned to him, moved by his excitement. Knew what?

You're Igbo, he said, smiling. He's Yoruba, half the people here are Yoruba yet I was able to guess correctly.

I lifted an eyebrow. Oh, I said, unsure how to respond to that. That's nice. I returned to my phone.

Sorry to disturb you o, he said. A brother was just trying to be nice.

I ignored him. Lanre was walking toward the bar. Let us talk, he said to me, asked for a glass of Hennessey. We left the bar, began walking, the silence between us engorged with awkwardness.

Nice trousers, he said.

I looked up at him, surprised. Thank you.

He nodded. I hope you're enjoying the party, he said, lifting his glass to a couple who had lifted theirs to him.

Well, I can see everything from the bar.

Good, good. We had walked away from the heart of the party, the sound of music floating down to us. The band was singing Aṣa. *I didn't understand you,* they cooed, *I thought your love was strange.* We were standing before sturdy glass barriers ringed by silver banisters; from this height, the whole of Victoria Island seemed to swarm with glowworms, cars and skyscrapers and apartment blocks iridescent, the ocean a black bed upon which all the city's lights slept.

I'd like to ask you a question, he said, guy to guy. No shame, no judgment.

Okay.

What sort of relationship do you have with Kayode?

We're friends, I said, not even pausing to think.

It's obvious. I'm asking if, you know, is Kayode gay?

I said nothing. I should have said no, berate him for even thinking such nonsense about my *mannest man*: he would apologize and say what was he even thinking and make me promise not to mention it to Kayode. But I said nothing. I looked down at Lagos, all that life, all that beauty, it was almost painful to watch, and yet I missed Nsukka.

Well?

I don't know, I said. Why not ask him?

But you're his guy.

That does not make me his mouthpiece.

There was silence. I held onto the metal banisters, my hands trembling.

See, he said, I have been in this business for many years. I have met people, made people's careers. These guys wey dey rock woman yansh up and down inside music video, you think say all of them straight? Many are gay, as in, them dey fuck man-ass. I don't care where a guy puts his dick, as long as he does not bring it near me. What I care about is the music, the business. And in this business, it's suicide to be gay.

Why are you telling me this?

We're not children—Somto, right? It is obvious what you are, you're not even hiding it. As in, look at your trousers, for instance. Don't get me wrong, they're dope. But they're too tight for a guy na, even you, reason am. Anybody sees you constantly with a guy like Kayode, and only one thing enters their mind.

Who I am is not your business, I said. If you have anything to say, say it to Kayode. Turning around to walk away, I thought I'd return to the bar, but instead I walked past it, feeling the fullness of Lanre's eyes behind me, and then the barman's, whose lingering gaze made me want to turn around and yell at him. I spent about ten minutes searching for the exit, the hotel was massive, and, when I found it, stood for a long time in the night draft, trying to flag down a taxi. In the back seat of the taxi, finally, I cried. Quietly, my face cradled in my palms. The radio was tuned to Cool FM, the presenter's voice smooth and low as she said, This next song is for all the people who are afraid to love, to be themselves, to speak out. E talk say we be wonderful, wonderful people, so no need to be afraid. All you wonderful Lagos people, Emeli Sandé!

By the time Kayode returned, I had cried out all the anger and self-pity, and I was listless. He flicked on the bedroom light, staring at me. You left early, he said, burped. Sorry. He kicked off his shoes, took off his wristwatch, his shirt, unbuckled his belt but left his jeans on. You should have told me you were bored.

I folded my arms, looking away. If I stared at his oblivious face a moment longer, I might say something hurtful.

Babe, he said. The bed dipped under his weight. Did someone say something to you?

I remained quiet, unmoving.

Talk na. Why are you pouting, eh? You know you look hot when you pout. See, I'm going to take a picture of you frowning and send to Ekene.

Oh my God, my phone!

What happened to your phone?

I looked at him now. I think I left it at the bar. I left immediately after talking to Lanre.

Don't worry, I'm sure someone will keep it. Let me try the number.

He dialed it. It's ringing, he said, placing the phone to his ear. And then, What did Lanre say to you to make you leave so suddenly?

He wanted to know if we're fucking.

Wha—wait. Hello? Who's this? Please, you have my friend's phone. Erm, what do you mean, *baby*?

As he listened, his entire body stiffened, as though he'd been given news of a sudden death. He held out the phone from his mouth: *Shit*.

What is it?

He tapped his phone's screen, the voice of a man filling the room. The man was singing Kayode's song gruffly, *Tastes like manna when I kiss you / Baby divine, meal for the brightest*. He snorted, a short, harsh sound. So na man be the manna wey you dey chop? he growled. "Meal for the brightest," olòshì.

It was the voice of the barman, Anthony. I buried my face in my palms, how endless the night.

What are you talking about? Kayode said. He was trying to keep a calm voice, I could tell, but his eyes showed that he was afraid.

You think I don't know your voice? See, I will crack this phone's password. Shebi that your stupid boyfriend thinks he's better than everybody, feeling big up and down? When my friends arrive and we crack this phone, your matter will be all over Linda's blog and Nairaland.

Cut the call, I said.

What?

Cut the call!

I snatched the phone from him and hung up. He looked at me and I looked at him. Are there pictures on the phone? he said. Of course, there were pictures of us, I retorted, stood up and began pacing the room, arms wrapped around my body, wrapped because I felt so weightless, I could be blown away. I wanted to be held and brought back to the center of things but the only person who could have held me was in need of holding, too.

Are the pictures on the memory card?

There's no memory card in the phone, I said. I use the phone's memory.

He nodded. And what is your password?

You know it na, my mum's birthday. But all my apps are locked with different passwords.

Jesus, babe, he said. He dashed across the bed and hugged me. Thank you, he said. Thank you so much.

I stood with my arms hanging by my side. This was not a time to celebrate, I thought. So much could still go wrong.

He moved into the house in Lekki and I remained in Festac because it was the smart thing to do. The story had gone around on blogs that we were dating (in the posts that were recopied from blog to blog, I was described as *the woman in the relationship*, the guy who saved Kayode's phone number as *Baby*) but without explicit photographs and screenshots of messages, it became another empty rumor that people debated in between work and idleness, a rumor that died down after only a few days. Still I had to deactivate my Facebook and Instagram accounts for two weeks because of the threats I received, so that the nights I didn't sleep over at Lekki, I stayed up, casting wary glances around the room, sleep annihilated.

I got funny stares at work, colleagues murmuring behind my back, and as I walked to the staff room after teaching one morning, the principal, Sister Monica, joined me, talking about the weather, the students, her new arts program. Eventually, she said, There are some rumors about you online.

People will always talk, I said. We paused under the awning of the staff room.

So true. And without conscience, too. What a serious lie to spread. She looked pointedly at me. A quick breeze ruffled her habit.

So heartless, I said.

I stopped taking the bus to work: Kayode asked and Lanre got a taxi driver who drove me to and from work and anywhere I wanted to go until the whole thing died down. He also called someone who hacked my phone and destroyed every piece of data in it. Arranged for Kayode to attend an event with a budding TV host named Jokè where they held hands and leaned into each other, whispering and laughing, someone's camera going *click*. For days, the pictures circulated the Internet. In interviews, Jokè said, Kayode and I are good friends, in the way that people do when they are withholding something tantalizing; asked how close, she merely smiled, pressing her lips together.

Lanre is such a great guy, Kayode said often. Like, many guys would dump me after this scandal. We're really lucky to have him.

Yeah, *we*, I said one evening.

What is that supposed to mean?

I don't know. Maybe I do not have the same experience of him, of any of your buddies. Does it ever occur to you? Of course it doesn't, seeing as you have chosen blindness lately. But, hey, anything that makes you comfortable.

The silence in the room was like a balloon blown to its elastic limit.

You can say your mind without being a bitch about it, Somto.

Excuse me?

You heard me, he said, blinking.

I said nothing at first—we'd never spoken to each other like this before. That was not us. And yet I looked him in the eyes and said, You don't realize how silly and naive you sound most times. You think Lanre cares about you? You think he wouldn't dump you if something concrete drops about us tomorrow? If you didn't learn something from this thing that happened, that nobody gives a shit about boys like *us*, then I'm sorry, you'll never learn anything in your life.

He stared at me, saying nothing, all the whites in the room reflecting in his eyes. He looked as though he'd walked in here only to find a stranger seated on his bed. He walked out of the bedroom. Soon, the sound of the television filled the house, This is CNN, a deep voice said. Kayode never watched the news. I remained seated on the bed, still unused to its wideness and softness, its spotless white sheets, filled with a shapeless sadness.

About an hour later, the sounds from CNN taking on a hollow timbre as the night stilled, I went to the living room with a blanket, knowing he would be asleep. He was, splayed out on the couch, one arm tossed carelessly to the floor, the other clutching the remote to his chest. He was wearing just his singlets and boxers and the AC was on full blast. I turned off the lights, took the remote control from him, and turned off the television. As I covered him with the blanket, tucking his arms gently under it, I looked at his face in the dim light of the appliances, anger in his brows. I thought of the evening, weeks after he first said he loved me, when, walking to Chitis, a group of guys called me *homo* and he marched up to them and made them apologize.

When I heard the shower running early in the morning, I rolled off the bed, having barely slept, and knocked on the door, then eased it open. He wasn't singing in the shower this morning. I'm sorry, I said. All those things I said, they were really mean.

He stopped rubbing his hands on his face, stood silently with his eyes closed, water running down his body. The sound of the shower drowned our silence. I stood there, waiting for him to respond. Kayo, I said, and still he remained silent. I turned around, was about to shut the door, when the shower stopped and he spoke: It's not what you said, Somto. I know I'm not perfect. It's the way you said it.

I turned around, our eyes locking.

It was almost as if you hated me, he said. Please don't do that again.

His album dropped on my birthday. The plan, he said, was to attend the launching, the small after-party, and then come home and party all night, just us two with our friends. It was the same day I met his mother and his sister, two funny women with whom I had spoken on the phone and on Skype countless times, meeting them finally felt like a reunion. You should come to Baltimore with us, his mother said, holding my hand and smiling so lovingly, it shocked me later hearing her say to Kayode, He's much girlier than I expected.

I'd gone out to get a haircut, my first in our Lekki estate, and had been excited to tell Kayode all about it, how the barber had washed my hair midway, massaging my scalp ever so gently, before working on my hairline, how painless the clippers were. Instead, I entered the kitchen to their shocked stares.

You're back, Kayode said.

I did not respond. I walked to one of the cabinets, opened then closed it.

I'm sorry you heard that, his mother said. I'm just worried about Kayode, especially seeing how distraught he was after he almost got exposed.

We don't need to talk about this right now, Kayode said, looking nervous.

She adjusted her dress around her shoulder. I'm simply expressing how I feel. When you told me you were bisexual and were with a boy, it was hard for me to swallow. Ìyá ẹ ni mo jẹ́, Kayode, I will not lie to you. But then your happiness is the most important thing to me. I don't want you to be miserable the way I was with your father.

So why all this talk now?

You've always been a happy child, right from when you were little. The only time I ever saw you truly unhappy was when your father stopped you from playing in that band. That was when I knew that music was your everything. Now you have been offered a chance only a handful of people ever have, to do what they love and still be successful, and at such a young age. I'm just saying, the two of you can find a way to make yourselves less obvious.

I like Somto just the way he is, Kayode said, glancing at me.

I did not know why, but I stood there listening to her in spite of my discomfort. At the after-party that night, his family already returned to their hotel room, I watched as one of Lanre's girls ran her hands all over Kayode's body, watched as Lanre and the other guys laughed, teasing him, You dey fear? Kayode glanced across the booth at me, his eyes pleading, almost frightened, yet I felt nothing, my body dulled by such listlessness, I imagined I was an empty hall in which someone screamed only to be replied to by the sound of their own voice.

I sipped my Smirnoff. She began to kiss him, right there in the dimly lit bar. The guys cheered. Kayode placed his hands on her face and kissed her back. I watched them, mesmerized by how seamless they were, how compactly their bodies moved, it was almost as if they were each created with the other in mind, her long Brazilian hair pooling over their faces as she sat in his lap.

There are bedrooms upstairs o, Lanre said, laughing. The girl stood up, held Kayode's hand, pulling him up. Somto's birthday party, he said, turning to look at me, shock and confusion in his eyes: he expected me to do something, stop them.

I think Somto understands, someone said. He's a correct guy. This is *your* night, live for once.

Lanre turned to me. Abi no be true? he asked.

I shrugged. Kayode followed her toward the reception, turning to glance pleadingly at me. The moment they disappeared up a flight of stairs, my listlessness dissipated, and I felt the weight of sadness in my chest. I glanced around the bar: it was me, alone with these men whose faces annoyed and terrified me.

People are waiting at home, I said, standing up.

You need a taxi? Lanre asked, and I stared at him, my heart full of nothing but hate. The smirk on his face, his cocky manspreading; this was a battle he'd won, a battle they had all won: Kayode was one of them.

I left without saying anything else. The taxi driver I flagged down said Three thousand to Lekki, an outrageous price, but I did not care. He was nodding to Kayode's "Baby Mi," mumbling, *This love no be Cinderella ati Snow White*.

Please turn it off, I said.

Sir?

I said turn it off!

He mumbled something in Yoruba and then turned off the radio, Lagos's cacophony rushing in where once there had been a melody.

Days passed, and though I said I understood, no, I wasn't angry, I stayed away from Lekki, moped around the tiny room in Festac, my body ready to snap. In school, a girl was five minutes late to her exam and I asked her to leave, don't even look back, I told her, and don't come to the staff room to beg. Sister Monica called me into her office and said, You're one of the best teachers we've ever had, friendly with the girls without being inappropriate, but lately there have been complaints about short temper, and, honestly, I'm worried. Is there something I should know? Do you need a break?

I needed a break, I told her. A break I spent baking meat pies and cakes and cleaning the entire house, raked by an absence of peace. Kayode came to Festac, but the nights he spent were wasted, like water on a dead plant. When he kissed me, I did not caress his face in wonder, and when he was in me, I winced and winced until, his eyes shadowed by worry, he pulled out. Sometimes he held me as he finished himself off, his nose pressed firmly to my neck, it reminded me of our beginning in Nsukka, the smallness of my mattress before he bought the bigger bed, the pleasure of his body pressed against mine. When he reached out to help me finish, I gently pushed his hand away, because if he did I might cry afterward, and I did not want that.

One morning, in the flat in Lekki, I told him that I felt alone, that he was doing his best, still I felt alone.

I browsed about it, he said. This sort of thing happens when one partner in a relationship becomes successful. It will pass.

So now I'm jealous of you?

That's not what I said. I want you to be happy, Som. Tell me what you need me to do.

He was standing by the kitchen door and I was standing by the sink, the morning bright with light. I'm sure you'd like that, I said, being the shiny knight who rescues me.

Fuck, babe, why are you suddenly finding faults in everything I do or say?

Maybe Google will give you an answer to that, too.

He stood there, silent, his face long with weariness. And then he banged his fist on the door and stomped out.

I stood there, quaking with anger and sadness, bloated with the load of all the things I'd kept away from Kayode, enamored and protective as I was of his innocence. I thought of Eunice and of Nnamdi, of the spellbound boys in Ekene's room and their looks of incredulity, thought of all the people over the years who, through words, actions, or prolonged stares, had questioned what a boy like Kayode was doing with a boy like me.

I left the kitchen, walked into the living room. Kayode was playing his guitar on the balcony. Really, he was thumping lazily at the thing, his body stretched out on the reclining chair, his eyes closed. The sun drew lines on his chest and stomach. I stood by the door, watching him, his face shadowed by a frown, his nose, his lovely pink lips. I watched the rise and fall of his chest. I wanted to collapse on his body and weep, wanted to hold him there, in the near serenity of that moment, forever. But I was thinking of James Bay: *When it's just too heavy to hold / Think now is the time to let it slide.* I would start with that, I would remind him that the reason we flee burning houses is not because we no longer cherish our home. I would pull a chair close, sit down and say, Let us talk, Kayo.

We need to break up, I said, instead.

He peeked at me. What?

I cleared my throat. I don't think we can make this work anymore.

He sat up. Don't do this, Som.

Kayo.

Som, please.

Something is always happening, I said. When it's not Lanre, it is the whole country. I am not happy, I am constantly angry at people. I have to know what it's like to be me again, Kayo, because this is not me.

You don't love me anymore?

Haven't you been listening to me, Kayode!

I have but you're not making much sense to me. All these things, we can fix them. You still love me, right? I know you do.

The look on his face, of blinding desperation. I glanced away, at the children riding their bicycles down the street. If this was love, I thought, why did I feel so mired, so squeezed out of air? Why had we wound up here, struggling to breathe, restless in each other's presence? It was strange, this: to imagine, now, that there were times, had been times, when we both felt content in each other's company.

I am tired, Kayode, I said, and began to cry. He stood up and held me. For a few seconds I let him, and then I shrugged off his arms.

I have to do this, for me, I said, turning away.

Ekene said, over the phone, That boy is heartbroken, Somto. The way he cried on the phone when he called to ask me to help talk to you, I've never heard anything like it before.

I said nothing, merely stared at my socks, black on one foot, gray on the other. I should clean the house, I thought, sort out my clothes.

Are you there? Ekene said.

What about me? I said. How do you think I feel? How is it that nobody is thinking about me? I love him, I fucking love that boy, yet I broke up with him, that was and is still hard for me. I am heartbroken, too, but let's talk about Kayode instead.

Come on, nna, it hasn't gotten to that level. Of course I am thinking of you. I've asked if you want me to come to Lagos and stay with you, because I will. You can come to Akure, too, if you need the space. JJ will be visiting next week.

When I hung up, I sat on my bed and stared at the wall. My phone began to ring, Michael Jackson's voice wafting through the speakers. Kayode was calling. Several times, I'd gone to my call settings to delete the ringtone, but each time I'd been unable to, had ended up tossing my phone across the bed, crying. I silenced the call, went into the bathroom to shower for the night. Coming out of the shower, I found that he'd texted me. *You have been my biggest joy, Som*, he messaged, *I can't believe I'm hurting this much right now because of you.*

I switched off my phone.

At about midnight, I woke up to insistent banging on my door. I sat still, my heart thumping. Open the door, Kayode slurred. I went to the door, unlatched it.

He stood in the hallway, resting his weight on the doorframe. His eyes were red, his shirt buttons undone, and he smelled of beer and weed. He waved his phone in the air, stepping into the room. Listen, he said as I latched the door. He tapped his phone. A song started to play, it was Tiwa Savage's "Love Me."

What is wrong with you? I said, a little annoyed, a little worried.

You don't remember this song? Our first dance?

He began to sing, swaying toward me, his lips close to my ears. *So ma fi mi si le*, he sang, burped and chuckled, *Oh I like it here.*

Kayo, I said.

After everything we've been through together, he said suddenly, a moment of sharp clarity in his drunken incoherence, it startled me. I turned on the light. He looked up at me, chuckling, his red eyes dreamy.

After everything, Somto, you want to leave me now that I need you most.

His hands flew to his mouth. He rushed into the bathroom. The sound of vomiting filled the room. I stood by the bathroom door. Are you okay?

Yes—retching, more vomiting. "Love Me" had stopped playing, now his voice swelled from the phone, filling the room with his song. *You be like fire for my pocket*, he sang, *Come lie down make we relate…*

I stood there, listening to his retching, to the song. Years later, when his songs would set the continent on fire, when I would stand by my window and look out into Lagos, wondering if leaving him was the biggest mistake of my life, it would be these sounds that I would hear in my memory, of a young man throwing up in my bathroom and a beautiful song playing in the background.

MICHAEL'S POSSESSIONS

Obinna did not expect this sort of generosity from Adanna. He'd expected her to meet him at the door with some of Michael's things; instead, she stands aside to let him in, saying hello and smiling politely, her gap-tooth showing. She is wearing faded blue jeans and a gray sweater, her hair bunched in a hairnet. Her eyelids are puffy, her eyes tired, the eyes of someone who has not had enough sleep. It's been three years since he last stepped foot in the house. The room is dim in midday. He wants to throw the curtains open, flood the room with afternoon light. She used to joke all the time that the only thing capable of coming between them were the curtains.

He'd hated the dimness, the laziness of Saturdays here on the sofa with the television on. On those days when, dissatisfied with himself, he'd thrown the curtains open, flouncing around the house with a bucket and a mop, riling her up, she'd say, "It has started again, your madness." He thinks of reminding her, as something to laugh over now.

He looks around like a visitor, which is what he is, although this had been his house before they got married, and he still pays the rent. So much has changed: the walls have been repainted a garish green, the pictures on the walls arranged in the shapes of hearts.

Their wedding pictures are gone, he notices, replaced by pictures of Michael, moments captured spontaneously. In one of them, Michael runs after a pigeon, his legs blurred in motion, the bird captured in the process of flight. He must have been three.

"Four years, actually," Adanna says.

"Huh?"

"He was four, Obinna."

He turns and nods at her, he did not realize that he'd asked the question out loud.

The floor is clean, the brown tiles glistening, if he squats, he will see his face on the floor. The sofas do not look as if anyone has lain on them today, the pillows carefully tucked. She had hated the color of his chairs, floral-patterned armchairs and a cream sofa, had thought even the material too delicate. "You are no longer a bachelor," she used to say, with a quiet insistence, something she said every time he resisted changes to the house, it began to seem to him that she had come into their marriage with a readiness to expunge every vestige of what she knew of him. But he'd lived in the house for two years before she moved in, had transformed it into his abode, and one can only give so much of oneself away; he'd allowed her to change the curtains, had even helped her tear down the wallpaper in his bedroom, his lovely gray carpet gone, too, in favor of tiles that were always cold, even in heat season.

He is surprised that the chairs have not been changed. He sinks into a sofa, forgetting himself in the surge of memories. She parts the curtains, but only slightly, sunlight squeezing in. He is already rifling through the carton she'd placed on a stool. He empties its contents on the floor, begins to repack, folding each shirt neatly before tucking it in, stacking the toy cars and action figures. When he gets to the pictures, he pauses, suddenly unsure he wants to remember.

In the first picture, Michael is seated on their bed, a curly haired cherub propped up by pillows, a strand of saliva hanging from his parted lips. His eyes are so bright, he must have been laughing at something, someone, in front of him. He is wearing a blue pinafore sprinkled with white polka-dots; Obinna remembers walking into Shoprite with Adanna, how firmly she gripped his hand when she saw the cloth, her excited Oh my God, it's beautiful! His grimace, Ouch, how strong she'd become since her pregnancy, he often teased her, Are you sure we're not expecting a soldier, making her spit out, God forbid. The horror in her eyes amused him, always. Her pregnancy had been the happiest months in their marriage, as was the one year they spent marveling at everything Michael did, his cute lopsided walk that first year, his stumbling. The morning he said his first word, *up*— lifting his arms, he'd said to Obinna, Up, Up—they'd shrieked into each other's faces, pulled each other into a tight hug. For the rest of the week they devised ways to make him repeat himself, applauding with renewed joy every time he did, whispering at night about it all, which made him think of their time together at Youth Service camp, when they had been just friends.

She is still standing by the window, looking outside, a cup of tea in her hand. He knows that posture, her deep-in-thought posture.

"So, how have you been lately?" he asks.

She glances at him, the cup pressed to her lips. She shrugs, she is again looking out the window, melancholic in the feeble light leaking into the room. He concludes that she does not want to talk to him, nods and returns to the pictures. When she speaks, her voice is so soft and so detached, moments pass before he realizes that she's talking to him.

"I was at church last Sunday," she says. "I don't go that often anymore but I decided to go last Sunday. I saw Buzo, God, he's so grown. You remember Buzo, Buchi and Gerald's son?"

She's looking at him now. He nods, he remembers Buzo, how could he forget a boy who had spent many nights in Michael's room, sharing his toys, running with him in the backyard, a boy he had tucked into bed so many times, it began to feel as though he were his own son? He's watching her, but not directly, not looking into her eyes, he's waiting for her to say something else. She doesn't. She raises the curtain and peeks outside, and then walks out of the living room, toward the dining area, where she pours hot water into another cup, her motions, her movements so delicate, it feels to him as though she is playing with him, the generosity he felt at first meant to drag out his disquiet. It was another thing about her, the quiet efficient way she could wage a war.

"Do you want something to drink?"

He shakes his head, no, waiting. She returns to the living room, settles into a sofa by the window, and crosses her legs. It is obvious already that she has no intention of continuing the conversation about Buzo; suddenly, it matters to him that she does, it seems more important than all the memories in the carton.

"How is Buzo? Does he still stammer?"

She looks up at him, eyebrow arched.

"I didn't notice." She shrugs. "Maybe a little, but certainly not as badly as before, otherwise I would have."

He nods, *I see*, even though he does not see, this is not what he needs to hear. "That's really wonderful," he says, then, after a moment of silence, "Does he remember Michael?"

"How am I supposed to know that?" She is looking away from him and frowning. It is difficult to remember that there had once been a time when she could discern his moods, the words hidden behind his words, a time, before their engagement when they'd merely been friends, when he too had felt as though he knew her completely, so much that friends and family began asking why they weren't dating. He wants to tell her that he misses her, that he had always missed her, but not in the way that she'd missed him in the beginning, in a way that drove her to his parents, her parents, their friends, his secret rolling off of her lips into their ears, so that he remained in Abuja for those three months, prolonging his trial, until he got the phone call about Michael.

If her missing had been an overwhelming fire, his is a dull but consistent ache, a longing for the friendship they had shared before their marriage, open and effortless. He thinks of the evening late in their Youth Service year when he told her he might like men. They'd been sitting quietly on the huge boulder near the gate leading into his lodge—she came every other evening, sitting with him while they talked about everything, or simply stared into their phones, lifting their heads briefly to share something interesting, funny, or outrageous. He'd been terribly sad that evening, and when he said, "Men are trash," she did not say, "I know." She clicked her phone off, asked if he was okay. He remembers how afraid he was as he told her he thought he had a crush on his platoon leader, how relieved when she said, after a surprised *Oh*, "But he's an asshole and you are so nice."

He wonders if there will ever come a time when she no longer hates him. He thinks of asking when she became a tea addict, to soften the air, but the air forbids familiarity. Maybe it is not merely the air but something in him that needs softening. It used to be easy, making her laugh, not just her but everyone else. What is left of him now, of his once brilliant charisma? Maybe that is the reason Martin left, he thinks, he must have been overwhelmed by the absence of joy, after all, they'd built their relationship on laughter.

He does not want to think of Martin, not here and certainly not today, but it had taken his leaving to bring Obinna here. He cannot say fairly that he did not see the signs, the oblique way in which Martin withdrew, in installments, into his own life, away from the one they shared: the extra hours Martin put in at work; all the time he spent laughing with strangers on his phone; and finally the long moments when, lying beside each other, no words or touch would pass between them. The night he found papers for a self-contained apartment in Lugbe that Martin had bought, he accused Martin of dishonesty, Martin accused him of trying to control his life, their tiny flat resounding with the bass of their anger.

On the couch later that night, Obinna had been unable to sleep, not because of discomfort—he was thinking that after the tragedy that befell him, he'd fallen too deeply into Martin, had encumbered him with the weight of his need, his son dead and buried, his parents and siblings taking his wife's side in the crisis that escalated after.

He returns to the pictures in his hands, rescuing himself from those memories. "I remember this," he says, waving a picture in which he and Adanna are squatting beside Michael, who stands between them, lollipop in hand. A pout darkens Michael's face. Behind them, a great expanse of water looms. "Calabar. You had refused to get him an ice cream, instead you got the lollipop." For days prior it had rained nonstop; trapped in their hotel room with a balcony overlooking the beach, Michael's restlessness and moodiness that only lifted the next day, under a sunny sky so tender, it seemed like compensation for the deluge of the previous day. In the next picture, Michael is standing alone, ice cream cone in hand, his face alight in smiles. "It would seem you relented," Obinna says, absently, he is staring at the picture with deep concentration, as though by doing so he can animate the image, thaw the frozen smile so that the living room resounds again with his laughter. Those days when, looking at Adanna, he doubted the essence of their marriage, that laughter had erased his doubts. He steels himself, he cannot cry here, not in front of her. "He is four here, right?"

"Don't ask me. He was your son, too."

He looks at her, shaken, first, by her clipped tone, and then by the ease with which she spoke of Michael in the past, *was*. It is not odd that she would, it has been three years, after all, but such is human nature that when we are trapped in a moment, we expect the whole world to stand still with us.

Those had been Martin's words to him; looking at her, he feels naked in his shock, just as he had felt in Martin's presence weeks before, flailing, a man who was about to lose absolutely everything.

"I think he is four," he says, he is determined to ignore the walls she has put up. "I remember that he'd just had chicken pox before we traveled. The spots are even fresh on his face, see?"

She is quiet for a moment, her face turned to the window. When she looks at him, her eyes are glistening. "I thought you came here to get some of his things?" she says. "Shouldn't you be returning to your boyfriend?"

"Where is this coming from, Adanna? I only asked a question."

For a moment it looks as though she will pounce on him.

"You have the nerve, Obinna! You have the nerve to come in here and remind me of things I am trying to forget."

He should keep quiet, he should say he's sorry, gather the things he hasn't yet tucked into the carton, and leave. But he will not. "How can you say that you want to forget, Adanna? Don't say that."

She looks shocked that he has spoken those words, opens her mouth and shuts it. She rests her elbows on the dining table, palms clutched together under her jaw, her little fingers frantically tapping each other. He remembers that posture, too, of growing anger. He decides to say nothing else, returns to the task at hand, placing the pictures in the carton, Michael's shoes as well, tiny shoes that he must have worn when he was two or three. He wonders what these will do for him, really. Objects are not words, they are not arms: they can neither console nor embrace. If anything, they will only sit on his shelves as reminders of a time in his life. Before rolling his bags out the door, Martin had said, "You have to forgive yourself."

Every January, Obinna transferred money into Adanna's account for rent, even though she never called to acknowledge it, even though she had a job that paid as much as his, he did it, religiously. Sitting here, he senses the shape of a familiar sadness, the same sadness that enveloped him for days after each transfer. He should leave, he thinks. He begins to close the carton. Just then, Adanna rises and walks into the bedroom; shortly after, the door swings open, and she rushes out, holding a huge travel box over her head. She charges toward him, for a moment he thinks, That box cannot kill me, her eyes are so wild, she seems capable of any grave act. She'd had the same wildness in her eyes the day he told her about Martin. I thought you'd changed, she'd said over and over, and then, You cannot just stand up and leave your family, it's not fair.

She empties the box over his head, releasing a rainstorm of clothes and shoes and photographs onto his body.

"You want me to remember?" she yells. "Well, here it is, everything I remember. I remember you waking up a year after that trip and saying you had fucked someone else. I remember you leaving us. I remember holding my bleeding baby and rushing to the hospital alone. I remember calling your number, Obinna, but where were you? Where were you?"

He does not move. The clothes smell so strongly of Michael, a whiff of baby powder and pureness. The clothes smell so strongly of Michael. The clothes. Michael.

She is still screaming, Michael would not be dead had you not left! He wouldn't have gone out into the street with Buzo because it would have been video game time with Daddy! She is yelling, What did you come here for? Did you come here to hear that everything was okay? I will not give you that, Obinna, she says, go back to your boy.

The day he drove to the house in a swirl of dust, she was standing at this very spot in front of him. From there, she would change his entire life. Yes, a hit-and-run had killed Michael as he played in the street, she said, and, yes, he had been buried already, what was it worth, keeping a dead child and causing oneself enormous grief? He looked at her, unbelieving; he'd never seen that part of her, heartless and tranquilly cruel. How could she do this to him? he said. His son was dead and he did not even get to see his corpse—how could she?

"Maybe if you did not disappear for three months, you would still have a son!" she said.

He had never felt as though there were something to forgive himself for, he was merely angry, he'd told himself, angry that he had not been allowed to see his son one last time, even though lifeless, that he was denied his right to an ending, and yet nobody stood up for him, not even his family. As though his anger were a candle burning steadily in the dark, its boundaries precise and definite. As though it were not an inferno. It surprises him now, watching her, the stillness he feels, how clearly he can hear those words that had for so long filled him only with anger.

She sinks into an armchair, elbows on her knees, face in her hands. "What were we thinking, getting married?" she says. She lifts her head, begins to wipe her eyes with the hem of her blouse. "I know—I wanted a good man." She chuckles, shaking her head, then looks at him with sad contemplation. "And you, what did you want? A cover?"

"We don't have to cheapen what we had, Adanna."

"You humiliated me. Do you even realize how betrayed I felt?"

"I had a right to say goodbye to my son and you denied me that."

"I went too far, I know, but I was hurt."

They sit in silence, sunlight slinking through the closed curtains.

"It's been three years," she says, "and we've gotten nowhere in our grief."

He places his hands on the box, ready to leave, but she stands up and asks if he would like some tea.

MOTHER'S LOVE

It was not a good time for Mma to visit: two weeks earlier, Chenna had moved out. Chikelu still felt the weight of the loss lodged in his chest like a smooth and perfect pebble, still shut himself in the house after work, still fell asleep to the sound of the television, his curtains closed, the lights turned off, all he wanted was to banish light, to be left alone—but what was all that to say to one's own mother? And so here she was, flinging the curtains open, murmuring about how badly the house smelled, like dirty boxers or, worse, a corpse undiscovered, festering in the open.

"Have you seen a festering corpse before?" he said, teasing her.

"Don't give me your sharp mouth," she said, hands on her waist, her eyes scanning the living room. "This was one thing I liked about Uchenna, that man knew how to keep a house!"

He opened his mouth to say something but decided not to. He dragged Mma's bags toward the guest room. Earlier, he'd gone into the room with a broom, ready to be assaulted by the things that needed cleaning, only to find everything in place, the old cartons he'd left there gone, the floor tiles sparkling, the ceiling white and clean of cobwebs. All he'd had to do was make the bed. He'd wondered when

Chenna tidied the room, if it was on the day before their quarrel or after. They'd known about Mma's visit since the hospital informed him of a date to see the cardiologist, but, as always, he'd let the little things, such as making Mma's bed, roam the boundaries of his mind. Looking into the clean room, he'd been filled with gratitude, had slipped his hand into his pocket for his phone, and then, remembering, he'd turned around and banged the door shut, only returning hours later to make the bed.

Mma was seated on the bed now, rifling through her handbag, her entire arm submerged in it. She looked better than the last time they had seen each other, she was almost back to how he remembered her, how he'd love to remember her for the rest of his life, plump and restless, always doing, always talking, always moving. Tiny cornrows crisscrossed her head in intricate whorls; he imagined her sitting for hours under the dogonyaro tree in Mama Emma's compound, getting her hair plaited, the conversations that swirled from woman to woman, the children running around, dirtying themselves in the sand, the occasional peal of a woman's voice in furious scolding, the grating rattle of Mama Emma's grinding machine as it crushed beans or tomatoes, the flies, Lord, the flies. It had been two years since he had last visited Kano.

"Wetin you dey find?" he said; she was still digging into her handbag, her arm now frenetic.

She knotted her brows, her nose scrunched up. His mother had such a perfect nose, full and round, his siblings' nose. He'd inherited Mpa's, so flat it was almost as though God had bored two holes into his face and then slapped on a ridge as an afterthought.

"It's the fidget spinners I bought for KC and Mmeso," she said. "Are you sure I didn't forget them in Kano?" She emptied the bag onto the bed: notebooks, pens, pieces of chalk, a small black leather-bound Bible, combs, talcum powder, a small hand mirror and, above them all, smooth and glistening in the light, the fidget spinners. "Ah, thank God. That's all they asked me to buy for them after they learnt

I wouldn't be sleeping at your sister's. I don't know what they are, but all the children are playing with them."

"Why didn't Anulika buy it for them?" he asked, absently, his eyes focused on the long notebooks on the bed, their red covers splashed with cursive whites. Growing up, their house had been littered with books like those, and whenever he thought about home, there was always an image of Mma bent over their low center table, scribbling into the books, for hours, weekend after weekend, sometimes her face split between shade and gold under the feeble light of a kerosene lamp. She was talking now, about how his sister wouldn't buy any more fidget spinners after the children lost the last ones. "Children are children," she was saying, "you punish them for a moment and then you relent. Punish them indefinitely and they forget the lesson you're trying to pass. But your sister doesn't listen. She's been a mother for six years and suddenly she's a king who would not be counseled."

"You came all the way to Abuja with your lesson notes," he said.

"Are you not listening to me?"

"I heard you, Anulika is stubborn." She would not look at him, she was gathering her stuff, shoving it back into her bag. "You said you were going to resign after last term. What are you still doing with lesson notes?"

"Leave me alone, Chikelu."

"Why are you so stubborn, eh?" he said. "Is it until you kill yourself that you'll listen and take it easy?"

She was silent, took her time zipping up her handbag, and then she looked up at him. "Resign and do what, Chikelum? Resign and do what?" She stood up, walked to the wardrobe where he'd kept her travel bags, and placed her handbag there. Sunlight filtered in through the curtains, it was so bright outside, so hot. She returned to the bed, lowered down. "If the first thing you do when I come to your house is to berate me, maybe I should pack my things and go to your sister's."

He stood there, staring at her. Mma was so stubborn, so stubborn. "It hasn't come to that," he said.

She shrugged. "What did you even say happened to Uchenna? If he were here, he would be having my stomach full of food by now."

"Mma, I was going to stop at a restaurant on our way home. You stopped me, now you're talking about food."

"I'm not hungry. I'm just asking if you didn't learn anything about being a good host after many years of being his friend."

"Well, he's not here," Chikelu said, slightly annoyed. "I'll let you rest now." He knew that what she wanted was for him to sit on the bed with her and chat about things, him about work and her about the street, whose daughter was marrying whose son and whose nwa-boy had been sent back to the village without settlement. He loved those conversations, had always loved them, even as a boy when he would stand beside her by the cupboard outside the house as she chopped ugu. But now he felt no excitement, only exhaustion.

He left the room, easing the door shut behind him.

~

Uzoamaka stood briefly in the alcove, watching Chikelu, the way the light fell on his body, blue and soft, the way it made him look sad. He was lying on the couch, fiddling with the remote control. The living room was only slightly illuminated, the television's light spilling into corners. He was not looking for something to watch, he was passing time, filling in the silence with light and sound. The last time she'd seen him in Abuja, he'd not been like this; she could tell even though she'd been sick, even though after three days with Chikelu and one with Anulika, she'd been rushed to the hospital with a swollen leg and racing heart. Uchenna had still not found his own place at the time and had shared a room with Chikelu—she'd moved into his for the duration of her visit. Every evening, he'd return home with roast corn and ube and sit on the floor with Chikelu, their backs against the couch, eating, laughing at things on the television, the living room bright and warm and lively. She would glance at them from her seat at the dining table, she would watch him, Chikelu, the way he stretched his legs in front of him, her son, owning his own house. And she would imagine a woman seated on the carpeted floor with him, sharing everything with him, hear the patter of little feet running around the living room, ruining things but making them all laugh. "Mma, are you sure you don't want another corn?" Uchenna would say from the floor, turning to look at her, and she would find herself loathing his presence, no, she was okay, she would say simply; a few minutes later, she would walk out of the living room, frowning and merely muttering her good night. He was a sweet man, almost like a woman in his attentiveness and care, yet she'd found herself unable to like him. She'd disliked him, in fact. She disliked his face, chocolate toned and pretty, too pretty, and the way he would walk into the kitchen and ask if she was absolutely sure she did not need any help. "You know this one is only good at talking," he'd say, punching Chikelu in the arm. He wanted her to like him, she could tell, but she could not stop blaming him for Chikelu's singleness; no woman, she thought, would take Chikelu seriously as long as he continued to live with his friend. She'd visited Abuja once more since this trip but had not seen Chikelu then, he had been unable to wriggle out of a work trip, so Chenna drove her and Anulika to the hospital for her labs; from the back seat of the car, she watched as Anulika became engrossed in a story he was telling, watched as she laughed at his jokes, as she slapped his arm playfully, saying, "That's crazy." When Anulika, still laughing a little, turned around to ask if she'd heard Chenna's story, she said, "I wasn't listening" in a clipped, apathetic tone that gave even her pause, and then turned her face toward the window, staring at the road without really seeing it, silence descending on the car.

∿

Mma was awake early. Her movements traveled to him on the couch, silverware clattering in the hollow morning air, the piquant aroma of stew, also. Chikelu had hoped to wake up earlier and would have set his alarm for four thirty, knowing what an early riser she was, that she would be up at five regardless of the day of the week, but he'd fallen asleep watching a movie he did not now remember. He had been that way for weeks, hazy and forgetful, like a person always suffering from a terrible hangover.

He rolled off the couch, grunting, and ambled to the kitchen, cracking the door open. "This woman, you no dey ever rest?"

"Good morning to you too, Chikelu," she said, stirring her stew, which sizzled in the pot, as though defying her with its rude little hisses.

"You too like fight." He walked into the kitchen now, gently closing the door. He wondered why he'd done that, close it gently, as though Chenna were still here, ready to campaign against slamming things. He thought of pushing it back open and slamming it shut, and he would have, were Mma not here. It would have given him a small satisfaction.

"Stir this for me," Mma said, moving aside so that he could take over. "It will be done in five minutes. Take it down then. I have to go prepare."

"Good. Because you take ages preparing."

She didn't take ages preparing, she was always out of the bathroom minutes after stepping into it. When he was a kid and the neighbors queued up to use the bathroom every morning, people would yell at whoever had gone in after her, saying, "You no fit do like Mma Chikelu? If you wan' dey born pikin inside bathroom, go rent flat!" Perhaps that was why she never missed an evening bath, not even in harmattan. She woke him up first each morning, letting Anulika, James, and Bobo sleep longer, not only because she needed him to help her fan the charcoals in the stove until they glowed fiery red, a miracle of wind, but also because she needed him to shower before the neighbors, hearing the noise she made outside, began to spill out of their rooms to start their small fires in front of their small doors and, eventually, yell at him to hurry up and leave the bathroom. He always lingered there, scrubbing his armpits, his soles, his face, and, when he discovered masturbation, his groin, ditching the sponge for just soap, ignoring the cemented floor and tiny walls green with moss, or the occasional cockroach peering down at him. When it was harmattan and he'd run into the house shivering, teeth chattering, Mma would look at him sideways and say, her Igbo coming out as a single string, "You didn't know you were cold when you were taking your time with whatever it is you do in there." He would mumble, "I no dey do anything," defensive, even though he never thought for once that she was referring to his one-man trysts, but by then she would have moved on, rushing Anulika to the bathroom: "Mee ngwa-ngwa, nnwa a, I did not wake up at five to queue up with these people!"

He wanted to tease her now, to tell her that she no longer needed to wake up early, especially now with the doctors still trying to figure out what was wrong, that the bathroom was inside the house and that his neighbors all had their bathrooms inside their houses. But he wouldn't have been able to pull it off, the teasing, because it made him sad, not her here, now, but the thought of her alone, in Kano, waking up early as though she still needed to boil water for anybody, as though it wasn't just her in the house now, a house he had bought and renovated years ago, so that, even though the neighbors still had to queue up for the bathroom, she had hers inside, right beside her bedroom.

She was at the door now. "If you like, let the food burn, Mister Sharp Mouth," she said, stepping out.

He took the ladle. The kitchen smelled nice, of fried plantains and spices and simmering tomatoes. It had been months since the kitchen felt lived in. For years, Chenna had made elaborate meals, filling the house with the smell of food on weekends so that for the rest of the week the refrigerator was swollen with containers of rice, beans, egusi, onugbu, stew. But then after Mma's last two visits, during which she stayed longer, he'd done it less and less because she did the cooking when she was around. After she left, he didn't really ease back in, and it did not strike Chikelu at first: he would open the refrigerator and there'd be nothing, and he'd order something online, or ask if Chenna wanted to go to Soup Kitchen with him. And then the evening came when Chikelu asked, casually, when next Chenna would cook, maybe they could drive to the market on the weekend, and Chenna exploded at him. He stood over Chikelu and asked, over and over, when he'd been turned into a houseboy; his words and movements seemed to belong in a previous moment, when he'd first begun to feel this way, but that moment had passed, and now his anger felt outsized. Chikelu sat there, too stunned to speak; one minute they'd been sitting on the living room floor, totally ignoring the couches like they often did, Chikelu typing into his phone, occasionally laughing, and Chenna watching a football match on TV, and the next minute there was the shouting.

Chikelu began to stay longer at work, taking on more pro bono cases than he was required to. Some evenings, driving home from the office, he'd look out the window into the after-work traffic of Abuja, the roads so wide and full of cars, so orange in the swirl of the streetlights, and it would occur to him that he did not want to go home. He would drive to Tim's Place and order a plate of pepper soup and bottles of beer, sometimes in the company of his friends Kene and Moses, but mostly alone, because they were both married and spent most evenings with their families, or in hotel rooms with boys from the state university. When he got married, they told him often, he would learn to make every second he spent away from home count. He would stare at them, so unrecognizable from how they had been in their university days when they'd marched in the same pro-democracy protests and attended the same parties and crushed on the same boys, all possessed by the same radical optimism, and he would feel savagely lonely, their lives so vastly different. He'd feel silly, too, his problems with Chenna paling under the relentless beam of their cynicism: "See, you have to forget this thing with this guy and settle down." Driving back home, the roads clear of traffic, so that the orange lights seemed to ripple on the asphalt and cars zipped past as though in pursuit of something, he would wonder if he was fooling himself, brooding over the tantrums of another grown man. But then he would drive into the estate, wave at the security man at the gate, honk back at his neighbor driving out with her family, perhaps on their way to night vigil, park in his garage, walk to the kennel to pet Jasper or bring him inside the house, open the door, and there would be Chenna, asleep on the rug in his shorts, the television's light blue against his bearded face, and he would think this was all he wanted, this person with whom he had moved around for years, from the one bedroom in Maitama to the flat in Lugbe that was always too cold in harmattan, and, finally, to this, a place of their own. This person whom he'd thought he knew perfectly, this person whom he was now trying to understand.

She took her time preparing. He stood outside her door after knocking and peeking in, after she said, "One minute, nna." He paced the alcove. He'd had breakfast and rushed through his bath, hurried into rumpled jeans, thinking that she would be waiting impatiently for him. Now, he was the person waiting: Who would have thought? He went and sat on a couch, dialed Anulika. She would be up, she and Phillip, and they would be getting the girls ready for school, getting ready for work themselves. Maybe they'd be saying their morning prayers.

She picked up. "See who's awake!"

"Shut up," he said.

"What's up na?"

"Mma is making up. Mma dey put makeup for face!" There was silence, he could hear the hollowness from the other end. "Anuli?"

"Oh, I dey here. I just dey wonder how I go take talk this thing."

"Talk which thing? What happened?"

"Calm down." She sighed, her breath coming down in a rush through the phone, her peculiar prelude to a long story. "It's this doctor. The last time she was here, when you were gone, we had some problems at the hospital."

"What?" he said. "Why didn't anyone tell me?"

"Because it wasn't that serious, just basic office workers' inefficiency. Anyway, the people at the lab were giving us wahala and the doctor in charge of Mma's file wasn't helping—you know, young doctor, smart and nice, but she no wan' step on toes—and this man, him go dey like late fifties, tall, fine, full body, like a proper daddy, he walks in and Mma just sit down there, stressing, you know how emotional your mother can be." She laughed. "Well, he come ask her what's up, why she keep face like that, so she told him. He asked her not to worry, that he'd talk to the people himself. I no know wetin him tell them, but he went into the main office and in less than fifteen minutes, them produce lab documents wey them say them no see before."

"And no one thought this was something I needed to know about?"

"Calm your temper, Mister Lawyer. Haba." He knew she'd just rolled her eyes. "It has passed. The fine doctor handled it. There was no need to bother you. Uchenna said we should tell you when you got back to town but I know my brother, you for give yourself unnecessary headache, so I asked him not to. Anyway, the doctor made sure from then that we were attended to without any delay. How you think say we take get early appointment to see the specialist?"

He wanted to ask if they were sure, absolutely sure, that the lab got the right test results after that entire brouhaha, but that was exactly the kind of question that made them hide things from him in the first place. He felt betrayed by Chenna as well, he should never have hidden something like that from him, and he wondered now what else Chenna had hidden, with whom else he'd allowed a higher loyalty, but how could he say this to Anulika without exposing himself? He needed to talk to someone about Chenna.

"So you think Mma has a man friend?" He laughed, tried to laugh.

"I no know o, but I know something is up. After that day, na so she go dey for phone everytime, laughing like one amaria. I ask her who she dey talk with, she say doctor. I was like, hmm."

He tried to collect his thoughts, to decide how he felt about this.

Did the doctor see her in that way, he asked, worried about his mother expending energy, hope, on a man who was not going to be hers.

"Your problem, Chikelu," Anulika said, "is that you worry so much about people, you begin to think everybody is an idiot."

"Haba, Anulika." He could hear voices now from her end, Phillip asking someone to put on their sandals, a child's voice raised in protest. "Is that Mmeso?"

"Yes." She said something but not to him. She'd said it in English, a language she spoke only when she was angry or making a serious point. "Phillip says hi. Mmeso is being a little troublesome this morning. I have to go."

"Okay."

"See you in the evening," she said, paused, one of her intentional pauses. "You have to stop thinking that Mma does not know what she's doing or what's best for her."

After she hung up, he cradled his face in his hands, and then stood up and went to knock on Mma's door. "Finished, finished," she chanted, and the door swung open. He looked at her face, a powdered brown, her brows penciled in, her lips a hushed red. He was sure Anulika would have done it better, but this was beautiful, she was beautiful.

"O gini?" She touched her face. "Too much brown powder?"

"No," he said, and smiled. "Who be this fine girl?" He put his arm around her shoulders and whipped out his phone, angled it for a selfie. She smiled, a wide, happy smile.

～

Of all her children, he was the one she trusted to understand. When she had announced to them a few years ago that she was leaving their father, they'd stared at her and at one another, as though they had not all been cosufferers. At the point of making her decision, she'd not seen her husband for a whole year. And then Chikelu rose, as though snapping out of a spell, knelt before her, and hugged her.

His instinct had always been to reach out, support, comfort. As a child, he'd rarely gotten into trouble, but his siblings always did, especially Anulika, who had come into the world with a heart so strong, a lifetime of scolding did not leave a crack. For a while, Uzoamaka's favorite punishment was to buy them ice cream and deny the offending child, but Chikelu always went behind her back to share his, sometimes rallying the others to do the same, and she had to toss that for more direct lessons, asking the offender to kneel down while she did things around the house, their waiting, more than the few strokes of their father's belt on their outstretched palm, the punishment. Even then, Chikelu would corner the sulking or crying sibling, massaging their palm, saying sorry, hugging them, sometimes it infuriated her and she would threaten to give him his own ration of flogging. But mostly it made her sad for a reason she could not name, and after a while she discarded that method, too, because she really did not have the heart for punishment, and she resented that their father had left the job of raising the children to her when she was often confused and afraid she was doing the wrong things. The older they got and the more she needed him, the longer he stayed away, for months at a stretch, for half a year. He would call weekly from Lagos and ask to speak to the kids, and Bobo would say "No," face buried in a video game on Anulika's phone, until Chikelu said, sternly, "Come on!"

She glanced at him now, in his car that was cool and in which a choir was chanting a psalm. When the Gloria came on, he bellowed it in his off-key voice, *Glory be to the Fa-a-ther*. She and Uchenna had joked about Chikelu's love for choral music and his total lack of a singing voice, this was long before Chikelu built his own house when the sight of Uchenna did not irk her yet. He'd sung in the parish choir when he was in secondary school, she told Uchenna, and he in turn told her that he'd quit in their third year in university. "You no dey go choir today?" the roommates asked him the day he quit, and he said, "Bro, them say my voice be like frog own." The way he said it,

Uchenna told her, without a slice of bitterness in his voice, that was what he liked most about Chikelu: he had a good heart, obi ocha.

She wanted to tell Chikelu about Maxwell, who had been to Kano once to see her. She'd wanted to tell him from the moment he picked her up at the airport the day before, but he'd been strangely quiet as he drove her home, and she decided that it was wrong, anyway, to throw something like that at him. She would do it after they settled down at home, she thought, but he'd remained in a mist of melancholy. She'd thought of asking if it was because Uchenna had moved out, but even now that it came to her mind, she almost laughed at the thought, the ridiculousness of it. Chikelu was thirty-four, not ten, and he ought to have said too many goodbyes at this point in his life to brood like a man who had recently been abandoned by his woman.

"Wetin you dey think about?"

"Eh?" She tapped her head, even though her braids weren't itchy. "Oh, nothing."

"You dey sure?" He glanced at her and then at the road, again, and again. She knew that look, worry. "Are you nervous about your appointment?"

"I'm fine, Chikelum, don't worry." She touched his arm, it was warm and covered in coarse black hair, like his father's. She knew he was afraid. She was, too. Thoughts of death had assailed her since she'd gotten sick. After everything she'd been through with and for her children, would she die suddenly just as their lives were beginning to glimmer?

The hospital had ruled out blood clots, and when Maxwell had referred her to the specialist, he said he suspected it was nothing serious. But the worry didn't go down with the swelling. She realized, then, that this fear also had something to do with happiness. She'd met Maxwell. He always listened, was always full of questions, his attentiveness and humor like a miracle. For so long she had been alone, all her laughter coming from her children, her friends, and so had forgotten the thrill of a man's loving efforts, little shocks of joy at his good morning texts. Each day since he first asked for her number, she'd felt herself inching closer to something definitive, but she would not think too far—even if it was nothing serious, what she was doing with him, it was an opportunity to beat loneliness.

"You dey think something, this woman," Chikelu said, his eyes curious and shrewd. "Oya, confess."

"You think I'm one of those your court witnesses?" she said and he slowly shook his head. Another psalm was ending, the Gloria gliding in the contained space of the car. He joined in, his voice like bumps in the smooth sound of the choir. Outside the window, the road was endless, cars speeding on the roads that crisscrossed underneath this one, high-tension poles glinting in the sunlight, the corporate buildings far off. Everything in Abuja, new and beautiful and futuristic. She tried not to smile.

~

The waiting room was long and full of natural light. Chikelu walked all the way down the hallway, found a spot by the door and sat down. He hated hospitals, their antiseptic smell reminding him of needles and tears. He wished he was in the specialist's office with Mma but he was also grateful that he wasn't; inasmuch as he wanted to be there to hold her hand in case of bad news—and he had faith that there would be none, he had to have faith—he also dreaded the possibility of that moment when a sentence from the doctor's mouth would change everything forever.

That was his problem, worry; he imagined the worst outcomes for most situations. Ironic, he thought, with an inward chuckle, that even in all their fighting, he never imagined that Chenna would leave him.

He let his mind wander to their last fight, Chenna saying, "When it comes to your family, especially your mother, you become absolutely blind, suddenly you who notices everything cannot see how unkind your mother sometimes is to me," his retorting, "Of course everyone who doesn't immediately hug you is unkind to you. That might have been cute in university but now it's just annoying."

He wondered now why he'd responded that way. Perhaps it was the suddenness of the accusation, the way a fight over chores became about his mother. Perhaps he'd thought Chenna's words an utter mischaracterization of Mma, Mma who always opened their doors to the neighbor's children, Mma who had no airs, no bitterness.

When he returned home from work the evening of that fight to find Chenna gone, the house stripped of the things that were his, the wardrobes looking robbed without his clothes in them, the clock loud in the yawning emptiness, Chikelu had called him, angry, but when he did not pick up, his anger had melted into a quivering fear, and he'd sat on the bed and cried. That night, Chenna sent a short message breaking up with him.

He'd promised himself that he would not think of Chenna now that Mma was here. He had to be fully present, just in case. He thought of what Anulika had said earlier, that he often acted as though Mma did not know what was best for her. Was that why Mma didn't mention her doctor friend, even in passing? Perhaps he was being too hard on her about work, but wasn't it reasonable, what he was asking? He had not asked her to retire entirely, he'd only wanted her to stop walking from house to house in the heat of afternoon, teaching people's children, burning herself out, after an entire day of sitting with those same kids in class. Maybe when he and his siblings were younger and they needed the extra money, it had made sense, but not anymore. The only person still in school was Bobo and as far as he knew, he and Anulika were doing a great job of making sure he wasn't broke like they had often been in university. Mpa had taken advantage of their newfound prosperity and slowed down, moving from Lagos to settle in Owerri, so that he was just a few miles to the village to which he returned every other weekend, sitting in the dusk with his friends, sipping beer and eating goat head. That was the secret to a long life, Chikelu had begun recently to think, to love yourself unabashedly, and Mpa had always done that, loved himself unabashedly, sending them money whenever he had it, saying he didn't have when it wasn't there, and toward the end of Anulika's university days, his refrain had become, "M ga-egbu onwe m? I cannot kill myself."

He thought of those weekends in his childhood when Mma would give her phone to him. "Call your father," she would say, "maybe he thinks I'm joking when I say there's no food in this house. Let him hear it from your mouth." He'd resented making those calls; he loved to help, to ease Mma's burden, and Mpa listened to him more than he listened to anybody else (to others, he would say, "Nna, there's no business happening here o," but to him, he always added, "Let me see what I can do, i ṇugo?"), and yet Chikelu hated making those calls. When he spoke to Mpa, he wanted to talk about school, about his new win with the debate team, he wanted to ask him when he would visit Kano—he did not want to talk about money. One time, he must have been in SS1 then, he refused to take the phone from Mma, he grumbled something about wanting to be left alone, and her face had changed, her eyes filling with tears as she said, "So I am the only one who should not be left alone, eh? You people have seen the person that deserves to die from stress." He had walked out as she spoke, he was full of a new and confusing rebelliousness in those days, and it didn't help that he could not stop thinking of Gee, who had a girlfriend and did not know he existed.

Nurses paced the long hallway, some brisk and purposeful, others lazily chitchatting, their white uniforms almost disappearing into the milky white of the walls. On the bench across from him, a man cradled his son's head on his lap, gently patting the boy's shoulders. He'd not noticed them come in. The man looked exhausted, as did the boy, who was in his checkered school uniform. Decades ago, Chikelu had been that boy, crying into Mpa's lap because the tetanus injection had hurt. Now, he threw his head backward and closed his eyes, the memory inching closer, Mpa's hand patting his back felt so real. After the hospital, he remembered, they'd gone to FanMilk and had ice cream, Mpa telling him how strong he was, hailing him "My boy, my boy," even though he'd cried.

He allowed his eyes to travel, glancing at all the people perched on benches, looking tired and desolate. He hated hospitals so much. He wished that Chenna were here right now. They would wander off somewhere together, maybe buy bananas at the stand outside the gate and chat with the seller, to kill time. Chenna would have convinced him, he would have said, "Bilienu, nna," in that languid and swinging way he spoke his Igbo, and Chikelu would have stood up and they would have talked idly as they strolled to the gate. He should have listened to Chenna.

He pulled out his phone from his jeans pocket and scrolled to Chenna's name. *Obi m*, he typed, *I'm so sorry, please come back home.* He deleted the last letter and the one before it, and then everything. He typed again, *I think Jasper misses you. He's been barking a lot more at night*, pressed Send, and slid the phone back into his pocket as though it were something hot. He cupped his nose and mouth with his hand and exhaled.

Mma came out to the lobby just as Chenna was putting his phone away. She was walking down the hallway with a man he immediately knew to be the doctor. Her lace gown, green with yellow patterns and loose, swayed, as did her black handbag, which she slung on one shoulder. They were talking. The man was tall and, even though Chikelu could only see his shape from where he sat, he could not miss the beard that Anulika had described, gray and coiffed. He wondered if this man had brought out a hand mirror in his office and, looking at it, arranged himself in preparation for this moment. Had he been in the specialist's office with Mma? That seemed unlikely, it would be unprofessional, wouldn't it? He should be happy, he knew, she'd been through a lot, but Chikelu did not like this man who had now stopped and was facing Mma, saying something that made her laugh. There was nothing inappropriate about their posture, no grazing of arms and, when he turned left toward the west wing and Mma continued down, no hug, no handshake, just a wave of hands, brief and formal. He knew, then, that whatever Anulika had imagined between them did not even come close to what they really had. He knew all the postures, the calibrated ways of being together in public without divulging the private. It had been that way with him and Chenna in the beginning, barely talking to each other when the roommates were around, until they learned eventually that the best place to hide was right under the sun. Mma smiled as she came closer, as she saw him sitting there, watching her. She spread her arms in a questioning way, still smiling, and he shrugged. She was okay, he thought. She would be okay.

~

KC and Mmeso left their fidget spinners on the floor and chased Jasper around the house instead. Uzoamaka still jumped whenever it rushed toward her, wagging its tail, but she was no longer afraid of it. She even played with it now, sometimes caressing its back, which was covered in soft fur, its head, never its belly, so damp looking. The first time she saw it, she'd told Chikelu and Uchenna that she could not stay in the same house as a beast that big. Now, it was even bigger, and sometimes, when it barked at night as it roamed the compound, the sound at once aggressive and plaintive, she almost pitied it. It loved being inside, with people, Uchenna had told her.

The girls were running away from it now, squealing as it chased them from the dining area into the living room, their parents sitting there watching TV, not at all alarmed. KC jumped unto her body, laughing, and Mmeso did the same, and Jasper bounded toward her and stood on its hind legs as it reached for them with its front paws. Uzoamaka almost died, she'd never seen it that way before, as tall as a twelve-year-old boy, and thrice as bigheaded. "Bịa, ụmụazị a!" she yelled, throwing her head back and closing her eyes while it pawed at them. Laughter erupted in the living room. Phillip came and took the girls away, Jasper following. "Let Mma rest," he said.

Chikelu looked away from the television and watched them as though trying to remember when all these people had come into his house. He checked his phone, probably for the twentieth time in the space of a minute, dropped it back on the stool beside him, and returned his gaze to the television. Uzoamaka continued to watch him, the way he sat, with his legs drawn together on the chair. "Chikelụ, kedụ ihe ọ?" she asked.

She'd assumed that, with the house full, and after the news that the specialist had found no reason to suspect the edema was caused by something serious, he would rise from whatever pit he'd been thrown in, but he looked worse now, duller in the light of all that laughter. She'd sensed him descending deeper after they returned from the hospital that afternoon, and she'd asked, finally, what the problem was, but he merely shook his head and said it was nothing. Now, he looked at her from that vacuous place, as though contemplating her. He smiled. "Do I look like someone who has a problem?" She did not believe the amusement in his voice, so blatantly false.

"Yes, you do. You've been moping around since I came here. If you have a problem, spit it out. Kwupute ya. If it's my presence in your house that makes you moody, tell me, so I can pack and go where I'm welcome. Ị fụkwaa!"

"Mma!" It was Anulika. The room was silent. The television droned on. Even the girls were quiet, looking at them with eyes naked with curiosity. Jasper was curled on the floor and KC was rubbing its neck.

"I don't know what you're talking about," Chikelu said, not in pidgin, not even in Igbo, but in English, and in that version of English he'd used during debates back in secondary school and, she imagined, in courtrooms now. She felt slapped, especially as he continued looking at the television, ignoring her. She stood up, snatched his phone from the stool. Is it because of that man, she heard herself say, is it because of him? Chikelu leaped up from his seat.

"Do you want to drag it from my hand?" She gripped the phone, tight.

"Mma, biko nyeghachi m foonu m," he said, arm outstretched, palm open. She moved back. Anulika was talking, Kedụ ụdịrị mkparị bụkwanụ nke a? Phillip was saying to the girls, let's go and play with Jasper outside. They were moving, the sound of the door unlatching. She stood there, unsure, the air between them soiled by her one reckless move. She could return the phone now and sit back down and let the air ferment even further, and they could all sit in the discomfort of it, wait for it to pass; or she could open his messages and confirm her worst fear, a fear she'd never let herself name because doing so might call it forth into reality.

She pressed the side button, the screen lighting up. The texts were right there, under a thread titled My Heart.

Obi m, the most recent message read, *I am terribly sorry, please answer your phone or flash me. I didn't mean to make you feel that way. I miss you.* The one before: *I think Jasper misses you. He's been barking a lot more at night.* Before that: *If what you want is a break, then why did you pack all your clothes? And why aren't you at least answering your phone?*

Prior to all that, My Heart had texted, *This is the most difficult message I've typed in years but it feels necessary. We need a break. I need the space to think about us, about me. I love you but increasingly you no longer see me, and it hurts. I don't feel like the most important person to you, and that is not okay for me.*

Before that, from My Heart—in response to, *Chicken or point-and-kill?*—*You know I can never resist point-and-kill!*

Uzoamaka's hands shook. She stared at Chikelu but saw only his reflection. Anulika snatched the phone from her and said, "Chikelu," her voice a whisper, a plea.

Chikelu stood up, took the phone. He stared at her. "You've seen what you're looking for," he said, "are you happy now?" A calm in his voice, the surface calm of a simmering underbelly. "I guess no more secrets between us." He walked toward his bedroom and slammed the door.

She felt empty, as though she'd witnessed her son die. He would never bring a woman home and show her all the love bubbling inside of him, all the attention she herself had felt and relished; and he would never fill the house with little replicas of him for her to dote on and spoil.

"What entered into your head?" Anulika was saying but words meant nothing to her. She sat on a sofa, she could not stand, she was shaking. Anulika held her shoulder. "Are you okay?"

"My enemies have laughed the last laugh!" She put her hands on her head. "Hei!"

"There are no enemies, Mma. I'm sure you've suspected for a long time."

She looked up at her. "Can you hear yourself? I na-anụkwa onwe gị?"

"You cannot stay here tonight. Come with me, I'll help you pack."

"I'm not going anywhere. We must finish this thing tonight. Ọ bụrụ church, we will go to church. Is it dibia? Doctor? We must get to the root of it."

"You're not getting to the root of anything, Mma, at least not tonight." She rubbed her shoulders. "Bịa, let's go and pack your things."

～

It felt like hours, but it had only been about twenty minutes, and the room was dark. Outside, night was descending, dimly blue. He sat with his back to the window, one leg stretched out, the other pulled up in an inverted V. He could hear his nieces laughing, their father saying, "That's enough for today, girls. Get in the car. I'll take Jasper to his kennel."

"What about Uncle Kelum? We want to tell him bye-bye."

"If you don't get into this car this instant!"

"You heard Mummy, enter, enter," Phillip said. Jasper barked. "You didn't need to shout at them, baby." Chikelu imagined him kneading her shoulders. He could see the girls' heads, their hair decorated in ribbons of bright colors, as they walked to the car, saw Phillip walk Jasper toward the kennel. Someone was knocking on his bedroom door. He pulled the duvet closer, covering his shoulders. He did not want to talk to anybody.

The knocking persisted. "I am not going to leave until you open this door," Anulika said, kept silent for a second. "Kelum, bikozienu, I cannot bear to leave you like this."

He stood up and unlatched the door, returned back to the bed.

"God, see as this place dark."

"Don't turn on the light."

"I won't." He could see her, dim. She was standing at the foot of the bed, peering down at him. She sat down. "I'm sorry." She touched his leg, briefly, gently.

He continued to look out the window. He could hear the girls singing, *Do you know Mummy? I know Mummy is the best!*

"Where is she?" he asked.

"Who? Oh." She brought her fingers to her face and flicked her braids off, her nails were long and painted red. "She's in the car. She's going home with us."

"Huh. I see she cannot stay under the same roof as her demon son."

"Come on, Chikelu. I made her come with us. She did not want to leave. And I'm sure you don't want her here either tonight."

When she goes away, I will be left alone!

"And you? What are you going to do? Will you stop bringing the girls over now?"

She looked at him, her eyes sad, or maybe it was the dying light. *Can you take a picture to represent Mummy?* "How can I, Chikelu? They love you and I love you."

He felt a throb in his throat, he wanted to cry. "And Phillip?"

"Phillip is not like most men," she said. "And even if he turns out to be, we will fight over it and I will win. You know me, I always win." She smiled, touched his leg again, this time leaving her hand there.

"Of course, you always do." He chuckled.

Can a picture do what Mummy can do for me? Oh no-o-o, Mummy is the best!

"You should probably find them a voice teacher as soon as possible," he said. "They've murdered that song."

"Just like you murdered it during morning assemblies in nursery school, so enthusiastic and confident in your off-key voice. Or you think say I forget?"

They both laughed. There was a brief moment of silence, and then the girls began singing a new song, but he did not know it and so could not make out the words. "I talked to Uchenna," Anulika said, and he sat up. "We spoke yesterday on the phone. I asked him why he left without telling us."

He did not know what to say. She continued. "You ever wonder why Mma never left Mpa all the years he was in Kano with her, cheating up and down? Ever wonder why she divorced him when she did?"

"Because she wanted us to grow up first."

"That, too," she said. "But something else, something more. Mpa was not the worst of men, he was in fact very good, by available standards. When he was around, he took care of us, bathed us, helped in the kitchen, not for once did he beat Mma. Mpa had those flings and it made them quarrel all the time at first, and when Mma was younger it made her so unhappy. But she learned to live with it, to ignore it. And then he left her all those years with us, never made an effort to help when things became tough, never acknowledged her sacrifices. And Mma realized that she could not handle that, it made her feel alone, like a widow." She paused; he sat in the silence, waiting. "What I'm saying, Chikelu, is that everybody has their breaking point, the thing that they finally say no to."

The room was darker. He breathed, deep. She stood up. "Will you be okay? I can stay while Phillip takes them home."

"I think I'll prefer being alone," he said.

She nodded, walked to the door, turned. "Don't think too much about what Mma did. She was just afraid. We all know you are her poison."

After she left, after the car drove off and he went out to bolt the living room door, he returned to the bed, got out his phone and texted Chenna: *Mma found out about us tonight. She's left with Anulika now. I pretended not to see the way she treated you in the past. That will change.* He paused, let his thumb hover again. *I am afraid but I am also sure now that you're all I need. I love you.*

He sent it.

~

The entire family had gone to bed. She tossed and tossed in hers. There was power and the ceiling fan was blowing cool air, yet she felt hot. Her phone beeped. She knew, even without looking at it, that it was another message from Maxwell, perhaps saying good night this time and could she please call or text him in the morning to let him know she was okay. He was like a distant noise in her mind right now. Now that her anger was gone, now that her shock was gone, she felt sorry for what she'd done to Chikelu. She could still see the hurt on his face, the surprise, as though he could not believe that she was doing that to him.

Weeks ago, he had called her at night to tell her that Uchenna moved out. She'd been asleep when her phone rang, and she felt in the darkness for it, flicking it on and checking the time. It was 11:00 P.M. "Chikelum, arụ adịkwa?" she said, and he simply sighed, one long breath traveling down the line like wind through a tunnel.

"I didn't realize how late it was," he said, laughing, a short awkward laugh. The silences, they were wide and deep. The gentle rasp of breathing. His words, that he'd had a misunderstanding with Uchenna and he'd moved out suddenly. She could not remember the last time Chikelu had needed her. Unlike Anulika, who would call with all her school and friendship problems, he'd kept his life, his hurts to himself. Instead, he'd always been the one to listen as she spoke, angry when she needed him to be, absorbing it all. As she listened to his breathing, she sensed that he needed her, and she was afraid to pry, afraid that he would say something if she did, something she'd always suspected but did not want to confirm.

"Yes, I was asleep," she said. "But call me back in the morning." She knew that when he did, he would no longer need her.

She should have been there, she thought now, sniffled. He'd looked so sad hours ago, and she wished she could return to hours before, when she did not feel so conflicted in her love for him.

~

He was almost asleep when his phone rang. Jasper was barking, the sound coming from the door instead of the kennel. He picked up his phone, stared at it, his heart thumping.

"I'm at the door," Chenna said.

ACKNOWLEDGMENTS

I have been a recipient of astounding love.

Mighty thanks to my teachers at St. Thomas' Secondary School, Kano, especially Mrs. Mary Nwoboshi, Mrs. Eudora George Imo, Ms. Georgina Nnaji, Mr. Ian Dennis, and Father Habila Musa. For the lessons and the praise and acts of encouragement.

Thanks to the Iowa Writers' Workshop, to Lan Samantha Chang, to Jan and Deb, and the Truman Capote Literary Trust. Special thanks to Adam Haslett and Charles D'Ambrosio for the gift of their time, for seeing.

My wonderful agent, Jin Auh, for ease and the feeling of security. And Austin Mueller. The entire team at A Public Space Books, for taking such good care of this book, for painstaking intentionality, and for being so good at this: Brigid Hughes; my brilliant editor, Megan Cummins; Cristina Rodriguez; Anne McPeak.

Thank you, Damon Galgut. And the AKO Caine Prize for African Writing, for those amazing two weeks in Gisenyi, without which we might not have met.

For reading and loving and believing in these stories, for witnessing my development, and for telling me the truth: Gbolahan Adeola,

Kelechi Njoku, and my dearest Otosirieze Obi-Young.

My beloved family: Ijeoma and Amechi Ifeakandu, my first storytellers, my heroes; my siblings Nonso, Udoka, Chiamaka, Ebube, Blossom, and all my cousins—the next generation, the shining generation—for inspiration and hope. Aunty Friday Ifekandu of blessed memory. Aunty Chigoziem and all the Ndumnegos, beautiful, upright, gentle people of whom I am most proud.

For care and words of affirmation, these friends: Ebenezer Agu, Chisom Orakwute, and Benard Takon Esise, my day ones; Prince Jacon Osinachi; Jeremiah Dala; Gbenga Adeoba; Matthew B. Kelley; Ada Zhang; Somto Chikwendu and Dandy Ogbonnaya (I cannot forget how excited you were about each early story, how eager you were to read the next thing I was writing—such fuel!)

Mrs. Rita Areghan, Papa's mum, for reading and praising my first short story ever, for sharing and talking books with me.

The Writers' Community, Nsukka, and Adaeze Nwadike, assistant custodian that year, our year: believers, fellow dreamers. For the passionate conversations and arguments. For the inspiration—to be better writers, better friends, better people. And for some of the most soulful writing yet.

For good music and for community: Mr. Jude Nwankwo and J Clef Chorale at the University of Nigeria, Nsukka; Dr. Ade Adeogun and Christ Church Chapel Choir; Dr. David Puderbaugh of the Camerata Singers at the University of Iowa. My dear uncle, Chidi Ndumnego, lawyer and choirmaster and father extraordinaire.

For support: Dominic Fritz; Leo Onyemuche Ejesu; Jonathan Lee; Salvatore Scibona; Magogodi Makhene.

The wonderful people at Black Rock Senegal, for the best summer yet.

And to everyone who has said a kind word, lifted a helping finger, all the names not here: thank you.

ABOUT THE AUTHOR

Arinze Ifeakandu was born in Kano, Nigeria, and currently lives in Tallahassee, Florida. An AKO Caine Prize for African Writing finalist and A Public Space Writing Fellow, he is a graduate of the Iowa Writers' Workshop. His work has appeared in *A Public Space*, *Guernica*, the *Kenyon Review*, *One Story*, and *Redemption Song and Other Stories: The Caine Prize for African Writing 2018*. *God's Children Are Little Broken Things* is his first book.